CW01498665

"An irresistible homage to the unsun
man and champion raconteur Larry

-Camilla Barnes

"Hooray, at last, an insight into the unsung hero, at the helm of making filming magic. This intriguing story illuminates the tightrope day-to-day tasks of a 1st assistant director and the crew, on and off a film set - that has never been touched on before. Mr Lamb pulls no punches. It is speedy, sexy and amusingly truthful.
I loved it."

-Celia Imrie

"Some of my fondest memories of being on the set of Gavin and Stacey were listening to Larry Lamb tell incredible stories.
He is one of the best."

-James Corden

Published and Manufactured by Softwood Books
EU Responsible person: Maddy Glenn
Office 2, Wharfside House, Prentice Road, Stowmarket, Suffolk, IP14 1RD
www.softwoodbooks.com
hello@softwoodbooks.com

EU Rep:
Authorised Rep Compliance Ltd., Ground Floor, 71 Lower Baggot Street, Dublin, D02 P593, Ireland
www.arccompliance.com
info@arccompliance.com

Paperback ISBN: 978-1-8381735-6-2

Printed and bound in Great Britain by:
CPI group (UK) Ltd, Croydon, CR0 4YY

All Wrapped Up

Lots of love to you Becky
from
Larry x

LARRY LAMB

SB

SOFTWOOD BOOKS
SUFFOLK, UK

INTRODUCTION
by
Larry Lamb

Turning the hundred or so pages of a screenplay or script into an on-screen experience is a very labour-intensive process involving a crew of specialists with a whole range of artistic and technical abilities, together with a company of actors that audiences actually see on the screen. The difference is that actors work on the scenes they appear in whereas the crew works on every single scene that makes it onto the screen, as well as the ones that don't.

Fifty years ago I was a very keen, young, amateur actor who got a great big break whilst supervising the reconstruction of an overhead power line system in Eastern Canada. With absolutely no planning involved, purely by chance, I became a professional actor. I dumped my former life and dived in. But as I started to move from theatre into film and television, I realised that as much as I loved the acting, what was gradually becoming obvious to me was that I also loved working alongside the crews of highly skilled people, who were often very similar in character to those I'd worked with before I jumped ship and got into 'the business of show'. People who design and make costumes, the makeup and hair specialists, the production designers, and their art department specialist-artists, who create the entire look and feel of a show, the production managers, the assistant directors, location managers who track down and secure real places to be featured. The cinematographers who manipulate the magic of light then film every scene, the sound engineers, the electricians, or 'sparks', who wrangle the practical side of lighting, the stunt men and women, the special effects teams, props men and women, the carpenters, or 'chippies', the construction managers, the riggers, the 'grips' who bring skilled high-precision muscle, the medics, the caterers, the drivers, the security men and women — the list goes on and on.

Of course, all those people and all their skills need to be harnessed and coordinated so that no effort or talent is ever wasted. What I gradually came to understand was that there is a person on the crew who is responsible for doing just that, and their title is 'First Assistant Director', and without their input and that of their team, there is no film or TV programme. As someone whose previous job had been very similar, I began to watch them to see how they work; see how they deal with emergencies; how they keep the production moving forward no matter what obstacles confront them, physical or otherwise. They are there to handle any and every situation, no matter how serious or absurd. The First is, in fact, the keystone to ensuring that when the final call to wrap up the show comes, the project is completely finished and, as they used to say, 'in the can'. That is the reason I started to think about telling this story.

The man I'm writing about had tried his hand at a lot of jobs before getting involved in show business. Even working on oil pipelines and rigs, however exciting they'd appeared from the outside, had proved far too dirty, dangerous, and repetitive to a young man looking for a well-paid job with travel and adventure thrown in.

It's a rather self-contained world and one he knew absolutely nothing of, and the chances of getting into it without connections are a bit slim. However, he spent hours talking to a woman, at a party he wasn't even meant to be at, who opened the door. She was determined to keep him at arm's length but interested enough in what he'd told her about himself, over the course of his relentless come-on chat, to suggest that a career in film and television might be worth considering.

Like most people, he'd assumed she meant being an actor and laughed at the idea, as any thoughts on being one of those had been completely knocked out of his system after being cast in a school production whilst still an arrogant teenager.

'No,' she said, 'I mean working behind the camera. Did you ever take the time to read the credits and see just how many people had worked on a movie or a TV show you'd just watched? Sometimes hundreds of them; far more than the actors. A girlfriend of mine is a production manager on films and television, and she's always on the lookout for people with potential.' His new friend wrote a name and number on a slip of paper and handed it to him. 'Here, tell her Maggie suggested you call.'

That slip of paper had set him off on a life he wouldn't have dared to dream of.

It's a business that runs in many ways along old-fashioned lines. People have started literally at the bottom, cleaning up after everyone on the set, and eventually gone all the way to running an international movie business in Hollywood. The sky is literally the limit. However, for a lot of people whose names roll over in the end credits of all those movies and TV shows you've watched, they simply want an interesting, constantly changing, and well-paid career.

If you don't go in with a specific artistic or technical skill, which may well have involved several years of specialised training, you might well start out with the assistant directors department as a runner, and if necessary, running all day and all night. As with every job in show business, at any given moment, the whole production can rest completely on the shoulders of the lowliest member of the crew, and if you're a runner, that may well be you!

LOS ZAPATEROS

CARIBBEAN SEA

NORTH ATLANTIC OCEAN

SAN LORENZO

MARINE LANDING BEACH

CASA SANTINI

NELSON

N
W   E
S

SCALE IN MILES
0   5   10   15   20   25

1

Day one of a movie shoot, and until the first assistant director calls a wrap on the final day, each second that ticks by has a big price on it.

In the wee small hours, just as trumpets and church bells in days gone by called the troops to action, bedside alarms are buzzing, beeping, ringing, and singing in house-shares, council flats, chichi penthouses, and suburban ranches. Every member of the crew is on the first team, no reserves carried; they're all hand-picked for the job, and as they go through their own routine in preparation for the coming days and weeks, not one of them, no matter how many productions they've been a part of, won't have at least a tiny flutter of nervy first day excitement nudging them towards their own front door.

At five a.m. on this particular day, Killian Wilde, the first assistant director on this particular film, is already awake as his alarm goes off. Fifteen years in the business, his adult life has always been early starts and late finishes, and twenty minutes after he's silenced the beeps, he's sipping the last dregs of his tea and watching Ted the unit driver haul his enormous bulk up the front garden path. They've worked together for years, and Ted waits under the porch whilst his pride and joy, a sleek, black, top-of-the-line Mercedes, sits at the kerbside in the orange-tinted street light. As the front door opens, Ted nods and smiles.

'Ready, Killy?'

'Yeah, you grab the two big ones and I'll lock up. Nice morning, Ted. Did you get the papers?'

'Yup, call sheet's with them as well.'

Killy slid into the backseat, made himself comfortable and checked through the two pages that he'd signed off the night before. 'Give Frank a quick buzz, Ted, see if he's got the Guvnor.' Whatever gender, the director of a film is also known by the crew as 'the guvnor'; it's one of the old terms that's stuck in the business over the years. But the morning evidently wasn't starting at all smoothly for the man in question.

Frank's voice came through on the speakers. 'He's just come out in his dressing gown, says he'll be twenty minutes. Baby crying all night or some old bollocks.'

Killy sat back, flipping through the papers and taking sidelong glances at suburban London coming to life. Normally by this stage he would have spent a lot of time with the director assessing potential locations, discussing every aspect of the script and the cast and crew, and planning out the shooting schedule. However, the man originally hired to direct the film had locked horns with Arthur Margolies, the producer, and left the project. His replacement had been parachuted in immediately. Ted brought him out of his reverie.

'This new director, you worked with him before?'

'No, never heard of him. Kramer walked and Arthur hired him the next day.'

'What's he done? I mean, I know he's had this big hit but

what was he doing up till then?'

Killian made eye contact with him in the mirror. 'Commercials mostly, music videos, short films. Then he got lucky with the one they're all talking about, which Arthur had seen, so when Karl bailed out, he offered him this on the strength of it.'

'Well, I tell you, Killy, Arthur let me have a peep at the script; loads of action but I couldn't make head nor tail of the rest of it.'

Killian, now gazing out the window, was drifting back into his own world and asking himself just those same questions. 'Yes, what the fuck is it? It's supposed to be an action-packed love story all set in the sixties; American diplomat's daughter kidnapped by guerrillas on a Caribbean island, gets rescued by US marines, and falls in love with the young captain in charge. But then it all turns political and it's finished up a total dog's fucking breakfast.' His phone was buzzing and HIS MAJESTY rolled across the screen.

'Morning, Arthur. Ted and me were just talking about you. Everything alright?'

'All good, sunshine, you on your way?'

'Yup, about an hour I reckon. How's the weather?'

'Been stormy today. It was boiling this morning but it's cooled off a bit now. Just to let you know, there's a bunch of tree-huggers that have shut down the local airstrip. Our plane will be waiting to fly you up as soon as you land but if it's still shut here and we can't use it, we'll have to drive you.'

'Well let's hope it all gets sorted, Arthur. I can do without four hours bouncing around in the mud. So what exactly is going on?'

'Some government development scheme. A lot of little farmers are being forced off their land, and now the fucking eco-warriors have joined in.'

Killy almost bit on that one, but lecturing Arthur on social and ecological advances would go nowhere, so he stuck to business. 'Why didn't Furio say anything about it on the recce?'

'That was my first question, son, but he reckons the government was keeping it all hush-hush.'

'That's bollocks, Arthur, he must have known, he's the fucking fixer for fuck's sake.' Killy paused and took a deep breath as this was all going nowhere. 'Anyway, Arthur, it's too late now — we're in too deep.'

'Yeah and I'm whacked. I'm turning the light off, I've gotta sleep. I'll see you when you get here, son. Safe journey.' and on that, Arthur ended the call.

Ted turned his head. 'How's it all going out there, Kill?'

'A few problems. Nothing that can't be sorted out, mate.'

'If you don't mind, Kill, I got a question. Me brother-in-law was round last night and I told him I was picking up the first assistant director this morning, so he's asked me what you actually do on a film, so of course I realise I don't know exactly what it is you do …? And all I could tell him was how it has to be important, cos your name is always the first one when the crew credits roll over at the end of the film. And that's after *how* long we've been working together?'

'Too fucking long, Ted!'

He laughed. 'Yeah but seriously, Kill, I told him I'd ask you.'

'Alright.' He took a long pause and really thought the way through his answer. 'OK. I make sure that every bit of kit, every member of the cast, and every person on the crew is exactly where needed at every moment of the shoot, twenty-four-seven.

And if anything from a heart attack to an earthquake occurs, it's my job to deal with it and ensure that no matter what it takes, the job gets done and the producer has his show. That's what I do, Ted: I make it all happen, mate, as planned. Much better on the set than in my own life.' Killy stared at his face mirrored in the window, his head shaking in disbelief and outer London far from his thoughts. Dispossessed farmers might be a cause he and all of his crew would support themselves, but now it was a real-life situation he was going to have to deal with whilst shooting the picture he was on his way to the Caribbean to make. He thought the news over, trying again to get on top of it. 'Furio had to have known. That's what we pay a fixer for — to smooth a way round anything that could affect us. I've got a disaster of a script to sort out, a promising young director I've never worked with before, a lead actor Arthur had to accept to get the picture financed, and now our fixer's been asleep at the wheel. Fucking job's already a nightmare, and I haven't even got to Heathrow.'

Julian Burford-Brown, the director, was deeply embarrassed about having been late, and as he and Killian settled into a quiet corner of the business class lounge, an hour before their flight, he explained what had happened.

'It's our second baby, Killy. The poor little thing was screaming until two in the morning and it took me forever to get off to sleep. Fortunately, my alarm started her crying again and that actually woke me, or I might still have been in bed. My poor wife's got six weeks on her own, with two of them!'

'It's a tough one, Guv. Anyway, it's only for six weeks.'

Julian smiled, realising it was gentle banter, and as his phone rang, he excused himself and wandered across the lounge to take the call. Killy watched him, studying his body language, and then went and made himself a very strong cup of tea, all the while keeping an eye on the man he'd be working with practically every moment of every day for the coming weeks. He sipped his tea. 'Here we go again, Killy boy. You about to take the reins and give the director everything he needs to make 'his picture', while you both are working for Arthur, who as the producer thinks of it as '*his*' picture'. Funny old game, making films. No wonder only insiders understand how it works.'

Whilst most people would assume the director to be the boss it is, in fact, the First who plans the order of the day's work and pushes it along, so that the director gets enough time to film everything he or she wants to complete, but also ensuring that they finish each scheduled day on time and within the producer's budget. The director and the First have to operate as a team and so a lot of directors like to work with the same First whenever possible. Building mutual respect is the key and once that's established, apart from the odd inevitable disagreement, then everything should run smoothly. And so when they haven't worked together before, opportunities for the two individuals to spend time with each other, even in an airport lounge, are extremely important.

Julian finished his call and walked back to Killy, looking very definitely troubled.

'Coffee or tea, Julian?'

'Tea please, Killy, I don't drink coffee.'

'Me neither.' So there was a little link already, something they had in common. 'So what's the news from home?'

'It's the baby, Killy, they're taking her into hospital. That was Angela, my other half.'

Killy had to be careful with this situation, as Julian was clearly torn as to how to deal with it. 'Look, Julian, you have to do whatever is best for you and your family. If you want to stay here and make sure the baby is OK, and then come on out tomorrow or the next day, then that's what you must do.' As he said it, he was calculating how much of a problem that would be, whilst making sure that Julian understood he would have the full support of the production. 'Think it through, Julian, and if you feel hanging on for a couple of days would be best, I'll get Ted back here right now and he can drive you directly to the hospital.'

They walked across to their seats as Julian weighed up the pros and cons.

'We had a lot of problems with our little boy when he was born, and Angie is really upset, obviously, but she's tough. We just talked about whether or not I should stay ...' he paused. 'No point beating about the bush, Killy. This movie is too big of a break for me to miss out on, so we've agreed that I fly with you today, but if it's anything really serious I come straight back.'

What Killy thought was 'thank fuck for that' but what he actually said was, 'I think that's the best call, Julian. Have they given your wife any idea of what might be the problem with the baby?'

Julian was shaking his head and clearly still torn. 'No, and when they heard the symptoms they dispatched the medics right away. Angela was calling me from the ambulance.'

'Which hospital will they be taking her to, do you have any idea?'

'Royal Free, we're just around the corner.'

Killy phoned Alison, the second assistant director, his right-hand woman, as he walked back across the room. 'Morning, Ali, sorry to wake you. I'm at the airport and we've got a bit of a ...' he paused and was about to say 'drama', but even though Julian was once again on his phone and probably wouldn't be able to hear what Killy was saying, calling it that didn't seem fair, as the poor man was doing brilliantly at not turning it into one. '… A situation.' was what he finally said. 'Julian's new baby has just been taken into hospital.' Killy stood by the floor-to-ceiling windows, filling her in on what had happened as he looked down at what was probably the plane they'd be flying out on, as the ground crew hustled and bustled all around it in the growing daylight.

Alison, Killy's unflappable 'Second', two hours before she was due to get up and having doubtless gotten through at least a bottle of Rioja the night before, was fighting to pull her brain together as she took control. 'Hospitals won't speak to anyone other than immediate family, Kill. Can you put Julian on?'

'Excuse me, Guv … Alison, my Second, is going to call you. Ring him right now, Al.'

As Killy ended the call, his phone was buzzing; it was Richie Robbins, the movie's stunt coordinator .

'D'you know where I am, Kill?'

'No, mate, no idea at all.'

'I'm in hospital, with a bad fracture of my right leg. I don't believe it, mate!'

Neither did Killy. 'What happened, Rich? You OK?'

'Fine right now, Kill; doped up on painkillers. Just come out of the scanner.'

'So when did it happen?'

'Couple of hours ago. Been on nights all week. We had one more shot on a crash sequence to finish, and the boy who was supposed to drive twisted his ankle on a cable. The director was havin' a shit fit so I had to do it myself, and it was all a bit rushed, and I overshot it, flipped the bastard thing twice, and here I am in

Harley Street. Really sorry, Kill.'

This was exactly the type of problem he was paid a lot of money to sort out. Richie was clearly being well cared for, so the first objective was to try and fill the huge gap he was leaving.

'You sure you're alright, Rich? Nothing we can do?'

'Nothing, mate, they're really looking after me. I'm just sick about letting you all down.'

'Don't you worry, just get yourself mended and get back on your feet. Anyway, if you're sure you're OK, the first question is: who do you reckon could do it?'

'Yeah, been thinking about that. If he's free, and I reckon he is cos I know he's just come off the *Bond*, Wally's definitely your best bet. You got his number?' He paused. 'Gotta put the phone off, Kill, going back in with the Quack. Call Wally now, he'll be up.'

'Good luck, Rich, say hello to the missus.'

This was a real body blow. A medium budget film with a lot of action sequences, in a difficult and remote location, with a South American stunt team, and the key man, one of the best stunt coordinators in the business, was out of action. His conversation with Ali finished and now clearly less stressed, Julian looked over.

'Everything OK, Killy?'

'All good, Julian. I've got a couple more calls to make, excuse me. Have they announced our flight yet?'

'No, I just asked. They're a bit delayed.'

'Good. Did Ali sort things out?'

'She's amazing! She's taken everything over.'

'All part of the service, Guv. Anyway, give me a couple of minutes could you?'

He didn't want to get Julian involved at this stage, so he

wandered over to the window as he made the call.

'Wally? It's Killy.'

'Yeah, you flashed up on the screen, mate. How're you doing, Kill? Long time.'

'It is. Have you heard about Richie?'

'Yeah, on our group chat. Poor bastard. He'll be out for weeks and he shouldn't 'ave been doing it, anyway.'

'Yeah, well, I'm at Heathrow with the director, on our way out there. I've asked Rich and we agree you're the best man to jump in for him. What do ya reckon?'

Wally took a long pause. 'Well I just had six months away, so it could cost me my marriage ...' He paused again. 'You reckon Arthur'd pop for a ticket for the missus to come over there for a week, soften the blow?'

'Mate, if he won't, I'll buy her a ticket myself!'

Wally paused a long time. 'Alright then, Kill. She's already fed up with me hanging round the house: next it'll be a list of jobs, then it'll be nagging, and then ructions. So yeah, I'm on. Just so long as they don't try and screw me on the dough.'

'No fear of that. I'll talk to Arthur. Thanks, Wally, you're a gem!'

Killy walked back to Julian, who was gathering up his bits and pieces.

'They just called our flight, Killy. Is everything OK?'

'Yeah fine, Guv. I'll put you in the picture over a nice Bloody Mary!'

2

Bloody Marys were going to take a few minutes to organise, so they would have to make do with a glass of champagne, which wasn't really the tipple of choice for either of them at that hour of the morning. However, with a reassuring text having come from Julian's wife, and as the steward was already standing next to their seats offering it with a great big smile on his face, they both accepted a glass anyway.

'Cheers, Julian. What does she have to say?'

'The baby is settled and sleeping soundly, and the doctor now is certain it was a bad case of colic.' Julian read him the rest of the message and, as everything was sounding positive and the baby was responding to treatment, Killy's mind went back to the job and how Wally was going to work out. He raised his glass to Julian.

'Great news, Guv, I'm really happy for you. And here's to your family. And the job.'

They clinked glasses.

'And thanks, Killy, for stepping in like that. We all really appreciate it.'

Their super-deluxe side-by-side bed-seats were facing each other, with a low partition between them. Julian set out his pile of notes and looked across to Killy, and asked what it was he had to tell him. Killy put him in the picture as to what had happened to Richie, and how Wally Cox had agreed to step in.

'Have you worked with him before?'

'Yes, but it's been a while. Rich and I did a job and really got on, and you know what it's like in this game — chance brings you together, and if you click you try to keep up the connection.'

'So I take it Wally is as capable as Richie?'

'Blimey, yeah. Richie got his start with him, so Wally actually outranks him if you want to put it that way. I don't know how many *Bonds* he's done, but that's a world of its own, whereas Richie's worked on dozens of different pictures all over the world. We were looking forward to this one as it's been a while since we were away on a job together. Anyway, Julian, you and I have got a lot to talk about before we land, so if you don't mind I'm going to get my head down right now for an hour or two, and make up for all the morning's excitement.'

'I'm absolutely shattered myself, Killy, and I definitely have a lot of catching up to do. I've dealt with a fair amount of action stuff on commercials but I have to admit I might need my hand held a little on this.'

Killy lowered his seat, put his earplugs in, and slipped on his sleeping mask, now reassured that if Julian was candid enough to even mention needing help, there was a good chance they would work well together. It set his mind at rest regarding the director, but it was as close to sleep as he got.

There were too many questions needing answers — and not just those relating to the job. As ever, when he'd closed the door on his private life and followed Ted and his luggage out to the car, it still clung on to him, goading him every second of every day, and desperate as he was to sleep, he couldn't shake it off. It was Susie, his beloved ex. They had somehow managed to survive the turmoil that his career had dragged them through but it was definitely a long way from a straightforward relationship. Three years under a shared roof had been enough to shatter any illusions they ever had of their marriage being a long runner. She was nine years his senior and had come with Martín, her son, both of them having dealt with the sudden death of a much-loved father and husband. Killy's own childhood had been a disaster, mainly due to an alcoholic father and then losing his adored mum in his early teens, but through family friends just as he was starting out in the business, he'd gotten to know Susie and Martin. Over the course of about ten years they'd gradually adopted him and he them, and even if he couldn't be the perfect partner, Killy was determined to be a good father, and so Martin had become the bond. However, a big, black cloud was threatening their little family's complicated but settled existence.

The day before he'd left, Susie's GP had called to say that her recent mammogram had shown some abnormalities and that the practice was organising a scan. The bottom was falling out of Killy's world. And the one he was flying to wasn't sounding much better.

He gave up on sleeping and found the button that brought his seat upright. Julian was obviously out for the count, so he walked along to the little First Class bar area where the steward was mixing drinks.

'I haven't forgotten your Bloody Marys, señor; I was going to bring them to you but I saw you were sleeping. Shall I serve them now?'

'Just mine, please. I'll have it here, if that's OK?'

'Of course. Do you like it very spicy?'

'Not too spicy, thanks, but plenty of salt and lemon.'

'Of course. May I ask if you are going to San Lorenzo for business or pleasure, sir?'

'Well, I've been before, so there's definitely an element of pleasure, but let's say a bit of both this time.'

'Aha. Where on the island will you be staying?'

'Up in the North. We're based at Los Zapateros, do you know it?'

'I certainly do, we used to go scuba diving up there. It's beautiful.'

'Do you know the island well?'

He grinned. 'Very well, señor. I was born there and it's not so big. That area is quite undeveloped, do you mind if I ask what you're doing up there?'

'We're shooting a film and that's why we chose it; it's exactly what we need.'

'Oh really? What kind of a film?'

'Action-adventure with a romance thrown in for good measure.'

They chatted for quite a while about the island and why it worked for the film, and then a lot about the business of film making in general, until the steward noticed that Julian was sitting up.

'Your colleague is awake, señor,' then he glanced around and carried on in a definitely more subdued tone, 'I shouldn't be asking you this, but I'm crazy about movies and I have some leave time owed to me. I would love to work on a film. Will you be hiring, what do you call them, 'extras'?'

'We used to call them that but now they're 'supporting

artists', and we certainly shall be hiring a lot of them. If you are really interested, I can give you a number to call? Your English is excellent and that could be a big help to us.' The steward beamed. 'OK, I'd better get back to my seat. My colleague and I have got a lot to do. Why don't you bring us each a pot of strong tea? English breakfast please.'

Julian was already arranging his notes. 'I slept like the dead, Killy, you?'

'Not a wink, Julian, but I've had a great chat with our steward who was born and raised on the island, and certainly seems to know a lot about it. Wants to be an extra.'

'Did you manage to put him off?'

'No point. He's a movie nut and he's really keen. His English is better than mine. So why not give him a go?'

'Why not indeed? I need a cup of tea.'

'It's on its way.'

Julian was looking through a list of heads of department. 'The director of photography, Enzo Valente. Italian, I assume?'

'Yeah, Arthur loves Italian cinema, and he's desperate to produce films there but they keep managing to make it very difficult for him, so whenever Enzo's available, he likes to bring him on board as the cinematographer as a way to get in over there via the back door.'

Julian gave a knowing nod. 'And I notice there are a lot of ladies on the crew.'

'Well I don't like to generalise, Julian, but they're really great to be around and Arthur feels the same; they work bloody hard, and fortunately things have changed big time in the industry, so it's much easier now for them to get into all departments and move up the ladder. Long overdue in my book.'

Julian scanned up and down the lists of names and departments. 'It's a bit of a United Nations, isn't it? I like it. Italian camera crew, Marta Klein doing costumes, and Gloria Banks on makeup and hair.'

'Marta works in South and Central America a lot, so she brings her key people with her from New York and hires a local team of cutters and seamstresses. Gloria has a couple of Cuban hair and makeup artists she always works with on jobs on that side of the water, and they speak really good English.'

Julian smiled as he found a familiar name. 'Paddy Graham. He was the sound recordist on a commercial I did. Nice guy.'

'Yeah, Paddy's another one Arthur likes to have around: good bloke, steady, great company. Have you worked with any of the art department before? A lot of them are London-based.'

'Couple of names I recognise, but not the production designer, no. Alain du Clos: must be French, yes? Does he do a lot of work over there?'

'Alain works all over the world. Never stops.'

'And this place we're using, Los Zapateros. What's the story with that?'

'Obscurely, Guv, it means 'the boot menders'. It was a top-secret American base built in and around a disused canning factory, surrounded by thousands of acres of pineapple plantations. The Americans basically ran the island and over the years, Washington would install their choice of president, pay him off in Switzerland, and do exactly as they wanted — until the early seventies when they didn't need the base any more, so they just abandoned it. But not the island. They never completely gave up control of it, and, after going through several more presidents, they finally hit on one with a bit more business nous, and he has actually managed to put the island on the tourist map — but focussed down at the southern end around Nelson, the capital. Up at the northern end where we are, it's old-style Spanish Caribbean; undeveloped, and with nice, friendly, country people. Very definitely on the mañana system. Perfect for us.'

Julian looked up from his lists and set aside the notes he'd been taking. 'So, what's the political situation on the island right now? I tried to read up on it but there's very little available. Is it still linked to the US?'

As Killy started to answer, it flashed through his mind that with whatever was happening anti-government-wise at their airstrip, things might have changed once they'd landed. He decided he'd carry that one, himself; Julian already had enough to deal with.

'Not officially, but in reality it's always been a listening post for political activity in the region, and unless you know what you're looking for, it appears to be just another little holiday hideaway for wealthy middle-class yanks and Canadians, right alongside the local families who own all the businesses and the agriculture.'

'Which consists of, Killy?'

'A lot of coffee and lower grade tobacco that's used as filler for Cuban and Jamaican cigars, and they still grow really high-grade sugar cane, from which they make a spectacularly good rum that you may find yourself developing a bit of a taste for. The upside of the undercover operation is that the island is virtually crime-free. Drug business just can't get a toehold. The minute they make any sort of an attempt, the local police, heavily backed up by US DEA agents, literally disappear them. So you can wander around at night and, apart from the risk of falling coconuts, you're completely safe.

'I first came here with an American TV series and loved it. If you can speak a little bit of basic Spanish, you're laughing. The people are lovely, beaches are spotless and, as I say, it's safe as houses. The food is simple: wonderful fish, fresh vegetables and fruit, and the best rum in the world.'

'Well, what can I say? Lucky me, eh, Killy? To drop into it right out of the blue.' He took a pause, then after a second or two, he came out with what was clearly on his mind, 'So tell me: why did Karl Kramer walk? I didn't seem to be able to get a straight answer from anyone back in London.'

'Karl's special, Julian, or so he thinks. He's not satisfied with just being the director; he fancies himself as a producer, as well. He gets a producer's credit in his contract, which is fair enough as he's done a few successful movies, and once they get to that level, it makes sense to get paid a producer's fee, as well. But Karl likes to think of himself as the boss and chuck his weight around. Unfortunately for him, Arthur won't have anybody stealing his thunder. His attitude is, 'yes you're one of the producers but it's *my* picture'. They were like two big old bull walruses rearing up at each other on an arctic beach, but in the end it was Karl who backed down and waddled off, and you got a break.'

Julian nodded. 'Thank you. Here comes our tea, so let's have a look at that proposed shooting schedule.'

3

They worked right through the flight, only pausing to drink the endless pots of tea the steward brought them, and as they left the plane, Killy handed him his card.

'Phone that local number and tell them I told you to call about being an extra, and that's my name on the front. Thanks for looking after us. Hopefully see you again.'

As they came into the gate area, Killy was expecting their fixer to be there waiting for them, and mouthed to Julian, who was deep into a call with his wife, *'Give me a minute, I'm going to find Furio.'*

Then he saw him, weaving his way through the throng of disembarking passengers and dressed as ever in one of the severely crumpled linen suits that he must have bought by the dozen, with his tattered old hat crammed down on the huge mop of frizzy and greying black hair. Killy stood to the side of the corridor as he came towards him, and the smile on Furio's face faded as they shook hands.

'Que tal, Killy?'

'Not very good, Furio, I'm afraid; Arthur said there's been some kind of civil disturbance and that we might have to drive to the location?'

Furio was clearly trying to make light of it. 'Ah, no, Killy, everything has been settled. Your plane is waiting here to fly you up to Los Zapateros.'

'So what's going on? Why didn't you warn us this might happen?' Furio started to repeat the story he'd told Arthur but Killy shook his head. 'Furio, you're bullshitting me. You never mentioned any development deal and you're getting paid a lot of money to make sure we know if anything like that is likely to happen. What the fuck is going on?'

'I knew about the deal but it was not due to be finalised until long after we finish shooting. I assure you, Killy, everything is under control and an agreement has been reached with the demonstrators.'

The flow of passengers was gradually thinning out and Julian was waving and giving Killy the thumbs up. It was clearly not the time to carry on with the conversation, so Killy walked back to the gate with Furio following him.

'Furio, this is our director, señor Julian Burford-Brown. Julian, this is our fixer, Furio Asante.'

Furio didn't quite jump to attention, but immediately extended a hand. 'Very pleased to meet you, señor Julian ...?'

Julian shook it and gave him a smile. 'Julian is enough, Furio; too many other names.'

They both enjoyed the little joke. Furio indicated the direction they were going and then almost immediately punched a code into a digital display by a door to their left, and led them into the backstage world of the airport. He seemed to know everyone as they passed through various offices, and nobody questioned the presence of the two obvious outsiders with him. After a few minutes, he stopped in front of a door and knocked. It was opened by a uniformed official, who ushered them into a rather sparsely furnished room. He shook Furio's hand and as they exchanged a few pleasantries, he just about cast a glance at Julian and Killy as he took their passports, stamped them, and then stapled the landing cards they'd filled out on board to the appropriate pages. He handed them back, nodded to them both, then shook hands with Furio and opened a door that led outside, where an airport minibus was waiting, the driver standing by its open side door with all their bags loaded aboard.

Julian was clearly very impressed. 'Blimey, Killy, you can just imagine this at Heathrow, can't you?'

'In your dreams perhaps, Guv. Welcome to the world of Banana Republics; anything and everything possible.'

Furio jumped in next to the driver, who took the perimeter road all the way round to the domestic side of the airport, where a number of small aircraft were parked in front of a couple of nondescript hangars and a scruffy little control tower. Furio broke off from his highly animated chat up front as they pulled alongside a small, blue-and-white painted twin-engine plane.

'This is your aircraft, gentlemen.'

Its side door was already open and a young man came down the steps, smartly turned out in a uniform of white open-neck shirt, black trousers, and shoes. He greeted Furio and then shook hands all round. 'Please go aboard, gentlemen, while we stow your baggage. But be careful, the doorway is very low.'

Both around six feet, they had to bend over almost double to make their way forward to their single seats either side of the aisle, right behind the open door to the cockpit. The captain turned and saluted them, and in broken English said, 'Nice to have you on board, gentlemen.'

Furio stuck his head in the doorway and called along the aisle, 'Have a good flight, see you at the weekend.'

Killy turned around. 'I think we need a talk before then, Furio. I'll get Monika to arrange something.'

Furio nodded and backed away as the young man climbed in and drew up the steps behind him, then, having secured the door, made his way forward along the aisle and crouched down between them.

'Gentlemen, would you please fasten your seat belts. There is no smoking allowed on board. We will be in the air for approximately twenty minutes, so please sit back and enjoy your flight.'

He climbed through the doorway into the cockpit and took the co-pilot's seat, then turned and presented each of them with a couple of boiled sweets and a small bottle of water. And that was it for safety formalities and catering.

The captain pulled his headphones over his ears and started the engines, and as the twin propellers began to turn, Julian and Killy were peering directly through into the cockpit and smiling like little boys on a school trip. The plane started to move gently forward and with a slight surge of power, they rolled quickly out onto the runway and then shuddered to a halt.

After a minute or two, during which he spoke over the intercom with the control tower, the captain finally gave the thumbs up and gradually pushed forward on the power control set above his head. The plane juddered as the engines roared fully into life and the smell of aviation spirit came wafting through the cabin, as they accelerated down the tarmac then lifted off in what seemed no time at all. Suddenly they were up and out over the airport, as a great blanket of deep, lush green spread itself below, with the bright, blue sea in the distance.

The noise of the engines was deafening, and Julian looked

up from his phone and shouted across the aisle, 'Brilliant news from home! The baby is absolutely fine! Angela says it's as though nothing ever happened. She asked me to pass on her thanks for everything. And that has to be the coolest arrival ever, Killy! Does everyone get that treatment?'

He shouted back, 'No way, Guv! Why do you think I flew out with you?'

Killy sat back as best he could in the small leather bucket seat, staring down at the countryside as his mind wandered over what Furio had said, but more the way he had said it. Something didn't feel right. The backdoor treatment at the airport had gone without a hitch, and evidently the local disruption had been resolved, but his problem-predicting radar was pinging loudly as they flew over the cane fields, the hills, and the endless coconut palms.

But then he started to question the way he'd jumped on Furio as soon as they'd met. Was that fair? He'd basically convicted him before finding out any more than Arthur had told him, and with an already complicated scenario opening up, he might have done better to give the guy the benefit of the doubt for the time being. And so it went on, all the way across the island; should have, shouldn't have … As they finally started to drop out of the sky, Killy looked down at the little airstrip and his eye was immediately drawn to a brilliant-white Lear Jet with the US flag and registration; it stood out amongst the collection of run-of-the-mill planes like a Bugatti in a Lidl car park. The aeronautical equivalent of Jeeps, they were powerful, reliable workhorses, nothing fussy, and most of them at least twenty or thirty years old. The little strip was owned and operated by the rich-to-very-rich residents; people who could afford one of the fabulous villas that lined the beautiful beaches and needed to be able to fly into the capital to shop or, whenever necessary, directly into Miami for business.

As the propellers stopped, the young officer bent himself through from the cockpit and along to the door, opened it, and lowered the steps. Killy and Julian both thanked the captain, who was obviously staying on board, then followed the young man out into the glaring sunlight.

'I hope you enjoyed your flight. The ground crew will take your bags to your vehicle. Have a good day.' He shook hands with them and then climbed back up the steps, and as they walked under the wing and turned towards the little collection of maintenance hangars and the control tower, there was Monika waving to them and looking every bit as tall, tanned, and trim as Killy remembered her.

She ran over and hugged Killy. 'It's lovely to see you, guapo! Welcome to Los Zapateros.'

'And you too, guapa! Julian, this is Monika Sanchez, our production manager.'

Julian put out his hand to take hers. 'Nice to meet you, Monika.'

'Welcome to Los Zapateros, Julian, lovely to meet you too. So, gentlemen, let's get your bags organised and show you to your new homes. I've arranged a little brunch, so we can all catch up and work out a plan for tomorrow morning.'

Killy was focussing on the Lear jet. 'Anything to do with us?'

She shrugged and drew a deep breath. 'Well, yes, in a way it is. Arthur flew in on it this morning with Nathan Bedford's business manager.'

He laughed. 'Arthur Margolies, coming to work in a Lear

jet? He's changed his style.'

'No, Killy, the plane is on charter to Mister Bedford and he's flown his manager here to check up on his accommodations for the shoot.' The two of them shared a look and then Monika went off to sort their baggage with the ground crew.

Killy smiled at Julian and slowly shook his head.

'I could smell Hollywood bullshit rising up from that plane, Julian. I knew it. I'd never even heard of Nathan Bedford, and now he's jetting his fucking manager out from LA to *check on his accommodations?* I mean, fuck me gently!'

Julian laughed out loud. 'Don't sit on the fence, Killy, speak your mind!'

Their air-conditioned bungalows under the palms were only a minute back from the beach, beautifully furnished, and each with its own well-equipped little kitchen. Killy dumped his bags on the bed, rooted out a pair of swimmers, and within five minutes was rolling around in the sea.

A swim, a quick shower, and a shave, and he was on his way to the garden restaurant by the crumbling old main buildings of the complex, and there under a beautiful banana leaf umbrella sat the boss; the man himself, their producer, 'King Arthur' Margolies.

'Hello, Killy boy!' His foghorn of a voice blasted its way through the glorious tropical midday air. 'How's it swinging?'

'Not too far and not nearly often enough, Arthur!'

'Load of old bollocks, son. Coupla weeks, and you'll be right back in the saddle.' They both laughed as Killy sat across the table from him and poured himself a glass of water.

'First thing, Arthur; I take it everything went alright with Wally? Monika tells me he'll be here tomorrow.'

'Yes. Well done for getting him, even though he stuck me for a pair of tickets for his missus and her mum. But all things considered we're lucky he was free, or I dunno who we'd have got. It's really busy at the moment, thank god!'

'So tell me: what's with the Lear jet and the manager, Arthur?'

'You tell me, son. It's all I need at half a million dollars plus exes; a reality TV star, who I hear can't act his arse onto a toilet seat, who's got around five hundred and fifty million teenage girls following his every move on social media, sending his oily rag down here to suss out his fucking digs! I ask ya! Monika just took him over to look at the villa. Gary's had his boys working on it for over a week now and it's the best there is anywhere on the island, but when 'Mister Bedford' got the video we sent, he decided he didn't like the décor, so he wanted the whole gaff completely repainted and a new kitchen put in. For two fucking weeks!? The owner's laughing his nuts off. Him and his missus only come out here for a month each year, so they're getting a complete refurb on top of the rent — and you really don't wanna know how much *that* is. I tell you, son, the movie game is getting totally out of control. Oops, here's the boss-lady!'

Monika was walking across the garden followed by Julian, as Arthur hauled his six-foot tall twenty-stone body up to greet them. He was dressed in a violently vivid purple tropical shirt, and ridiculous matching shorts that set the whole thing off disastrously; their beloved boss in all his tasteless glory.

'Julian, lovely to see you. I'm happy to hear things have calmed down with the family. You must be relieved. There's nothing worse than being away on a job when something like that's going on back at home. Sit next to me. What would you like to drink? Monika, darlin', get someone to serve us would you please? And where's our manager friend?'

She gave him a look of disgust. 'Our *friend*, Arthur, is having a quick shower. Then he'll join us, but only for a drink. He wants to be on his way. It now appears his master, Nathan Bedford, wants a pool for his children because they're too frightened of sharks for them to swim in the sea. And it has to be a minimum of fifteen metres long! These people are insane! Excuse me, Arthur, but would you mind telling the gentleman that I had to go back to the office and then as soon as he's left, I'll join you?' She stalked off, calling out to the kitchen to send someone to look after them.

Arthur was so incensed by what she'd said he was having trouble breathing. 'Excuse me, gents. Got to have a little chat with this guy.'

Killy looked at Julian. 'Great start, eh, Guv?'

4

According to Monika, Arthur's 'little chat' with Bedford's manager had started with him almost battering down the door to the man's room, and then got more and more heated as it carried on into the car that drove them both out to the airstrip. As she spoke, the three of them sitting in the shade, tucking into a by now very welcome meal prepared and served by the local family who ran the kitchen, heard the distinctive sound of the Lear jet taking off.

Jumping out from under the umbrella, Monika pointed up over the trees behind them. 'There he goes, the little *hijo de puta!*'

Julian looked at Killy inquisitively, as he mouthed, *'Son of a prostitute, Julian.'*

Arthur roared into the garden, 'That fucking little shyster! Monika, get Nick on my private line will you, please? This has got to be sorted out right now. What's the time in London?' He looked at his Big Ben-sized watch. 'Yeah, he should still be in his office — and if not, get him on his mobile. Nathan fucking Bedford! He's bringing his wife, two kids, a nanny, and his personal fucking chef. And now he wants a pool! Sorry, boys, enjoy your lunch. I might not see you this evening, but I'll drop into the HoD meeting and say hello to everyone — if I don't have a fucking heart attack first. Monika, darlin', get the kitchen to serve mine in my office, please.

See you later, fellas.'

Arthur scooped up a handful of some tasty little add-ons to their meal and thundered off, with Monika close behind him. As they got to the other side of the garden she turned and smiled, shaking her head with a, *can you believe this?* expression lighting up her face.

Julian was chuckling. 'Is he always that animated, Killy?'

"*Animated*'? Yeah, animated's good, Julian. 1 mean, I have actually seen him more fired up, but this wasn't a bad example of King Arthur in pissed-off mode. Pretty fucking scary, eh? I bet 'Mr Manager' won't forget his little ride to the airstrip for a very long time. This wine's a bit corky. Happens a lot here; they don't take proper care of it unless it's top of the line — which Arthur won't stretch to, other than for special occasions. So, what's the latest from home? Is it good?'

'Very, but they're going to hold on to her and Angela overnight, just to be absolutely sure, and they should be home in the morning. What a relief. We were terrified we were going to lose her. Please pass on my thanks to Alison.'

'Thank her yourself, Julian, she's coming in on tomorrow's flight. D'you fancy a wander round the grounds a bit later? Might as well while we have the chance. Maybe meet up back here in an hour or so?'

'Good idea, yes.'

'I'll get them to bring some beers over. What's your house number, Julian?'

'I think it's thirty-nine.'

'My age,' Killy thought.

A couple of minutes after Killy got in, the young lad who had done most of the waiting at their table was tapping on his door with the beers. He tipped him and sent him on to Julian's, set his bottle on the stand by the bed, kicked off his shoes, and by force of habit — to avoid any unpleasant surprises — called Alison back in London. 'Hello, beauty, are you packing your bags?'

'All done, Kill. Is everything calming down after Hurricane Arthur? I had Monika on; sounds like it's going to be fun.'

'It'll be fine. Gary'll build the pool and Arthur will find a little loophole in the contract and chisel the cost of it back, plus a grand or two for his trouble. He's got Nick Lombard on his side, so Bedford's management are going to get a lesson in why not to mess around with the toughest showbiz lawyer in London. Is everything else sorted?'

'Yes. I'm going to have a nice, slow evening, a couple of bevvies, then a really early night, and that's it. Ted's picking me up first thing and moaning me all the way to Heathrow, so hopefully I'll see you at lunchtime tomorrow.'

'Good girl. And well done on sorting out the director. He seems a lovely bloke. Still got to see him under fire, but so far so good. Safe journey, Al. Lotsa love.'

Assured all was well on the job front, he called home and checked in with Susie, who wasn't up for a chat because, despite his efforts to get out of the house unheard, Ted's foghorn of a voice had managed to penetrate her cocoon and she'd need at least a day to get her humour back. Her tone when she answered was enough to tell him to keep it short and to the point, so he just checked that there was no more news on her scan, apologised for Ted, said goodbye, and left it at that.

Then Arthur called. 'What do you think about Julian: can he handle it? It's going to be a tough one, I can smell it … Killy, you still there? Tell me what you think. Is he going to cut the mustard?'

'He's going to be fine, Arthur. From what I've seen of him today, he's not full of bullshit and he's been around enough to have a good idea of what's in store. I like the guy, and if he shapes up the way I think he will, I reckon you picked a winner there.'

'Lovely, son, just what I wanted to hear. See you in the morning.'

Their look around the gardens didn't happen; Killy got deep into preparing for the HoD meeting, and Julian fell asleep.

...

They met up on the beach at seven the next morning. The water was beautifully cool; a perfect start to what was going to be a long, hot day. Both jet-lagged, they were drinking tea in the garden as the kitchen clattered into life.

'Julian, I'm thinking after breakfast, rather than sitting around here discussing everything all morning, it might be an idea to take a drive over to the old base so you can start to familiarise yourself with it. Alain's been here for a month already.'

Julian nodded. 'Alain du Clos, yes, our globe-trotting production designer?'

'Spot on, guv. He can give us the grand tour, then you can have a wander round and check if there's any areas of the place that look interesting to you, shots-wise. What do you think?'

'Sounds like a plan, Killy.'

'Right. I'll get Monika to sort out transport. Here's the glamour girl herself. *Buenos dias,* señora.'

Dressed in a chic linen safari suit, she came across the garden like a model striding the Madrid catwalk, where her movie-making career had begun. 'Good morning, gentlemen. Everything

41

alright with your accommodations?'

Killy made a sad face. 'Don't we get our own swimming pools?'

They stood up to greet her and were rewarded with warm but business-like kisses on both cheeks.

'Mine's perfect. Thank you, Monika.'

'You're welcome, Julian.' She smiled at Killy.

He nodded. 'Mine too, thank you. So we thought it would be a good idea to spend the morning over at the base and that way Julian can get some time with Alain, and I can familiarise myself with everything before the meeting. Could you sort out transport?'

'The driver's outside; I read your mind. And the London flight is delayed, I'm afraid, so by the time they all get here and settled in, it might be sensible to push the meeting back until tomorrow morning; which would suit me better and mean that everyone can have a chance to acclimatise after the flight. What do you think?'

'Good call, darlin', it was all going to be a bit rushed anyway. Shall we have a look at the buffet?'

She led them over to the long, wooden table in the centre of the garden, beautifully dressed with banana leaves, flowers, and big baskets of fruit. 'It's fresh-squeezed orange juice, fruit, eggs, and toast until we start shooting, and then if you want it English-style, they'll be serving bacon and eggs. If you'll excuse me, I've got to get back to the office, so I'll leave you to it.'

Half an hour later, they were sitting in the rear seat of a four-wheel drive, bumping along the track that was all that remained of the old plantation's main road — and which was now a real third-world extravaganza. The locals lived in simple shacks with corrugated steel roofs, that lined the route along both sides of what had become a disastrously rutted trail, and at that hour of the morning everything was coming to life.

Charcoal was the local cooking fuel, and in the cool morning air the smoke from it formed a thin, eye-level, horizontal cloud across the track. A lady selling bread was wandering along, calling out her wares at the top of her voice, with little loaves piled on a woven tray she carried on her head. They passed a stall selling what was obviously meat but completely covered in a heaving, crawling coat of fat, black flies. After every dozen or so huts there would be fruit and vegetable stands, stacked to the roof with amazing arrays; anything in the way of fresh-grown produce that anyone might want.

There were packs of kids grinning from ear to ear running alongside them, holding out their hands and asking for pesos, as the driver did his best to steer the impossible road and not run them over, while they laughed and shouted as the vehicle bounced all over the place, amusing them even more.

Julian was popping off photos right and left. 'I promised Angela some pics, and I know she'll love seeing these boys and girls and all the shops. Is anyone selling fish? I don't see any.'

'You won't, Julian, they sell it straight from the boat. You can go on your day off and get it cooked right there on the beach, if you like.'

They slithered to a halt as a goat parked itself directly in their path. Their driver was blasting away on the horn and yelling a stream of wonderful Spanish obscenities at the top of his voice, presumably to get it moved. There was nothing to do but laugh and go along with it.

'Day one, Guv! Only a couple of months, and we'll be on our way home.'

Julian looked up from the notes he was trying to make. 'Is it a dirt road all the way?'

Killy asked the driver, who assured him it was only about another few hundred metres and they'd be on a concrete road that the 'Yanquis', as the locals called the Americans, had built to take heavy trucks to the base. They drove onto it after a few minutes and then, apart from some massive potholes and a couple of points where the road edges had sunk into the boggy ground, it became pretty smooth going.

The old plantation they'd been driving through now had reverted to tropical forest, which over the years had started to encroach upon the cleared right of way either side of the concrete. In places, there were trees overhanging and low, bushy undergrowth growing right along the roadside. Julian looked up from his notes.

'Uncle Sam found a great place for his secret base but now Mother Nature's claiming it back. Killy, tell me: when do the extras start arriving? Particularly the ones who are supposed to be the American marines? I'd like to see if they look like military men.'

'They'll be up here tomorrow.'

'And what about their costumes?'

'Tomorrow, too. Marta and her wardrobe team will be bringing them up by boat.'

Julian was nodding. 'And the armaments?'

'Tomorrow as well, hopefully. Getting about a thousand imitation rifles and machine guns, and about fifteen tons of blank ammunition, all cleared through customs in this place could take you a lifetime. Furio's got it all sorted, cos if you don't pay them off, they inspect everything down to the very last bullet. I speak from bitter experience.'

They pulled up to the weathered red-and-white barrier that was lowered across the entrance to the base, and the driver jumped out and pushed it up. The derelict guard post still carried the faded warning in English and Spanish:

Private Property.

All visitors report to security.

The base had originally been completely enclosed by three fifteen-foot-high parallel razor-wire fences, now badly rusted, with old skull and crossbones signs showing they'd been electrified.

Julian was like a kid in a toy shop. 'This place is incredible! Obviously it's been here for years, but who actually put us onto it?'

'Furio. He'd been mates with a cousin of the president at university. As soon as he saw it, Furio knew it would be perfect for film and TV shoots, so when Arthur told him what we were looking for, that was it.'

'Somebody should turn this whole place into a studio, Killy. You could do all kinds of things here. I'd bet Spielberg would buy this in a heartbeat!'

'Good idea, Guv. Why not phone him? Anyway, back to reality. The southern end of the island is doing very well out of tourism, but this end needs a massive infrastructure upgrade: roads, electricity, water — you've seen what it's like. The president's cousin is just sitting on it, they're in no rush. He's agreed to unofficially lease it to us through Furio and give us a good deal on the fees, which are not cheap.'

The driver let them out by one of a line of massive hangars, around thirty feet high, with curved concrete roofs at least two feet thick, and all completely grown over with vegetation.

Julian stood staring up at the plant cover. 'Designed to

be undetectable from the air and to take anything other than an atomic bomb.'

Killy nodded. He was peering into the hangar as Alain came walking towards him, his arms spread wide.

''ello, Killy, mon vieux RosBif! Good to see you, my friend. Welcome to my cavern — it's wonderful, *non?*' They hugged each other and did a lot of back slapping.

'Salut, Alain, you froggie bastard. Come and say hello, Julian, Alain's here!'

Julian was up on the roof waving at them. 'Nice to meet you, Alain, I'll be right down.'

Alain waved back up to him, clearly charmed by Julian's childlike joy in this big, new toy, and when he'd scrambled down they shook hands and it was immediately obvious to Killy they were going to work well together. Alain; a fit and very young fifty, with years in the business of creating the look and feel of dozens of films, and Julian; a director, bright enough to realise that filmmaking is a team effort and that no matter how brilliant everyone says you are because it's 'your movie', it's every member of the cast and crew working together that brings the director success and a reputation. They were a great match.

'So, Alain, what're the chances of you showing us around?'

'Of course, Killy. The sets for the flashback scenes are almost finished, so follow me, gentlemen.'

He led them into the hangar's cool, dark interior, where supported on a framework of scaffolding were two lines of prison cells facing each other across a corridor. To the naked eye, even close up, it was a steel-barred, high-security cell block, but in fact was made entirely of plywood, paper, plastic, and paint. Alain's team of artists were putting the finishing touches to the bars as

Julian wandered around introducing himself and shaking hands with them. There was no real hustle or bustle, everyone worked away quietly on their own sections; a real artist's workshop in the middle of a tropical rainforest. Alain was clearly impressed by his appreciation of the team and their work.

'Are you ready to move on, Julian? I'd like you to see my favourite, over here.' They followed him across to another, much taller set.

'Oh wow, Alain! The torture chamber! This is brilliant!'

Julian stood in the middle of what looked like a huge, dank, and deep underground dungeon. There was a terrifying-looking stainless steel operating table in the centre, with manacles, chains, ropes and pulleys hanging over it, and a huge circular saw blade set in a slot running right along its length. Alain was standing by a bank of big, antiquated electrical switches.

'Please come over here next to me, I want to show you something.' They joined him as he pressed a real switch, hidden behind the false ones, setting the table's blade spinning and gradually moving along its length.

Killy shouted above the screeching din it was making, 'You fucking French weirdo! You really love all this stuff don't you?'

Alain switched it off, laughing as the blade stopped. 'Eat out your heart, Monsieur Bond!' He gave them a truly grotesque grin. 'Killy, you like sports but I find pleasure in other things. Perhaps you'd like to join me on our day off?'

'I'd like to think you were joking, Alain, but Julian and I are respectable Englishmen. S&M for you, maybe, but definitely M&S for us!' Killy's phone was buzzing. 'Excuse me, gents, it's Monika. I think they have a branch in Paris now, don't they, Julian?' He ran back across the vast concrete floor and into the sunlight. 'Hola guapa! Yes, I can hear you now. Is everything alright?'

Monika's voice had stopped breaking up. 'Yes, everything's fine, and the London flight is back on time. Do you want to go ahead with the meeting later today, or stick to plan B and do it in the morning?'

'No, let's do it in the morning. I think Julian would prefer to spend the day here, we've only looked at a couple of the set builds. So yes, straight after breakfast. Anything else?'

'Carmen says someone you'd met called the office about being an extra? A steward on your flight?'

'Ah, good! I hoped he would. He'll be a bit wasted as an extra, though, his English is perfect. He's mad about movies, so I was thinking if he did show up we should give him a go as a runner if he fancies it? He'll certainly get to see a lot more of how it's done. Tell Carmen if he's interested, to get him on the crew boat in the morning. What do we have in the way of accommodation?'

'I'll get him a room in the men's quarters. Do you want me to bring him to see you?'

'If you could, that would be great. I can't even remember if I got his name.'

'It's a traditional one: Gustavo. You won't forget that.'

'No, not run into that one before. So yes, for sure; look after him. If he comes, that is.'

5

Alain drove out of the hangar in an ancient four-wheel drive with Julian in the passenger seat.

'We're going to see the work at the exterior guerrilla camp, Killy. They're starting to build the shelters and digging the escape tunnel. Are you coming?'

Killy jumped in and Alain drove them along the road to an opening in the fence, and onto a meshed steel temporary road surface that had been rolled out for a couple of hundred yards through really dense undergrowth. He parked where it ended, in a line of medium-sized trucks and a small trailer-mounted generator, that was powering cables laid along a narrow pathway leading further into the bushes.

'Follow me, gentleman. And stay to the sides of the cables, please, so we keep disturbance to a minimum for when we start shooting, as it's all supposed to be completely untouched.'

They followed him through about fifty yards of bushes and small trees, as occasional shafts of sunlight broke through the great tropical canopy above. The set was a part-cleared space, where two of Alain's team were supervising a group of young local trainees fashioning a jungle hideout.

Julian was right beside Alain. 'I see they leave a lot of the smaller trees as they clear the place. Is that how it's done, Alain?'

'Natalie, the lady in the green T-shirt, spent ten years in

Colombia with the FARC building and living in camps just like this, Julian, and it's exactly how it's done.' He called over to her and she turned and gave them a gentle smile and a nod of the head, as Alain continued, 'This is Natalie's project; she chose the best spot and cleared only what was necessary, saving everything else for the roofs and those little sleeping platforms.'

Julian was nodding, taking it all in. 'So, no walls necessary in this climate, just somewhere off the ground to sleep and a roof to keep the rain off?'

'They throw these camps up really quickly. Everything you need is there as long as you know how to use it. If you come over here, you can see how they're creating the exit from an escape tunnel.'

They followed him into the clearing where a team of local workers were laughing and joking as they dug and, judging by their sweat-stained shirts, they'd obviously been at it for some time. Alain pointed down the hole.

'We've lined the shaft with planks purely for safety, Julian. In reality, they would weave small branches into a long, very strong tube to retain the soil. We replicate that in fibreglass and paint it, so it looks to the camera just like the real thing, and then slide it down into the shaft with ventilation tubes to provide fresh air for the actors.'

Julian interjected, 'Alain, what about the tunnel sequence where our hero chases the guerrilla leader; are you building a false one of those?'

'We'll start that next, Julian. I need to speak to you and Enzo about the dimensions you'll need it to be. But yes, it will all be done where we're going next.'

Alain then drove them to the second of the hangars, where

an exact copy of the camp they'd just left was being built indoors. He pointed up into the roof. 'The riggers have suspended a gallery up there to take the lights, and beneath them a network of hoses so we can have our own indoor weather system. The afternoon rains will be starting soon and in this way, if things outside get too difficult, we have controllable rainfall inside. What do you think, Julian?'

'Perfect. A lot of the guerrilla camp scenes are at night so, if necessary, we can shoot all of them in here and just use the exterior one to establish it — and then for the big attack sequence with all the explosions. It's brilliant, Alain, thank you.'

'You're welcome, Julian. So, gentlemen, let's go to the cannery.'

This was right on the shore; a huge, rambling expanse of old brick, crumbling concrete, and rusting steel, with a long rock jetty that ran out into the sea for about a hundred yards.

Julian opened his door and left them. 'I have to get some pictures of this place from out at the end.'

Alain sat at the wheel smoking and chatting in French on his phone, as Killy watched Julian popping off pictures all the way along the jetty, enjoying the way these two key creatives had hit it off.

But as ever with Killy, reflecting on the positives only served to start him thinking about what wasn't going well. Whilst it was Furio they had to thank for the whole extraordinary facility they were working on, the fact was that Furio had exposed them to what might turn into a serious political situation, and as the First, would mean him having to get them out of it. But as Julian walked back along the jetty, clearly very content with what he'd been gifted as a key location for the film, Killy had to force himself out of the gloomy place his thoughts were taking him.

They thanked Alain and were picked up by their driver, but were slowed down almost immediately on the way back by rain that came out of nowhere. The trail rapidly began turning into little more than a river of sloppy, rich, red mud which splattered everything as they bounced and bucked their way along — but without the kids, the bread lady, and seemingly everyone else.

Julian peered out through the mud-smeared windows. 'Now I understand why you wanted me to experience what driving to work everyday would entail. It would render me insane, Killy, and you'd certainly never get crew buses along in this. That reminds me: have you had any word on the location for the party scenes?'

'Well, with it having to have gardens and be ritzy inside and out, and be close enough to the capital for the supporting artists to drive to in a couple of hours, max, that's a very big ask, Julian. There's obviously places on the island that would work but from what Monika tells me, they're either too expensive to hire, geographically wrong, or just unavailable. I'm not losing sleep over it yet, but if it doesn't get sorted soon I very definitely will be.'

The driver dropped them off outside the production office. Julian gathered his notes.

'Fuck that for a game of soldiers, Killy! Definitely a once-in-a-lifetime experience. I'm going to have a shower and make a few calls. Do you fancy meeting up later on for a bite of supper? I'm starving.'

'Yup, I'm going for a dip right now. See you in the garden around eight?'

About half an hour later, as he finished his swim, a man was paddling a canoe towards the beach; a big guy with an amazing physique, like a lot of the locals who were descendants of the slaves brought by the Spanish to work on the sugar plantations. As he jumped out and started pulling the boat up onto the sand, Killy helped him.

The man grinned. 'Americano?'

'No señor, ingles.'

'Ah!' He seemed pleased. 'Bueno.' He pulled a netting sack full of fish from the back of the boat and Killy pointed towards it.

'Es posible comprar pescado?'

The man's face broke out in a huge, questioning smile, 'Claro, señor!' and a look that said, *of course you can buy them, what do you think I caught them for?* which made them both laugh. He emptied them out onto the sand, about a dozen of different colours. They looked beautiful lying there, glistening in the sunlight, and Killy pointed at a big, bright blue one. 'Cuánto vale el azul?'

The man picked it up by its now sand-covered gills, felt the weight, and held up five huge fingers. 'Cinco dólares.'

Realising he had no money with him and he needed a couple of minutes to run back to the house, Killy held up his hand. 'Momentito, tengo plata en la casa. Dos minutos, por favor.' He turned and jogged back through the trees and into the house, grabbed his wallet, then ran back and gave him the five dollars, thanked him, and carried off his prize by the gills.

'Do you fancy this for supper, Julian? Fresh as a daisy.'

Julian stood in his doorway, obviously amused. 'Where did you get that? It's a beauty! What is it, some kind of grouper?'

'No idea, I already stretched my Spanish to breaking point getting this far. But it's straight from the sea, and I'm going over to the kitchen to ask them to cook it for us this evening. You still good for eight?'

'Perfect. What will they serve it with?'

'Anything you like, I'm sure. Sweet potato, rice, salad?'

'All of those, please! Thanks, that's really kind.'

Things were busy in the kitchen. Killy laid the fish on the counter and called to the lady in charge. She laughed out loud and mimed using a fishing rod, as she asked him in her almost impenetrable local Spanish accent if he'd caught it himself. He laughed and luckily remembered the Spanish for fisherman.

'No, señora. El pescador.'

'Ah, Papon!' She took it from him and judged its weight admiringly. 'Muy bonito.'

That was the easy part, and Papon was the fisherman's name, so now came the technical bit. He knew the key words, 'cook' and 'oven', and 'director' was the same, so he took the plunge, 'Señora, es posible para usted cocinar en el horno para mí y el director?'

She smiled and nodded. 'Si, señor. A que hora?'

Clearly she'd understood, and the time, eight o'clock, was easy. 'Ocho horas, por favor.'

'Con patatas y ensalada, señor?'

He gave her a big thumbs up for potatoes and salad and then remembered Julian wanting rice. 'Y un poquito arroz, por favor. Muchas gracias, señora.' He was so delighted he'd sorted it all out, as he turned to go he realised he hadn't asked her name. He pointed at himself. 'Perdona, señora, me llamo Killy. Y usted?'

'Rosalía, señor … señor Killy!'

'Gracias, Rosalía. Hasta ocho horas.' So that was an eight o'clock supper organised. His phone buzzed as he walked indoors. It was Monika.

'How was the recce, Killy? Is Julian happy?'

'Very happy. Especially as he gets a ten-minute walk by the sea each morning and doesn't have that drive. See you in a minute, I just need to shower and change.' He saw a missed call from Arthur and phoned him.

'Hello, son. I spoke to Alain and he reckoned everything had gone well with Julian. Really liked him.'

'Yup, they clicked instantly. Julian had a few suggestions, all of them workable, he loved the set builds, and he's potty over the cannery. Very good day, all in all. Had any joy with the party location?'

'No, son. And there's no way the budget will stand a build like that, we're miles over already. I think we might have to stage it somewhere a bit less opulent.'

'Funny you should say that, Arthur, Julian mentioned he'd been thinking along those lines on the way back. So, if push comes to shove ...?'

'What time are you eating tonight? I might join you.'

'Yeah, do. Eight alright?'

'That's a date, son. I look forward to it.'

The production office, or 'Production' as it's known, was housed in the buildings that had been the old cannery's school; in a far better condition than everywhere else, and very comfortable for the team who were responsible for everything from a quarter-of-a-million-dollar camera, right down to a dummy bullet in a leather bandolier across an extra's chest.

Monika was on the phone at her desk and motioned for Killy to sit opposite her as she ended the call. 'That was another possibility for the party location, but it's too near the airport. This is becoming a real pain, Killy. If we don't find something soon, it's going to upset the whole schedule.

'Surely Furio must know people who own the type of property we need. Have you spoken to him?'

'Yes, he called to say the flight had arrived on time and that he'd got everyone organised. I told him that none of the location leads he'd given me for the party had worked out.'

'What did he say?'

'He said he'd make some more calls as soon as he had time.'

'Well, let's hope he has some time soon, we're certainly paying him enough for it. Are you eating tonight?'

'No thanks, too much to finish. Maybe a beer later?'

He went and knocked on the production accountant's door and walked in. 'How are you doing, Chris? Everything falling into place?'

'Slowly but surely, Kill. All the usual last-minute dramas; money transfers going adrift, wages to locals held up for lack of dollars. Same old, same old. You?'

'Not too bad, thanks. I'm having a bit of supper with Julian and Arthur. Fancy it?'

'No thanks, mate. I've already spent hours locking horns with his majesty over the budget, so that's enough for today.'

Killy wandered down the corridor, trying to imagine himself doing a job like Chris': keeping on top of every hour worked by every person in every department, from day one until they wrapped; every item purchased, every penny spent; whilst shut away in an office and with a boss like Arthur, who at any moment of the day or night might want to know exactly how much of his money had been spent or was spoken for. As he stepped out through the main door, walking towards him was Gloria, the tall, glamorous ex-model and highly respected head of the make-up and hair department. Killy walked towards her.

'Hello, beautiful!' They gave each other a hug, then stood back, hands resting on each other's shoulders. 'How was the flight?'

'Funny you should ask, Killy. Excuse my French but it was fucking terrible, thank you! That airline we flew out on is completely useless. All my kit arrived but they've lost my suitcases! Turns out they're still sitting in terminal five!'

'Don't worry, G. I'll get it sorted, promise. Let's have a little bevvy and a catch up after dinner, yeah?'

Still with her hands on his shoulders, she cocked her head to one side and stared at him. 'Wally Cox on the picture, Killy?'

His jaw dropped. 'Oh fuck, G! I didn't think! We were so relieved to get him! I don't know what to say, love …'

'Well that's a first, Killy Wilde. Thank god *she* didn't come to see him off. I might be lying dead in the airport, along with my luggage.' She smiled to let him know he was off the hook. 'Don't worry, Kill, we talked it through on the plane and we'll handle it. You should have seen us at the check-in, I don't know who was more shocked. Anyway, I need to sort out a few bits of drag to see me over; is Monika in her office?'

Killy nodded, still rendered almost speechless. 'Yeah, straight down to the end, G.' She gave him a wink and marched along the corridor, leaving him shaking his head in disbelief. 'How could I have let that one past me? You fucking idiot, Killy.'

Wally had been stunt doubling for the lead actor on the film that had gotten him and Gloria into trouble. They were spending a lot of time together as she fitted him with a wig to match the star's hair. They discovered they shared the same birthdate and that got things moving, but it was the wig fittings and rather a lot more of them than was usually required — that lead on to romance.

They'd managed to keep it all under wraps, or so they'd thought, but were spotted together on a day off, holding hands across a table in a little restaurant miles from the location, and the word got around amongst the crew. By breakfast the next day, in fact. Gloria got a call from the married director she'd been having a thing with, to say he'd just called Wally's wife to tell her the news. It was that quick. These things can happen with film crews away from home often for weeks, or indeed months, but this particular affair hadn't ended well for any of the people involved. Gloria was dumped by the director and Wally had come very close to divorce.

...

Killy picked up Julian on the way and as he'd hoped, all the gang who'd just flown in were already eating at tables around the garden. It went a bit quiet as the two of them arrived, so he grabbed the bull by the horns.

'Evening, everyone, lovely to see you all. I'm going to walk around with Julian, who some of you already know, and say hello to everyone in no set order, so no bitchy stuff thank you. Leave that to the talent.' Enzo, the director of photography, was sitting with two of his camera crew, a man and a woman, at the closest table. 'Buona sera, Enzo! How are you my friend?' It had been a couple of years since they'd seen each other.

'Lovely to see you, Killy. You're looking very well.'

'Enzo, I'd like you to meet Julian. Julian, this is Enzo.'

They shook hands, and Julian had obviously done his homework and watched one of Enzo's best known films, so that got things moving nicely between them. Then, Italian gentleman to a fault, Enzo introduced the two of them to his crew members, both Italian and whose English, judging by their response to a little crack Julian made, was pretty basic. But as camera crews dwell in their own separate world, so long as the director of photography speaks good English, all is well. Arthur made his entrance at that point, dressed in his usual understated way; with a lot of fluorescent purple featuring and topped off with a brand-new Panama he'd definitely paid a fortune for. A round of kisses, hugs and big 'hellos' followed his entrance, and things gradually turned into Arthur's welcome party. Killy walked Julian across to where Wally was sitting deep in conversation with Gloria, who'd obviously calmed down from their earlier meeting and jumped up and gave Killy a big hug.

'Julian, this is Gloria Banks.'

Julian, on maximum charm level, put out his hand. 'Lovely to meet you, Gloria. I think we have a friend in common, don't we? Erik Grant?'

'You know Erik? I haven't seen him for ages, how is he?'

'Very well. We did a little job together earlier in the year. Lovely man.' Killy let them chat for a minute or so, then introduced Wally to Julian. 'I'm so grateful to you, Wally, for getting us out of a big jam, but I have to say on a strictly personal note, I'm a total *Bond* nut! I'll be picking your brain about all the ones you've worked on.'

Killy left them to it and turned back to Gloria. 'Did Monika sort you out? You look fantastic.'

'Certainly did, Kill. What a sweetie.' She spread her arms and gave her head a bit of a shake to show off a spectacular pair of earrings that perfectly matched her deep green eyes and Monika's beautiful silk sarong. 'We're exactly the same size; she's going to have to fight me to get this lot back.'

'Yeah, and if it came to it, I don't know which of you I'd bet on!'

She loved that and grabbed him for another hug, and whispered directly in his ear, 'Don't worry, everything's working out fine; we both still fancy each other, so I think it's going to be fun!'

At precisely that moment, King Arthur burst amongst them. 'Ms Banks! Come and give your poor old boss a hug!'

Killy glanced at her, then seized the moment to move on, gently putting his hand on Julian's shoulder. 'Wally, mate, excuse us will you? I have to get Julian over to Paddy and then all the art department ladies before we starve to death. Julian, come and say hello to Paddy, our sound recordist. Didn't you say you'd worked together?' They walked across and joined them.

'Yes. Lovely to see you, Paddy.' From the way they greeted each other they'd clearly gotten on, and then Paddy took over introducing Julian to the ladies.

'This is Celia, our props buyer; Eliane, set decoration; and I hope I get this right, Angelica, set dresser; and..?' Killy could see Paddy needed help, as it was pretty clear he'd already been introduced to the lady in question and she didn't know whether to prompt him or not, so he stepped in.

'Paddy, you're losing it mate. It's Cath!'

Arthur exploded onto the scene again, grabbing Paddy in a bear hug. 'How come you're always surrounded by a gaggle of beautiful women? What have you got that I haven't?'

Killy was really tempted to suggest it might be dress sense but thought better of it and as Julian was doing a great job talking to the ladies, he walked across to the kitchen and told Rosalia they were ready.

She nodded. 'Sí, señor Killy. Dos minutos, la mesa del frente.' As instructed, he sat himself at the front table, waved to the waiter, and asked him to put his coldest bottle of white wine and half a dozen beers in a bucket of ice on the table. He sat back and watched the whole scene playing out before him, smiling to himself at the sight of all these familiar and not-so-familiar faces getting together.

Rosalia came out, holding up the steaming blue fish on a big serving platter so everyone could see — which of course they did, as film crews rarely miss anything to do with food. King Arthur saw it first, from over the shoulder of whoever it was he was hugging, 'What's the occasion, Killy?'

'You're here, Arthur!'

'Don't give me that old codswallop, I invited myself!'

Of course everyone had already eaten but had to taste the fish, which was so delicious Julian and Killy barely got any of it. Arthur certainly bagged his share, and was having such a great time he got completely carried away and bought champagne for everyone. Two of the boys from the kitchen were musicians, so out came a guitar and a set of bongos, and pretty soon everyone was up and dancing. Rosalia brought out several bottles of the local rum, which proved very popular, and the whole thing in the end became fondly remembered as the Blue Fish night.

Relieved that the Wally/Gloria scenario appeared to be under control, Killy's thoughts switched to the Furio situation, but that had to wait until they were face-to-face. The one thing that would lift the biggest load from his mind would be positive news from Susie, but as he checked his phone yet again, there was still no word.

6

Killy stood in front of the heads of department in a room next to the main production office, pointing to the very simple map he'd drawn on a white screen set up on a tripod.

'OK, so this is where we are right now and this, just along here, is where most of us are going to be working for the majority of the shoot. The site has had multiple uses over the years and a lot of it is in a very poor state, so please keep to our marked-out areas as it's a long schlepp from here to the hospital; and none of us want any of that, for ourselves or our people.'

He pointed to a line linking the two sites. 'This is laughingly known as a road. In fact, as Julian will tell you, it's little more than a cart track, which as the rainy weather comes on can become impassable. In theory it should be five minutes by car, but it can take an hour at this time of year, so we're all going to get a lovely ten-minute walk to work along the beach every morning. Regarding transport, we have two larger boats for general use, and three smaller but much faster launches to ferry artistes, crew, and equipment to the two locations not on this site. We're calling this the studio base, and the caterers will be located here once we start shooting, serving breakfast and lunch as per the call sheet, and an evening meal for the military extras. Supper for cast and crew will be served in the garden restaurant until ten-thirty pm.

'Wardrobe, hair and makeup, camera department, all the electricals, armoury, props, stunts will be accommodated there with full twenty-four-hour security. I think, as you will all want to have a look around your assigned areas, we can adjourn this meeting now and head straight over there, and go through all the questions you will doubtless have *in situ*. By the way, Marta and Ali should be joining us back here this evening, and of course there will be a health and safety briefing at the site. So, thanks very much. I'll see you all there.'

The meeting had gone smoothly. Arthur had said a few words of welcome to kick it off, then he'd introduced Julian, who'd told everyone how delighted he was to be doing the job with such a great bunch of professionals. There'd been a few general questions touching on accommodation, expenses, and wages for locals and so on, which Monika took care of, then she, Arthur, and Julian had gone off to a budget meeting with Chris. What Killy had to say was over pretty quickly, and now they were all moving off to get started.

What Killy didn't know as he made his way to the base, and indeed wouldn't hear about for another twenty-four hours, was that down in the capital Furio had run into a serious snag. He was with the armourer and his assistant, who'd flown with all the imitation weapons and ammunition from Mexico City overnight on a chartered aircraft, but try as he might he could not get the consignment cleared through customs. Assuming it was the low-ranking functionary he was dealing with seeing a chance for a nice backhander, it was definitely something that couldn't be sorted out over the phone.

Furio made the armourers comfortable in a little bar

owned by a friend of his, just across from the customs hall, then drove through the morning traffic into the centre of the city to see his old college friend, Alonso Perez, the president's cousin. The pair of them were having a gentle stroll around the lush tropical park next to the presidential palace, and though they might have appeared relaxed, in actual fact, Alonso was terrified by what Furio was telling him. All the required bribes had been paid to the relevant officials and by that time, the equipment should have been cleared through customs, loaded onto trucks, and under armed guard, well on its way to Los Zapateros. Alonso smelt a rat. But his problem was not knowing who to approach to sort it out, and whilst his position made it simple for him to pay off the right people up the chain of command, the current situation appeared to be caused by somebody down the chain. He made a call, Furio didn't know who to, but in fifteen minutes they were joined by a well-dressed young man who led them to a black Range Rover and drove them to a nearby office block, where they left Furio and walked inside. Ten minutes later they were back, laughing and telling him everything had been sorted, but Furio sensed from the way Alonso sounded that he was really shaken but doing his best not to show it. They dropped Furio back at his car, so he didn't get a chance to question Alonso as to what had transpired. As he drove away, he was still in the dark.

An hour later, a still very unsettled Furio had walked into the bar and picked up the armourers, then led them back across to the customs hall, where all the paperwork was signed, stamped, and handed over to him; in theory the show was back on the road, but of course it wasn't as straightforward as that. Furio had kept his phone on silent throughout his dealings in the city and, once he'd made sure the trucks were actually on their way, he could see at least half a dozen missed calls from Monika. He had to decide what to tell her and in the end he'd opted to bluff it out. When they'd finally spoken she'd seemed quite inquisitive as to why he hadn't answered her calls, but he was sure she believed the story about his phone and the 'peon' breaking his balls to get a handout.

Killy, meanwhile, had finally finished discussing space allocations with all the department heads and walked back to the jetty, where Monika was waiting for him with the young steward. 'Gustavo, good to see you! So you decided you wanted to have a peep at the movie business, eh? Very wise. Has Monika sorted you out with a place to stay?'

He nodded. 'Yes, sir.'

'You can forget all the 'yessir' stuff; I'm Killy from now on. Go and get your room sorted out, have some supper, and I'll see you first thing tomorrow for a proper chat. I'm delighted you're joining us. Have a good evening.' Killy put his arm around Monika's shoulders. 'Right, beauty, I can see something is bugging you.' She took a long pause and then out it all came.

'I spent more than an hour this morning on the phone with the shipping agent in Mexico City. He was really concerned that he'd had no notification that the armaments had cleared customs here. When he'd eventually got through to his Armourer, the guy could only say he was with Furio and dealing with a problem. When he called me again, I told him I'd make some enquiries and get back to him, but Furio wasn't answering his phone. I tried all morning, and then around two o'clock I got a call from the agent to say he'd received the notification.'

'OK, so what's the problem? Half a day late in this place is really good going.'

She was shaking her head. 'No, Killy. Furio eventually

called me at around two, with some ridiculous story about a tricky customs guy, and how he'd left his phone in the car. I know he was lying; he doesn't go anywhere without his phone and if somebody was giving him a hard time, he would have gone to his car and got the goddamn thing and made a call to his contacts. And *then* called me.'

'So, I'm a bit confused, darlin'. What are you saying? He was doing what he's paid to do and dealing with a problem. And anyway the gear is in the country now, so job done, no?'

'Yes, the job is done, Killy, but he was lying to me about his phone. And why was there a problem in the first place? This was all organised and paid for days ago! Something went wrong, and he's trying to keep it from me.'

'Have you said anything to Arthur?'

She shook her head. 'He's been onto his lawyers in London all day fighting over Bedford's swimming pool. And anyway, Killy, he pays me to deal with this local stuff. I want to tell Furio what I think but it has to be face-to-face, which I'm certainly more than happy to do, but I can't move from here at the moment.'

'Right; let's get him up here. Organise a meeting for tomorrow morning but tell him it's to nail down this problem with the party location, which needs resolving anyway. Once we've covered that and he thinks he's in the clear with the customs hiccup, we can both go for him. Colonel Kubitt is flying up here in the morning to choose the marine landing beach, isn't he?'

'Yes, he's due here at nine.'

'OK, get Furio on the plane with him and schedule a meeting for ten to brainstorm this location thing, and decide whether or not we'll go for an alternative solution. Then, once Arthur and Julian are out of the way, you and I can get Furio on his own. How's that?'

'OK, good scheme. I'll call Furio now and organise it. And you're right, that location has to be settled. By the way, how did it go today?'

'All things considered, pretty good. I need a couple of hours to go through my notes, then I'm having supper with Julian, so I'll call you just before I go over there. I've already got a list for you a mile long.'

It was a beautiful evening so Killy was working at the table out on his porch when his new recruit came wandering along the track. 'Good evening, Gustavo. Out for a stroll?'

'We only ever came up to the beaches here by boat, Killy, so I thought I'd have a look around the whole place to familiarise myself.'

'I'm just off to the kitchen for a beer, you want one?'

'Thank you, yes please.'

'Sit yourself down.' Killy came back out and handed him a bottle already opened, and clinked it with his own. 'Salud. So what are you doing about your job? How much leave do you have?'

'I quit. I have been trying to escape from it for about a year now. I never really liked it, but I'd given up my studies and my father insisted I work.'

'What were you studying?'

'I come from a medical family so there was no choice. But medicine never interested me and I didn't see the point of all those years of study just to maintain a tradition.'

'So why cabin crew?'

'Family connections, and I'd studied English from childhood and it seemed like a chance to travel. But it's all a facade.

I hated it, so here I am.'

'Well done, I like your attitude. What did Monika tell you? Did she say what you'd be doing?'

'She said you wanted me to try to be a 'runner', instead of being a supporting artist. She explained I would be working with your team of assistant directors and that I would have a lot to do.' He smiled. 'And that I would be busy all the time, that my English would be very useful, and that was it.'

'Right, Gustavo. If you're really interested in working on movies, this is the way to learn how they're made.'

'If you don't mind, Killy, I'd prefer it if you called me Gus or Gussy. Gustavo is a name that runs through generations of my family and I have hated it since I was a kid, and I am twenty-seven years old.'

'Welcome aboard, Gussy! In the morning, I want you to start in the production office. Be there at ten to seven and, here, take this with you. It'll give you an idea of what this game is all about.' He handed him a sheet of A4 with a couple of printed paragraphs titled *The Realities of Filming.*

As he started down the porch steps, Killy realised that there was something worth asking a local middle-class boy from a good family. 'Gussy, hang on a minute. You might be able to help us find a really important location. We're looking for a big, traditional home with gardens. Any ideas?'

Gussy was smiling. 'My mother is the one to ask, she knows everyone on the island who owns that sort of property. I'll call her this evening.'

'Please do. I'll see you tomorrow. And read that sheet.'

Killy's phone was ringing in the kitchen; it was Martin, his stepson. 'Hello, stranger! How are you? Lovely to hear from you.'

'Hello, Daddy-o. Behaving yourself?'

'Oh yeah, I'm a good boy these days. How's things in Geneva? Are you still saving the world?'

'Things are good. When're you coming for a visit? There's someone I want you to meet.' That was definitely big news.

'Oh yeah? How long has this been going on?'

'Actually about a year now. She's with UNICEF and she's away a lot, so it's taken a while for us to finally get together.'

'Where's she from?'

'She's French, from the south.'

'Whereabouts?'

'Marseille, but her father's a diplomat so she grew up all over the place.'

'Une petite Marseillaise, eh? What's her name?'

'You never change, do you? You want the ins and outs of everything! Hélène, actually. I think you'll like her. Anyway, the other reason I called is: do you remember the French family we used to meet at that campsite in the Ardèche, with the boy who was my age?'

'Yes, I certainly do. Cédric wasn't it? You crashed his moped?'

'That's him. Well, having completely lost touch, we bumped into each other at a great big UN jolly last week and by the weirdest coincidence, it turns out he's working with the French delegation in New York.'

'Blimey. I remember you had a lot in common but what're the odds of that happening?'

'Amazing, eh? Anyway, he was asking about all of us, how you and mum were and wanted to know everything, so we finished up going out for a beer and yacking for hours. Anyway, to cut to the chase, it turns out he's become a total film nut and so, of course, wanted to know what you're working on. When I told him where you were, it was almost as though he didn't know whether or not to say something, so I prodded him, and obviously it's very hush-hush, but he told me that the island you're on is part of his patch and there are rumblings of a potential regime change about to happen and he thought you should know ... Killy? You still there?' He definitely was, but his mind was racing through everything that this news had suddenly shed light on. 'Killy?'

'Yeah, sorry. I am, Mart, very much so, and I think you might have answered a question that I was going to have to ask someone I'm working with, so thank you. Tell Cédric I really appreciate it, and that it will stay strictly confidential. Look, I'm sorry to cut this short, mate, but I've got a meeting I'm already late for. Let's talk soon. Please give my best wishes to La Belle Hélène, and tell her I'll be coming to Geneva to meet her as soon as this gig's done.'

'OK, great. Let me know if there's anything I can do, OK? Cédric told me to tell you to call him in New York, if you need a chat. I'll text you his number.'

'That's great, Mart. Cheers, speak soon.' He ended the call and stood staring out through the kitchen window. 'Holy fucking shit, the president is going to be booted out! So, where the fuck does that leave Furio? And us?' He called Monika.

'Just spoke to my boy in Geneva. A UN colleague in New York has heard there's moves going on down here to replace El Presidente. You can bet your life that's what's causing grief for Furio. I take it you've spoken to him?'

'Yes, and he's not happy about having to come up here in the morning, but understands why. I didn't mention his customs problems. Should we call Arthur? What do you think?'

'Well, he needs to know, that's obvious. But the customs thing will have him way past boiling point in about two seconds, and I'll bet Furio is busy trying to find out what's going on, so best leave him to it. If Arthur thinks he's in trouble and isn't saying why, he'll make the poor bastard drive here right now, and we'll be up all night doing what we can do just as easily in the morning after a decent night's sleep. I'm going to have a bit of supper with Julian. Why don't you join us?'

'I'll see you in an hour or so.'

7

Killy's hunch had been spot on, and whilst he and Julian were sitting in the garden tucking into fresh lobster, down in the Capital, poor old Furio was in the back seat of his car with Alonso. The two of them were so panicked, the only safe meeting place they could agree on was the underground car park at Furio's apartment block.

Alonso had arrived in a taxi and was buzzed into the building by a very jittery Furio, who told him to take the fire escape stairs down two floors from the lobby and meet him at parking space AA12. Alonso was shaken up so badly by the time he found Furio, he was having trouble stringing sentences together. Evidently, the young man who'd driven them in the Range Rover was a contact in the local CIA station, however Alonso had known that he'd been bluffing and that was just adding to his fears, as there was nobody else that could help him.

They'd agreed that all further discussions would have to be person-to-person, and so they arranged to meet back there two nights later. Furio gave Alonso enough time to make his way out to the street, and then ran up the stairs to his apartment and prepared for his morning flight to Los Zapateros.

...

Monika had joined Killy and Julian as they were finishing their meal. 'I'm sorry about the meeting tomorrow, Julian, but we have to get this party location fixed and need to know whether you would consider—'

Julian jumped in, 'Killy and I discussed this yesterday, Monika, and I've been going through the photos and videos of the possibilities we already rejected. So yes, if it comes to it, I can make that disused hotel work; we agreed the gardens there are the problem, so it would mean rewriting the final scene as an interior, which would be a great loss visually. The alternative, which I would definitely prefer, would be to trick it and use a suitable garden somewhere else. In that way we can all move on.' He stood up. 'And anyway, I need to get on with my notes but just to say, I'd really rather skip the meeting as my day would be much better spent assessing potential landing beaches with our military advisor. So thanks, guys, I really appreciate it. See you tomorrow.'

Killy looked at Monika. 'Blimey. I wish they were all as flexible as that!' She leaned over, pulled her laptop from her bag and started to tap something in, then stopped and smiled at him.

'A little surprise for you now Julian's gone. Just before I came over, I got a call from the man you now call Gussy, but I still know as Gustavo, and he asked me to tell you he'd spoken with his mother and explained what we're looking for, and she suggested that we might like to consider their family's country house?'

'Yeah? So what did you say?'

'Well, it seems a few years ago his parents went through a very unpleasant divorce, and one of the big problems was actually the property in question, which came from his mother's side. Her lawyers had instructed her to prepare to sell it, to force a settlement.' She turned the laptop towards him, like a magician pulling a rabbit out of a hat. 'Here's the sales dossier!'

He took one glance at the cover photo and that told it all. 'It's a palace! Look at this! And the gardens.' Killy was flipping through the seemingly endless photo display. 'And it overlooks the sea! Is she up for us filming there?'

'Definitely, according to Gustavo. As long as we can agree on a fee and pay in cash, in dollars, she'd be delighted. So I told him to tell her I would arrange for our director to visit by the end of the day tomorrow. What do you think?'

'Incredible piece of luck is what I think. Good on you, Gussy! Where is it? Please don't tell me it's down the other end of the island.'

She turned the computer back to her. 'Here's a locator map and look, it's perfect; it's about thirty minutes by boat down the coast from here, and about the same distance from the capital, and it has its own docking facility.'

Killy was staring into the screen, shaking his head at their luck. 'Right. Julian and the colonel should have seen all the potential beach landing sites by mid-to-late afternoon, so I'll take Gussy and pick the Guvnor up from whatever beach they're on, and go straight to the house.'

The following morning at the meeting, Arthur took things much more calmly than they'd expected. They'd planned their order of attack over breakfast; Monika took the lead and told him about the house and showed him all the pictures and then broke the news that if the house didn't work out, Julian would be amenable to using a location that they'd previously rejected. A win-win scenario, which definitely pleased Arthur.

Stage two was to put him in the picture *vis-a-vis* Furio's behaviour the day before. Monika talked him step by step through the story, making sure he understood that she questioned only the way Furio had handled it, not what he was actually doing, and that rather than blatantly over the phone calling him a liar, she'd felt instinctively that as the producer, Arthur needed to be party to whatever came next. Then it was Killy's turn. Arthur listened, sitting bolt upright behind his desk. He considered Martin his 'Godson at the UN', and so every detail of what he'd said to Killy carried a great deal of weight. Then, as if on cue, there was a tap at the door.

Arthur called out, 'Is that you, Furio? Hold it open a second.' He bellowed, 'Ana! Bring us a pot of coffee please, and make tea for Killy. Thank you! Furio, come in and close the door, son.' Furio shook hands all round and sat himself down facing His Majesty. Never one to beat about the bush in situations such as this, Arthur came straight to the point. 'Right, Furio, I understand you had a problem yesterday with customs. What was that all about? Did they want more money?' Furio was clearly unsettled as this was not the way things were handled in his world, where a great deal of bushes would have been beaten about before any discussion began. He looked down at his hands and then started.

'Arthur, as I told Monika yesterday, it was simply a case of a peon in the front office trying for a few dollars.'

Arthur was starting to bristle. 'So, why did it take the whole morning? Surely you could have cleared it up with a phone call?' Really in the hot seat now, Furio drew breath and started to give Arthur the same story about his phone but he stopped him dead. 'Furio. You and I have known each other quite a while, am I right?' Having never been on the receiving end of King Arthur moving into attack mode, he could do little more than nod. 'You're flannelling me Furio, like you tried with Monika, telling her you'd left your phone in the car. Tell me right now what the fuck was going on!' For a Latin American man to be confronted like this was bad enough, but in front of a female colleague it was too much.

'Arthur, can I speak to you in private, please?'

'No you can't, Furio! We're all in this together and you clearly have a problem, which means we all have a problem. So tell us what's going on!'

Furio squirmed in his chair then took another deep breath. 'My contact's CIA connection said there had been a customs alert covering all air shipments from Mexico and that someone had made a mistake. However, my man didn't believe him. When we spoke yesterday evening, he still had no idea what had caused the problem, and so we are meeting again tomorrow. But I have to tell you, Arthur, he is very worried about this.'

'Is he? Interesting. Well, let me tell you, Furio, he's not as worried as I am! I've got a great deal of money riding on this picture, other people's money, and just yesterday a connection of mine at the UN in New York happened to call me because he knew I was shooting a picture down here and felt it his duty, in the strictest of confidence, to tell me that it appears Washington is unhappy with the way this place is being run, and that there are plans afoot for a new occupant of the presidential palace. They're switching horses, Furio. How does that grab you? Because I tell you, I've got a crew of technicians and a cast of actors in my care and had you been doing your job correctly, and putting me in the picture as to what is going on here, we would have gone somewhere else to make this fucking picture! As it stands we're stuck, with no possibility whatsoever to move somewhere else.

'And let me put you wise to something you should know, my friend; the people who are fronting up the money for this picture are, shall we say, a 'bit on the heavy side', and when they find out how their investment has been put in jeopardy as a result of you not doing your fucking job, I can't be responsible for how they might respond. Do you understand?' Furio looked absolutely poleaxed. He could barely speak. Monika and Killy managed the slightest flick of an eye between them. Arthur leaned further across the desk. 'So, Furio, does this make any sense to you?'

He finally nodded. 'Yes, Arthur, it certainly could help explain what happened.' He was obviously trying to think this one through on the spot but it was massive, and his face couldn't hide it. 'I need to get back to the city right now, Arthur. Here, I can do nothing.' Ana tapped on the door.

'Coffee and tea, señor Margolies.'

'Thank you, Ana, just put it there please. The plane that came up this morning; is it still here?'

'It is still here, señor. Yes.'

'OK. I want señor Asante driven out to the strip right now, and put onto that plane, and then get it back to the capital. Off you go, Furio, and I want to know exactly what's going on as soon as you do. There's a boat coming up here every morning now, so be on it the day after tomorrow, OK? Any problems, call me.' He stuck his hand out. 'It's a team effort, son, just remember that. See you soon, and good luck.' Clearly shattered by this episode, Furio barely paused to say goodbye. Killy looked at Monika and they both looked at Arthur, who was running his fingers back through what used to be a rather full head of hair. 'We come to a nice, quiet Banana Republic, to make a film about a revolution, and we finish up in the middle of a real one! You couldn't fucking write it could you? Talk about life imitating art! Monika, pour us a cup of coffee please, love? Help yourself to the tea, Killy.' He opened a drawer in his desk. 'Here, have a digestive.'

8

Making movies does have occasional little perks, such as lounging on the very wide and comfortable red leather rear bench seat of a big and extremely powerful launch, as it skims across a flat calm sea on a beautiful, sun-drenched Caribbean afternoon. And getting paid to do it! However, they only come from time to time and, bearing in mind the morning they'd had, Arthur and Killy were enjoying every minute of it. So was Gussy as his family had used the company's boats before, and he sat up front next to the skipper chatting and laughing all the way. He shouted back to them and pointed along the shore ahead, where their boat's twin was sitting near the edge of the sand. Giving the engines an extra burst, the skipper sent them hurtling along, almost flying over the water, and finishing with a big flashy turn, then cutting the engines and letting them drift in a little way behind the other boat.

Colonel Regis Kubitt, their American military advisor, was walking towards the water's edge, watching them coming in. Having seen action in Kuwait, Iraq, and Afghanistan, he'd taken early retirement in his late forties and now worked on film and TV productions all over the world, ensuring that everything representing US military subjects was correct down to the last detail. With his steel-grey crew cut hair, suntanned, chiselled cheeks, and perfectly ironed short-sleeved khaki shirt and slacks, he was the image of an American military man from top down to his light tan deck shoes. Killy hadn't seen him for a couple of years, but he was certainly showing no sign of wear and tear.

'Good to see you, Regis! Arthur and I were remarking how fit you're looking. How do you do it?'

'Clean living, Killy. You should give it a try sometime. Hello there, Arthur! Are you guys coming ashore, or moving straight on?' Now that their boat had settled, Arthur stood up,

'We're going down the coast, Regis. Lovely to see you. Where are the others?'

'They're just up above the beach, checking camera angles.' Julian was coming out from the trees, followed by Alain and Enzo who were deep in conversation.

Killy called out, 'Hello, Julian, are you ready?'

'Yup, this is the beach we're going to use, Killy. So let's get going.' Julian rolled up his very smart chinos, threw his shoes onboard and climbed right over the front, with Gussy giving him a hand to steady him. Alain and Enzo boarded the same way, and in about twenty minutes they were mooring behind a smart-looking red speedboat tied up to a very well-maintained, teak-decked, stainless-steel jetty, that ran for about fifty yards from the water's edge. They all got out and followed Gussy across the beach towards a striking-looking blonde woman, probably mid-fifties, in a blouse, boots and jeans, standing by a big twin-cab pickup truck. Arthur was struggling to straighten his rather dishevelled, fruit-themed beach shirt but without a lot of luck, as it was at least two sizes too small. Gussy did the introductions.

'Julian, this is Lydia, my mother. Ma, this is Julian, the film's director.' They shook hands, then it was Arthur's turn.

He took her hand and gave a very gracious nod of the head. 'Lovely to meet you, Lydia.'

'And this is Killian, my boss. And Alain, the designer. And Enzo, the chief of cinematography.' With greetings complete, Lydia ushered them aboard.

'Gustavo, darling, why don't you climb onto the back to give our guests more space?' She was obviously being diplomatic, as Arthur filled the double seat next to her.

The road was steep and led straight up for about a quarter of a mile through coconut and banana trees. It was a good, solid road, which Killy noted would be a big plus. At the top of the slope the road levelled off, and a few hundred yards further on they turned into a rather grand entranceway all finished in bright white Adobe, with 'Casa Santini' in black-painted wrought iron letters set overhead. They rolled along a wide, stone-flagged driveway, lined on either side with beautiful, tall palm trees all matching in height and girth, with immaculate lawns that ran back for at least a hundred yards in both directions. Dotted here and there were huge clusters of flowering bushes.

Julian said what they were all thinking, 'I hope you don't mind me saying, Lydia: the pictures you sent us were good but they don't do your home justice.'

'I have to say, Julian, they didn't impress me either. There, you can just see the house peeping through those trees.'

'When was it built, Lydia?'

'In eighteen seventy-eight, by my half-Russian-half-Scottish great-great-grandfather Sergei Sholto Santini, who'd made a fortune trading in coffee and timber and wanted to entertain in grand style. A 'Victorian party house' I suppose it would be called now.' They finally pulled up under a pillared portico that could shelter at least a dozen or so large cars, or the horse-drawn carriages it had been built for. Gussy and the two young men who had come from inside the house were all laughing about him arriving on the back of a truck. Lydia walked ahead into the cool, calm, rich interior of what was, with no exaggeration, a palace. 'Welcome to our home, gentlemen. Gustavo, darling, can you tell Othello we'd like some refreshments on the terrace? The sun will be off it soon. I'll take everyone this way, then we can wander on through and see the rest of what I think might be useful for the filming.'

She led the way into an enormous Victorian ballroom that had a frescoed ceiling at least thirty feet high, with an enormous crystal chandelier at its centre, and a whole wall of French windows giving out onto a terrace and gardens.

Alain, not someone easily impressed, finally broke what was becoming a bit of an embarrassed silence, 'Madame Santini, I have to say, I find your home exquisite. May I ask who built it? The craftsmanship is magnificent and it's untouched. Incredible!'

'Thank you, Alain. The British Architect, whose name escapes me, brought over his family and his entire team of craftsmen. The finest of materials were shipped from all over the world to the little dock you arrived at, not exactly that one obviously, and the whole thing took five years to complete. It's so nice to be amongst people who understand and appreciate such things.' Arthur had seated himself at the keyboard of an aircraft-carrier-sized Bechstein Grand on a raised dais at the far end of the room. It had evidently been played to accompany Italian Opera divas who'd crossed the Atlantic by steamship, vamped on by jazz stars of the nineteen forties flown in from New York, and now Arthur Margolies, cockney boy made good, was playing a Bach sonata that stopped them all, the hostess included, dead in their tracks. It seemed impossible that someone who appeared to be so rough could perform so beautifully. They all listened completely enraptured, and then applauded him until he'd closed the lid over the keyboard and taken a final bow.

He held up his hand for silence. 'Señora Santini. Lydia. I think it goes without saying we all agree that your beautiful home would make the perfect setting for the opening sequence of our film and ...' he paused and looked at Julian, 'very likely the closing scene, as well.' Julian was nodding and smiling as Arthur went on. 'So, Lydia, if you think that might be possible, I would appreciate a little chat with you so we can discuss terms.' Lydia looked charmed.

'After a performance like that? Of course, Arthur. Let's all go through onto the terrace, shall we? Othello is waiting to look after you.' Othello, the butler, looked as though he might have come over on the steamship that carried the five hundred tons of Carrara marble the house had gobbled up. He was ancient, tanned, and erect, and impeccably turned out in a very well cut three-piece grey suit with a matching silk bow tie. He shook hands and greeted them all, as Lydia introduced each of them by name, and position on the film, without a falter. A table had been set with a variety of tasty-looking little nibbles, laid out on a linen tablecloth so smooth it might have been lovingly ironed every week since the place was built. Othello served them an excellent, perfectly chilled Pinot Grigio and then with a gentlemanly nod, tottered off back into the house.

Arthur was getting stuck into a dish of nuts as Julian, who had walked out onto the lawns with Alain and Enzo to look back at the house, called for him to join them. Lydia had excused herself and so, checking that it was just him and Killy at the table, Arthur emptied the entire contents into one of the big pockets of his now completely mashed shirt and, still munching away, walked over to join them. The view out from the terrace was stunning, encompassing a great sweep of the gardens and across to the sea.

Killy was savouring the delicious wine when Gussy finally reappeared. 'Well, Mister Santini, if your mother and Arthur can agree on the fee, you just moved up a rung on the ladder. Well done! And thank you.'

He looked over Killy's shoulder. 'Hello, Ma, I think we ought to be getting back to the boat. Am I right, Killy?'

'Sadly, you are. Arthur! I think we're going to have to make a move pretty soon.'

He walked back to them across the lawn, wiping his mouth with a linen napkin, 'Could we have our little chat, Lydia?'

She nodded. 'Of course, Arthur. Let's sit on the bench by the cedar.'

In less than an hour they were on their way back up the coast, the now moonlit sea a flat calm, and with the engines running at full power they skimmed across the surface. Arthur and Killy were back on their banquette at the stern. Killy leaned in close and spoke directly into his ear, 'You look like the cat who got the cream. Good deal?'

Arthur turned towards him nodding. 'A good deal indeed, son. Both parties are very content.' Arthur wouldn't have been nearly so happy if he'd had even an inkling of the news he was about to receive. As they stepped off the boat and started the walk along the lantern-lit pathway to their bungalows his phone rang, and he excused himself to answer it. He mouthed '*Furio*' to Killy, and walked on.

Julian turned up the track to his place, as he planned to eat indoors and catch up on the notes he'd made. Alain had invited them all for a drink but only Enzo had taken him up on it, so those two split off as well. Killy stopped to watch Arthur make his way up to his porch and felt instinctively he should follow him, but decided that whatever it might be, if Arthur needed him, he would be summoned immediately anyway. He asked Gussy if his mother actually lived at the house and the pair of them walked on.

'No, she stays in the city and Othello brings her out there in the boat, for weekends. She only came today to meet us, so they'll be on their way back soon. Although she will be at the wheel, as she no longer trusts Othello's eyesight at night — and neither does he.'

'How old is he?'

'Seventy, I think. He's been with us for about twenty years. My parents were in Venice to buy the red boat down at the jetty and were staying at the Gritti Palace. Othello was the butler on their floor and they took to him immediately, and by the end of their stay they'd persuaded him to come and work with them here. My mother had to fight hard to keep him in the divorce. And the boat, too.'

As they walked into the garden, Ali got up from the table and came bustling across. 'Give me a cuddle, Killy, I've missed you. What a day! Those little planes! That one this morning rattled so much. I just hate them!' All that blasted into his ear as Alison hugged him to her copious bosom. 'And this must be the famous Gussy?'

He put out his hand. 'Very pleased to meet you ...?' All the instant familiarity, using first names of people on first meeting, was something he was going to have to get accustomed to.

'Alison, Killy's Second AD,' she said, grabbing his hand. 'Ali. No formality on this job. Fancy a beer? Come and sit down and tell me about yourself. Have you eaten yet, Kill?'

'No and I'm starving. What are you having?'

'Paella, and so's Monika. She'll be back here in a minute. Do you fancy that? What about you, Gussy, you joining us?'

'If that's OK?'

'Course it's OK, this is work. If we don't want you around, we'll tell you.'

Killy's phone buzzed in his pocket; it was Arthur. 'Come over here now, will you, son?'

And that was it. Killy put his phone back in his pocket. 'King Arthur calls. I'll have the paella. And Gussy, you choose whatever you want and put it on my bill. See you.'

As he turned to go, Monika was coming towards them. 'Killy, que tal? Good day?'

'Well it *was* all good, but I just got a summons from his majesty, so we'll see.'

Arthur opened the door, his face ashen. 'Furio was watching his contact getting out of a taxi right outside of his building and two guys on a motorbike drove by and shot him. He's dead. He was a cousin of the president, did you know that?'

It took Killy several seconds to take it in.

'No, Arthur, I didn't.' He paused again. 'How's Furio taking it?'

'He's in a terrible state and he wouldn't say too much over the phone, so it was all a bit cloak and dagger, but he reckons the police are saying they have proof that the guy had been in regular contact with a Mexican drug mob.'

'I reckon this could link back to Furio's customs cock-up,

Arthur. Is he still coming here tomorrow?'

'Yup. What's left for him to get through?'

Killy was running a mental tally of crucial personnel and gear that would likely need Furio's help. 'The Prof and the special effects team and all their paraphernalia coming in from Miami, definitely, and the generators and all the lighting gear is ready to ship from there as well, so between those two departments there's plenty of potential for customs to cause us problems. Let's hope he can get it sorted.'

Arthur nodded. 'OK. We'll sleep on this, son. We're too much in the dark to make any decisions, and there's fuck-all we can do anyway. Fortunately, we're insured up to the hilt, so if we can't get somebody else to smooth things out and there's a delay, at least we can try and claim for lost time. Let's go and have something to eat, I'm starving. What's Rosalia serving tonight, anything special?'

'Yeah, they're all having paella. And Ali's arrived, so we'd better get a wiggle on.'

9

Killy ate too much and was awake into the early hours. He finally dropped off and slept until about seven-thirty. He was sitting on his porch with a cuppa thinking about Furio, as a messsage from Martin flashed up, and unusually using an encrypted text:

Due to yesterday's shooting, Cédric is flying down to San Lorenzo to ensure his local personnel are not in any way impacted and would love to see you. Lotsa luv M.

Killy typed a response: *All good here Mart. I'll get in touch. Cheers mate. Kx.* Then he texted: *Martin tells me you're coming down this way Cédric? I could meet you in the capital, or if you'd like to visit us here to see what we're doing I can arrange transport, and accommodation if you'd like to stay over? Let me know, best wishes Killian.*

Killy stared at the screen of his phone. He'd worked in a lot of weird and wonderful places all over the world, but he'd never been faced with a situation that couldn't be sorted; usually with a wad of cash. Movie fixers' inside knowledge of the area they work in and the people who run things pays dividends all round, but a breakdown in the chain such as Furio was experiencing could be potentially catastrophic for everyone involved.

'OK, Killy boy. Worrying is what a First is paid to do, and in the end it only boils your brain, and revolution or no revolution you've got a film to make, and we haven't even started shooting yet.' He fired off the text, jumped into the shower, then went off to face the day. His fisherman friend was loping along the pathway as he came down the steps, and fortunately he'd remembered his name. 'Buenos dias, Papon. Qué tal?' Papon's smile was worth getting up for.

'Muy bien, señor. Muy bien, gracias.'

Killy pointed to the bulging net of fish he was carrying. 'Eso es mucho pescado! Has tenido mucha suerte.' He was hoping what he'd said meant that Papon had had a lot of luck catching so much fish.

He'd got it right and Papon was definitely feeling lucky; he hoisted the net trophy-like, way above his head. 'Sí, señor. Mucha suerte.'

Killy tapped a finger on his temple, hoping it would indicate that he needed to think through what he was going to ask him. They were scheduled for what would be the only weekend off for the entire shoot, and he wanted to do something special for the crew, so he plunged in. 'Nosotros tenemos este fin de semana libre, así que podrás cocinar pescado en la playa? Mañana en la tarde, pequeña fiesta, treinta personas?' His mangled and simplified version of *we have this weekend off, so could you cook fish for about thirty of us for a little party on the beach tomorrow evening?* seemed to be getting through, and Papon simply nodded.

'Sí señor. A que hora?' Seven o'clock was easy: Killy held up seven fingers,

Papon smiled and walked on, calling over his shoulder 'Hasta mañana, señor, a las siete, la fiesta!' He did a few outrageous dance steps, roaring with laughter and looking back over his shoulder, swinging the day's catch in his net.

Killy smiled and waved him goodbye. 'Adios, Papon!'

That little chance encounter, and setting something up for his crew, had really kicked Killy out of his mental slump, and brightened him up as he walked along to Arthur's and tapped on the door. 'I've got a bit of news. You up?' Arthur opened the door with his phone clamped to his ear. He was draped in an enormous, nineteen twenties-style, black and white silk dressing gown, with a huge pair of matching silk slippers Arthur referred to as his Thames Clippers. He flicked his head to usher Killy in, and carried on with his call.

'Alright, Chris. Yeah, I know but if you can't, we'll just have to take it off somewhere else, OK? Yeah. OK, Chris. Killy's here and there's a couple of things we have to sort out, so I'll come in and see you as soon as.'

He slid the phone into his pocket and shook his head with a *please help me* look. 'Fuck me, Killy. Chris is the best accountant in the business, but he could nag the bollocks off a bull elephant. He's worse than my old mum, god bless her. So what's your news, son?' He picked up his coffee and started towards the door. 'Had any overnight brainwaves? I barely slept.' Killy followed him onto the porch.

'No, but I got a text from Martin just now and due to the murder, his UN mate in New York is on his way down here to see if everything's alright with his local staff. So I said I'd meet him in the city — or here, if he wants to visit. What d'ya think?'

'Good, yeah, he might be able to tell us a bit more about what's happening.'

'Exactly. Let's see what he says. Have you heard anything from Furio?'

'Not a sausage, mate.' He lifted himself from his chair. 'Tell you what, I'd better get over and see Chris; he's having a bad one with the hire charges for the generator trucks coming in from Miami. They know there's nothing here on the island the size of the gennies we need, so they're really sticking it to us for the two big ones. Fucking pirates. They charge like a wounded bull. See you later.'

The production office was still far from the way it would be once they started shooting, definitely the calm before the storm. As the production manager, Monika ruled the roost, and she had Gussy running here and there doing just about anything that needed to be done, but without him having to deal with any of the shouting and bad tempers that can erupt as the pressure builds. Alison was in a side room meeting youngsters who wanted to work as runners; about ten of them, all film students, were waiting in the general office. With Ali's complete lack of Spanish, it was really a case of picking the ones with the best English, and she needed at least four to help with all the extras throughout the shoot. In the room with her, giving all the supposedly bilingual candidates a good chance to sell themselves, was Victoria, an experienced third assistant director from Buenos Aires who, like Gussy, could switch between English and Spanish with no hesitation.

Killy had asked around and everyone was up for a party, and he was about to walk through to see Ali when Cédric responded with a text saying he'd love to come to the set. He stuck his head in Monika's office. 'Hello, guapa. Arthur and I have a visitor coming here tomorrow. He'll need a boat to pick him up, say, mid-morning, and be back to the city early evening. I'll text his details. When's Marta due?'

'She should be docking with all the costumes at the studio jetty soon.'

'Great. See you later.' He knocked on Alison's door.

'Ready to roll, Al? Where's Gussy?'

'He's going to meet us over there. You're dead right: he's good. I think I'm going to have him running for you on set. Victoria will definitely need some back up, and he's really useful. Let's go.'

At just about five feet tall, and weighing a good eighty kilos, Ali had Killy in stitches as he manhandled her up off the beach into the boat and steered her, wobbling all over the place, to the back seat and lowered her down onto it.

'My little legs and feet can't cope, Killy! And to think, my father was in the navy. He'd have had me keelhauled.'

'I don't get it, Al; surely he took you out on boats when you were a kid?'

She shook her head with a dismissive smile. 'Afraid not Killy, I was meant to be a son, not "another bloody daughter". He was away at sea all the time and my mum was a complete landlubber; all hunting, shooting, and fishing. The two of them were a total mismatch, so we girls got lost somewhere in the mix and, when they finally split up, we were all packed off to boarding schools. How far is it, Kill?'

'We're almost there. I told the skipper to take it really slow. I figured you'd prefer it to walking ten minutes each way every day.'

'No, I'll walk, thanks. Bit of exercise instead of sitting glued to my chair.'

'OK, whatever you like. Anyway, what was it you were saying about the guy hiring in the extras, did you sort him out?'

'Not altogether, no. We had a little bit of a *heated discussion*, but we're stuck with him. A nasty piece of work. Which reminds me; I didn't tell you I got rid of that guy I was with, the engineer? You were right, he was just looking for cheap London lodgings.'

It came as no surprise to Killy, but he was impressed that she'd dumped him.

'You're OK though, eh? Went on for a while, didn't it?'

'Yes. But even though he was living rent-free at mine while I was on a job in Ireland, he couldn't be arsed to come out and see me — *and* I'd offered to buy his ticket, cos he was broke. Just as you said; a sponger. But of course, now I'm on my own again and I hate it. How many times, eh, Kill?'

'Yeah, this game looks glamorous but in reality it's hopeless for your private life.'

'Yeah. You go away to work for weeks or months, surrounded by people who become your family, and then the job ends and everyone goes back to wherever they call home. And if you're single, you're 'Billy no-mates' again. Too depressing, Kill. So even if it is just a 'someone', it's better than no one being there. Does that make sense? I wish I could find the right bloke to share my life with.'

'But can you share your life, Al? I certainly can't. Every time I give it a go, it always ends the same way. Belly up.'

The skipper had taken it so slowly it seemed they'd hardly moved, until he edged the boat right alongside the jetty. 'Here we are, Al. Not so bad, was it?'

'Maybe not for you, but it makes me nervous just being on the water. Give me a hand, will you? And thanks for listening to me groaning on. Anyway, I'm not going to spend six weeks crying in my beer. Look, Alain's come to meet us. Hello, you old French weirdo! How are you?'

'Not so much of the "old", Alison, please!' Getting her onto the jetty went quite easily with Alain pulling her up the steps. 'How are you, you fabulous creature? Come here, I want to drown in your beauty.' Alain was down on one knee, and the pair of them laughing like kids. 'Come and say hello to my friend Hortense, she's looking forward to meeting you. You too, Killy!'

One of the bigger boats was approaching, and gave them a couple of loud blasts on its foghorn. Killy waved to Marta, standing with several of her wardrobe team under the canopy that sheltered the whole front deck. It was crammed with rack after rack of costumes, together with huge stacks of cartons filled with boots, belts, and military paraphernalia filling every available space.

Marta Klein, as she always put it herself, was "a tough old New York broad". Her second language was Spanish, and she said something about Killy to the ladies standing around her just at that moment, and they all cracked up. She jumped off first and gave Killy a hug.

'How are ya, gorgeous? You're lookin' great. Show me where you're puttin' us — and it better be good, or I'll bust your fuckin' balls.' Killy hooked his arm through hers and led her to one of the less dilapidated buildings close to the jetty.

'Here you go ma'am; I saved it specially for you.' She let go of him immediately and called across for her team to begin unloading and follow her, then disappeared through the front door. The rain started at that moment, so everyone set to work draping sheets of plastic over the racks of costumes and wheeling them down the little gangway, and laughing all the way into their new workshop. The four or five local young men working with them began unloading the heavy equipment that kept the wardrobe department functioning. Off came several big industrial washing machines, then dryers, ironing boards and irons, followed by about a dozen industrial sewing machines, all in their cases. Then off came work tables, mannequins and work lights, then bundles and bundles of what appeared to be rolls of assorted fabrics.

Marta appeared back in the entrance. 'This is great, Killy! You did well. Your crown jewels are safe, baby! And there's so much more room than on a truck. It's perfect, thank you, and my ladies love it. Could we get a couple of air conditioners?'

'All part of the service m'am. They're on their way. Anything else I can do?'

'Tell me where the restroom is.'

'Down at the very end.' She disappeared again just as a van pulled up, and two ladies from the art department proceeded to hang a big, beautifully hand-painted sign over the workshop entrance: *Wardrobe/vestuario. Prop. Marta Klein. NYC*

This was typical of Alain, and they had just finished putting it up when Marta came back and laughed out loud. 'Alain! I love him. Where is he, Killy? I wanna give him a hug. Thank you, gals, *muchisimas gracias!*'

'He's gone with Ali.'

'Great! I'll get everything organised, and let's go find him.' Calling out a stream of instructions in Spanish, she disappeared inside and then came back out. 'Let's go, Killy Boy.'

By the time they arrived, Hortense, one of Alain's artists, a six-foot tall Haitian lady, had hit it off with Ali, and so with Marta's Spanish and Ali's limited schoolgirl French, and Hortense's ease in all three languages, they were very quickly getting in a party mood. Killy got a beer and a crafty wink from Hortense just as his phone buzzed.

It was Cédric. 'Hello, Killian. Sadly, I'm not going to have time to visit you. And we have so much to talk about …' He paused a tiny bit too long, Killy thought, almost as though he was hinting at something. 'As a result of the incident, there's a great deal of tension in the capital, so I've decided it's better for me to stay here. Could you possibly come to the city this evening? Perhaps we could have some supper at my hotel?'

'Let me organise somewhere for us to have a meal together, Cédric. Do you still eat everything?'

He chuckled. 'Yes, I haven't changed.'

'Great. Shall we say eight o'clock?'

'That would be perfect, Killy. Thank you.'

'I'll sort somewhere for us and text you the address. See you later.' Gussy was walking towards him as he ended the call and clearly with something he wanted to say, so Killy signalled to him just to stay where he was, and called Monika.

'Hello, beauty. New plan. I'm going to pick up a change of clothes and then go and meet our guest this evening. Would you get a boat to pick me up at the jetty and take me down to the city, then bring me back first thing, please? Ask Carmen to book me a room for tonight, will you?'

'OK, but please be careful, Killy. And make sure you take your passport.'

'Yep. Let Arthur know what's happening, and I'll see you at the fiesta.'

Call ended, Killy turned to Gussy. 'Right, what's up?'

'I just wanted to ask you if I can do anything to help with the party?'

'No, but thanks for offering. It's your first day off, so all you have to do is get to know everyone and have a good time, alright? Rosalia and her boys are on it. There *is* actually something; I'm meeting an old friend in the city for supper tonight. Can you recommend somewhere private but not too fancy, where we can eat well and have a quiet chat?'

'Of course. Casa Salvador. My family have used it for years. What time?'

'Eight o'clock, for two.'

10

They were inside the harbour in under an hour, and tied up alongside the massive stone walls that had sheltered ships for centuries. This was old colonial Spain in all its glory. Killy ran up the steps onto the quayside. There were no officials, and boats were coming and going, but through the gates out on the street, Killy could see things were different. There was a line of huge armoured cars surrounded by dozens of riot police in full combat gear, smoking and cooling off under the trees, all armed and looking ready for trouble. As he walked towards the gateway, an aggressive-looking uniformed policeman stepped out.

'Pasaporte!'

He handed it over and the man flicked through it, and checked the landing card that Furio's tame official had stapled in there, what now seemed like months ago, then handed it back. Killy would normally have walked to the hotel but he needed to shower and change, and didn't want to be late for dinner, so he crossed the road to a line of taxis and opened the rear door of the first one in the queue.

'Hotel Royale, por favor.' The driver turned and smiled at him as he pulled out into the traffic.

'You English?'

He laughed. 'Yeah. You been there?'

'I was born there, mate! Mum was booted out and sent back here, so we came with her.'

'When was that?'

''bout ten years ago now, I was still a kid. What you doing here?'

'Making a film.'

'What, here in the city?'

'No up the other end of the island.'

'Another world up there, mate. Roads are murder. What sort of film? Got any stars in it?'

'Nobody you've ever heard of. So, how's life here?'

'Not too bad. I make a living. The old grandad has a little bit of land, so we're all out there with him. It's not really a farm but he's got a few animals and chickens, and you can live cheap here if you can grow stuff yourself. He's brilliant, the old boy, so yeah, it's probably a better life in that way. But I miss London. Who d'you support?'

'I'm Islington.'

'Gooner, eh?'

'Yup, all the way. You sound south?'

'Lambeth, yeah. I'm Chelsea. Here you go: Hotel Royale. Have that one on me, fuckin' Gooner!' They both laughed. 'Here, take me card. It's a bit battered. If you're coming over here again give me a shout. I'll pick you up at the airport, and you can pay me then. Have a good one.'

Killy got out but paused by the driver's open window. 'What's this I hear about the government grabbing land up in the north; do you know what it's all about?'

He was smiling and shaking his head. 'You learn to keep your nut down here, mate. Don't make trouble, and keep your fingers crossed they don't nick your patch of ground — or anything else they fancy. Those poor bastards up there were unlucky cos the developers finally got the deal they wanted from the government, and there's absolutely nothing anyone can do about it. It's "Island Rules" here, mate; but don't quote me. See ya, Gooner!' He put his arm out to indicate he was pulling into the traffic, and was gone.

Killy stood staring after him, thinking about what he'd said. 'We spend a small fortune on a local fixer and I get more information and a free ride from a taxi driver.' He looked at the name on the card and smiled. 'You said it, Enrique Edmonds. "Island Rules", indeed.' He slipped the card into his wallet and, nodding to the very scruffily uniformed doorman, he walked up the steps and into reception. The Hotel Royale had definitely seen better days, but with dozens of their people coming in and out over several weeks, Monika had done a very good deal, meaning bookings could be made and changed as and when necessary with no charges, which was a big plus. They were all very friendly on the reception desk and when he came back down, the young lady who'd checked him in gave him a local map and marked it up with the way to the restaurant, and assured him it wasn't worth taking a cab. The strangely quiet city was starting to cool down as the night came on, and there were police and soldiers on every main intersection; he passed a couple of roadblocks where cars were being pulled over and checked, but nobody stopped him.

Casa Salvador was simple-looking and tucked into a side street just off one of the main boulevards. The elderly maitre d' greeted him very cordially and walked him through the main room, which was quite busy, and showed him to a little corner booth in the smaller back room, where the only other customers were a well-dressed, rather portly, older gentleman and a much younger lady. He'd just made himself comfortable when the teenage boy he'd kidded and teased, now a very well-turned-out young man in his early thirties, was walking across the room towards him. He was wearing a smart, white linen suit and an immaculate blue shirt.

'Cédric! Lovely to see you.' He stood up to greet him.

Cédric's handsome, very fine-featured face, which hadn't really changed much, couldn't hide his pleasure at this reunion any more than Killy could his as they shook hands.

'And you too, Killy. Such a long time.'

'So, where do we start?'

The conversation ranged through their lives and family histories since they'd last seen each other. Killy's career and where it had taken him, Cédric's parents and how and where they were now, and it wasn't until the waiter was serving them coffee that Killy realised not one word had been spoken about what he'd thought his companion had wanted to say.

He asked for the bill, which Cédric insisted he pay, but with a very courtly inclination of his balding head, the maitre d' quietly announced that everything had been settled.

'You are guests of the Santini family, señores. Would you like me to telephone for a taxi?' Cédric looked a bit taken aback. Killy smiled.

'People we're working with here. Very nice of them.'

'Very generous, Killy; would you please pass on my thanks.' Then, in response to the offer of a taxi, 'No thank you, señor, I have a car waiting for me. Can I drop you at your hotel, Killy?'

'I'm fine, it's very close. I'll walk you to your car, though.'

They were the last to leave. Killy shook hands with their host and palmed him a twenty-dollar tip, which was gracefully and gratefully received. As he bade them goodnight and locked the door behind them, a big car with a very prominent UN sticker in the windshield came gliding along the dimly-lit, deserted street and stopped right by them, its motor purring as the uniformed driver jumped out, saluted Cédric, and opened the kerbside rear door for him. Cédric nodded to the driver.

'Killian, are you sure I can't drop you at your hotel?'

'No, I'll stretch my legs for ten minutes.' Cédric pulled a business card from his top jacket pocket and handed it to him.

'This has all my personal details. If you come to New York, please be my guest and stay with us.' They hugged goodbye and he climbed into the car. The driver closed the door behind him and bade Killy goodnight, before sliding behind the wheel and driving slowly away.

Killy looked at the card and held it up in the light of the restaurant windows. Cédric Boisjoly. He remembered how they'd all laughed at its English translation, and "Prettywood" still made him smile. Then he flipped it over, and in very neat handwriting there was a message:

Regime change pending, replacement designated, assassination part of plan, theoretically peaceful transition, possible my phone being monitored even when not in use.

Killy had heard about phones being vulnerable in that way, but whilst never having been averse to a scrap, he preferred keeping that sort of stuff in front of the camera. There were still police and soldiers everywhere on every intersection, just the odd taxi cruising slowly touting for business, but again nobody stopped him. He ran up the steps and tapped on the glass of the Royale's old revolving doors. The ancient night porter shuffled his way over from the desk and welcomed him in. 'Buenas noches, señor, qué número?' He gave him the Spanish for 1066 and was tempted to make a joke of it, but immediately realised that it wouldn't work anyway. The old man handed him the key with its enormous brass fob and led him to the lift, opened the doors, and leaned in to press the tenth-floor button. 'Hasta mañana, señor.' Killy slipped him all the local change he had. As the old man took it, he smiled. 'Gracias, señor. Buenas noches.'

But the *noche* was not *buena*, at all. Killy finished up leaning on the balcony rail, looking down on the deserted street for what felt like hours. He finally gave up and turned in. Then, suddenly, his phone alarm was going mad. He was certain he'd spent the whole night in an intense and really emotional conversation with Susie, that she'd started by asking him what he would do if her cancer proved fatal. He was totally exhausted.

11

With no time to lie there reliving the whole thing yet again, Killy was up, showered, and dressed in a few minutes. He downed a big glass of freshly squeezed orange juice in the breakfast room and grabbed a banana for the journey. He dumped his key on the empty front desk and walked out onto the street, slung his backpack over his shoulder, and jogged towards the docks. There were still police and troops everywhere, but the morning air was cool and it felt good to be on the move. However, having explained that he'd had a sleepless night to the skipper, who appeared to have had a very good night himself, Killy stretched out across the back seat and slept until Arthur's voice came booming at him from up on the jetty at Los Zapateros, 'I can't get the staff anymore. Get up you lazy bastard! Come on, I got them to fix us a full English. You hungry?'

It was a feast, laid out beautifully on the table of Arthur's porch in little covered earthenware pots. 'So tell me, son, how were things in the big city? And, more importantly, how was your friend?' Arthur was pouring out questions, tea, and coffee all at once.

'Crawling with police and military, and Cédric was just as I remembered him. He gave me this as he left. We'd spent the whole evening catching up; he never said a word about anything else.' He slid the card across the table.

Arthur read it several times, then passed it back. 'More tea?'

'Yes, I will. It's good.'

'Not really any wiser are we, son? More or less everything that might go wrong has already, so how much worse could it get?' They stared at each other over the remnants of breakfast, both knowing that all they could do was wait and see. On a normal day off, they would have wandered down to the beach for a dip but there were too many unknowns. Arthur picked up his phone. 'Monika, Killy and I need your advice please, sweetheart. Would you? Great, thanks.' He put his phone back down on the table. 'Have you spoken to Furio?'

'No. I felt a bit funny not asking him to the party tonight and there's a standby boat here that could go and get him.' Arthur called him.

'Furio, Killy's organised a fiesta for this evening. We'd like you to come. Yeah, we know, we'll send a boat down.' He dropped the phone back into his top pocket. 'Get that sorted will you, son? I'm going to have a shower and change. See you in a bit.'

Monika managed to arrive exactly as Arthur reappeared in full monster tropical beach attire, with yellow and red parrots featuring strongly, and his Panama set at a very jaunty angle. She stood back to admire his sartorial splendour.

'Dressed for the party, Arthur? Little early, aren't you?'

'Yeah! Ready to rock and roll, beauty! Well, I will be. I've been indoors all week. Let's all have a wander along the beach and find a nice spot in the shade for a chat.'

They certainly chatted; for four hours non-stop, until eventually Furio came walking towards them through the palm trees, definitely looking a lot smarter than usual, his customary linen suit appearing to have been pressed instead of slept in. Arthur dragged himself up and gave him a hug and a slap on the back.

'Just in time, Furio. We're going back to mine and ordering a bite to eat, so tell Monika what you fancy.' They ambled along as though this were a normal Saturday at the beach, whilst Monika rattled off their requests to Rosalia. She held her phone away from her for a second.

'Does anyone want wine?

Arthur butted in, 'No need, darlin'. Plenty of that tonight. Just tell her to mix us up a couple of big jugs of orange and lime, and plenty of fizzy water.'

They sat around the kitchen table, and Arthur placed Furio opposite him. 'Right, what do you know?'

He was obviously prepared. 'A very senior security contact assured me, Arthur, that the story about Alonso being involved with a Mexican cartel is just exactly that; a story, a fabrication. This was a political act, carried out by a professional killer. However, it appears that your informant was correct, and the president very shortly will retire for "health reasons". The current vice president, Amerigo Reyes, will replace him.

'"Foreign interests", as it was put to me, who have a great deal of influence on the island, have been pushing for the president to go for some time, and Alonso's death has forced him to recognise the implication that it could well be him next.'

Arthur leaned back in his chair. 'So, anything else?'

'It's anticipated, indeed assured, that due to his popularity as vice president the whole process will go smoothly, and that with the president having departed, as Vice President señor Reyes will immediately begin serving out the remaining two years of this current presidential term. Good news for us is that the head of the Customs department is a very old friend of señor Reyes, so he will be retaining his position. But unfortunately, Arthur, his price has increased by ten percent.'

'Why? I'm already paying the bastard a fortune.'

Furio made an elaborate, very Latin, *what can one do?* gesture with his hands. 'It would appear, Arthur, that what we have been paying wasn't what he was receiving.'

'OK. So basically what you're saying or, in fact, *not* saying, is that your mate Alonso was taking a cut, am I right?'

Furio raised his eyebrows and nodded. 'Yes, Arthur, that would appear to be the case.'

Arthur shrugged. 'OK. Pay him what he's asking for. We don't have much choice, do we? Anything else?'

'That's it, Arthur. That's everything.'

'Alright then. So well done, son, meeting's over. Let's have a nice lunch and then go and have a bit of fun, eh?'

A brief downpour suddenly started and almost as quickly ended, and so Arthur ushered them all out onto the porch to enjoy the view of the sea through the trees and breathe the now cooled afternoon air. When lunch finally arrived Rosalia had sent, with her compliments, a bottle of her best white wine along with the soft drinks. As their meeting was now over, Arthur opened the bottle and poured a drop for Monika to taste and then, as she gave it a nod of approval, it was glasses all round. They toasted each other and the movie they were about to make, drank a glass, and ordered more. And then a lot more. The well-intentioned orange juice sat abandoned on the side-table as lunch went on and on until, more or less unnoticed, the sun had completely set and they could hear faint music coming from along the beach as the party was getting started. Monika ran off immediately to get changed but Killy, still in the same clothes he'd put on back at the Royale, was too far gone to worry about how he looked. Arthur and Furio were deep into a musical conversation about the wonders of Beethoven, and as they went back and forth about a composer they both clearly worshipped, Killy led them through the trees down to the sea, so they could walk along the beach for the hundred yards or so to where things were taking shape.

They were the first to arrive and the lovely, simple Latin American dance music playing from a speaker up in the trees set the whole scene off perfectly. Down near the water's edge, Papon was building starter fires in a long barbecue next to a wheelbarrow full of charcoal. Killy walked over and asked him where the fish was, and he pointed his huge, soot-covered hand towards a big, old-fashioned zinc bath at the foot of a tree next to a battered picnic table set out with all his cooking tools. Above it hung an old oil lantern to work by and it shone directly down on the bath, which was full of fish packed in ice, and right on the top was a massive blue one.

Rosalia's team had rolled grass matting onto the sand from the water's edge right up into the trees, and placed chairs around little tables each decorated with flowers and stubby candles that they'd already lit. There were two big fridges set behind a bar fashioned out of driftwood and palm fronds, and decorated with seashells. Tiny fairy lights wound in and around it, and up and out amongst the trees. Gussy, in a beautiful, white cotton Cuban shirt with hand-embroidered pockets, came walking across the mats. 'Buenas tardes, señor Wilde! Welcome. Can I get you a beer?'

Roughly fourteen hours later, with no assistance from

his alarm but with a pounding in his head so intense he didn't dare open his eyes, Killy tried to string together the images of the night's festivities in some sort of order. The whole thing was kaleidoscopic snatches of scenes that started with Gussy serving him the beer, then everyone in the crew dancing the conga, then Hortense grabbing him and trying to teach him the merengue, Julian and Wally deep in a discussion about Bond film stunts, and then Arthur, having not once stopped dancing with everyone on the crew, staggering off to his bungalow. And that was it; all accompanied by an incessant banging he couldn't control.

12

King Arthur was sitting in the garden with a pot of tea as Killy finally joined him. 'Morning, son, how did it go, you stay late?'

'No way. Was already too whacked out. Had a little dance, made sure everything was going alright, and that's all I can remember. Pass me the milk will you, Arthur? Has Furio gone?'

'Yeah. Just grabbed a coffee, said he'd had a great night, and off he went. What d'you reckon? He's not bullshitting, is he?'

'Well, those trucks are being loaded onto the ferry over in Miami right about now, Arthur, and they'll be docking down in Nelson at five tomorrow morning, so fingers crossed.' Killy's phone buzzed. It was 'Bunny'; Freddie Bunton, the chief electrician — or the 'Gaffer Sparks' as he's known in the business. 'Morning, Bun. How you doing, mate? Where are you? Everything alright?'

'All good here, Killy. They've put us in the Royale; is Arthur going skint? I mean, I've stayed in some dodgy hotels in my time, but this gaff takes the fucking biscuit, mate. Anyway, me and Pete are here, safe and sound.'

'Great. So, give me a call in the morning as soon as the boat arrives. Have a good day, mate.'

Arthur had guessed what Bunny had been saying. 'Is he going on about the Royale? He still lives in the same block of council flats I came out of, and it doesn't matter how many stars it's got, there's not a hotel in the world that he hasn't moaned about! And it's me that has to pay the fucking bills.'

Killy was shaking his head. 'Sorry, Arthur, I really overdid it; gotta lie down.'

'Go on, son, I shan't be long behind you.'

Killy slept all day and woke just as the sun was setting. He reached for his phone; it was six-thirty pm. He texted Ali. '*Hello beauty. Get Gussy to bring me my big work folder will you please? And tell him to let me know he's here.*' He had a shower and then, as he pulled on a pair of shorts, there was a knock at the open door. 'Hang on, Gussy, I'm just coming. Hiya, how are you?'

'Good, thank you. It was a great party. Everyone was so friendly. Do you do this every week?'

'No way, and this was special getting a whole weekend off. You'll soon see; after six days, everyone's so exhausted all they want to do on the day off is sleep. But we'll certainly have a big one when we wrap.'

'Yes, I keep hearing this *wrap*. What is it?'

'It comes from way back in the early days of cinema, when they used reels of proper film. W.R.A.P. stands for wind reel, and print. It signified that filming was over for the day, and all the shots that the director had chosen to save could be developed in the lab and printed.'

'Thank you! And thank you again for the party. And thank you for your notes on movie making; I'm already beginning to realise how different this business is.'

Killy smiled. 'Good. You'll really get it once we start. The picture becomes your world for those few weeks, nothing else matters. It's like emergency surgery; life and death, there isn't anything that can be allowed to interfere. It's the same ethos as the theatre. It doesn't matter what happens, 'the show must go on'. You have to give yourself up to it entirely; family and friends have to take second place. I think you're going to do well. I'll know soon enough. Anyway, on another note: the situation in the capital. Is it likely to go on for long?'

'I'm not the best person to ask, Killy, but I could make some enquiries?'

'Can't do any harm. Would it be easier if you went down there? I can spare you for a day or so.'

He thought about it briefly. 'Perhaps it would be better to see people in person. Yes, why not?'

'OK, go right now. Take the standby boat and if it makes sense to stay a bit longer, just call me.' He watched him walk down the steps, opened his work folder, but then closed it. He'd managed to sleep off most of his hangover but paperwork could wait. He needed to eat and then hit the hay again.

On his way to the jetty, Gussy let his mother know he was going to be home for a couple of nights 'as his new employers had asked if he could shed any light on the current unrest, as it was already impacting on preparations for filming'. Lydia was instantly on the case and suggested she might have a few old family friends round for a little supper the following evening, 'to let them catch up with you and your new career.' The skipper was overjoyed to be getting another unscheduled night at home and, having refuelled, he let Gussy take the wheel, stretched himself across the back seat, and slept the whole way.

Killy's phone rang just before five the following morning. Finally feeling in full working order, he answered it on the first ring.

'Morning, Bun, everything alright?'

'Yeah. Boat's arrived a bit early, Kill, they're about to start getting it all off. I'll call you back when everything's unloaded ...' He went quiet. This wasn't what Killy needed.

'What's up, Bun?' Killy could hear him breathing.

'I dunno mate, hang on.' The line went quiet again and then Bunny came back on, 'I just started to follow Furio down the ramp and one of the customs blokes waved me away. Now he's holding his hand up and shakin' his head.'

'Just stay on the line, Bun, will you?'

'Yeah. Furio's talking to the customs geezer who seems in charge, and they just went behind the first truck.'

'Tell me as soon as you can see them again.'

Killy was on the phone at that hour of the morning because Enzo and his camera crew, together with probably well over half a million dollars' worth of state-of-the-art camera equipment, with a huge daily rental charge, were ready to start filming. However, without the generators and the truckloads of lighting equipment Bunny was waiting to unload, nothing could happen. Killy's anxiety level was rising steadily.

'Can you see 'em yet, Bun?'

'No, still can't.'

There was another long silence, then Killy started to panic.

'Still nothing, Bun!?'

Then silence again as Killy started to take long deep breaths.

'No ... Oh. Hang on, Kill ... Yeah! Yeah, he's there, and they're waving us down. Come on, Pete! I'll call you back, Kill, when we've got it all off. Alright?'

Breathing a great deal easier, Killy made a cup of tea

and sat down at the kitchen table. It was far too early to go into the office, so he spent the next couple of hours bringing all his paperwork up to date. Then Bunny texted: *All signed and sealed. Furio in the bar having a drink with customs fellas and we're on our way. Two jeeps full of guards, all tooled up with AK forty-sevens! Like Ilford Lane on a Saturday night! All best, Bun.*

At just around the same time, in the centre of the city, Gussy was having coffee with a close school friend who was currently doing an internship with a member of the island's Congress. She'd been completely shocked by the news of the assassination, but had no insight into what might be going on regarding the seeming state of emergency. He then met with one of his oldest friends, who was working for a lobbying company and spending a lot of time playing tennis with senior politicians. He'd made enquiries and had it on good authority that two weeks before he'd been killed, Alonso had been secretly photographed at a big wedding in Miami, laughing and joking with two notorious drug barons, but as to the current situation on the island, he couldn't tell Gussy anything new. That evening, only slightly better informed, he put on a jacket and tie and joined his mother and her guests for dinner.

Señor Felipé Asturiano-Barbera's ancestors were traders who had come to the Americas in the wake of Columbus. Through very close family connections, Don Felipé, as he was respectfully known, had, as a young man, become Lydia's godfather, and a generation later he'd happily taken on the same role when Gussy was born. 'Uncle Philip', as he liked his godson to call him, especially once he'd started to excel in English, had always followed the boy's progress with great interest. When Lydia called to let him know that Gussy at last appeared to have found a promising job, he'd happily accepted her supper invitation. He was every bit the classic Anglophile Spanish patrician, immaculately turned out in a Saville Row suit, with his rich, thick, now-greying black hair worn lightly oiled and swept back. His magnificent Roman nose and hooded, steely-blue eyes accentuated his warrior heritage but beneath it all, he was a gentle and loving man who adored both his godchildren and, great raconteur that he was, he pepped up the evening's somewhat stuffy, high-toned Spanish table talk with one or two rather risqué anecdotes, coincidentally concerning the current president's peculiar peccadilloes.

The two other couples making up the party were old friends of Lydia who'd known Gussy all his life, but they were mere set dressing, as Lydia knew only too well that if anyone could illuminate the current political situation, it was Uncle Philip. Once supper was over, he suddenly switched to his quaintly-accented English.

'Gustavo, please come with me out onto the terrace while I smoke. I have to be in London next week and my English is so rusty, I need some practice. Come.'

So while his godfather trimmed and lit his cigar, Gussy told him that the production had already suffered some hold-ups due to what had gone on, and asked him directly if they could assume that things might settle back down. Without any hesitation, Uncle Philip assured him that it certainly would and that the change of leadership was definitely imminent, but that any military action would most likely be confined to the capital and the surrounding areas.

The following morning, Gussy sat opposite Killy completing his debriefing.

'So your uncle reckons that up at this end of the island we should be alright then, yes? Anything else?'

'He asked if he might be able to come with my ma and pay us a visit once we're filming, but told me not to hesitate to call him if we thought he could help us further in any way.'

'Good old Uncle Philip. A proper godfather, eh?'

Monika called. 'Killy, I've just spoken to Furio and all the special effects equipment has cleared customs, so once Colonel Kubitt and his military assistant arrive, we can get everyone together at the landing beach. What do you think?'

'Definitely. Bunny and his Best Boy should be there, too, so they can get some idea of what's needed to cable it all up. Okay, yeah, see you later.'

Gussy was clearly wanting a question answered. 'Killy, please what is this *Best Boy?*'

'OK, the chief electrician is called the Gaffer and his second-in-command is the 'Best Boy'. I'm sure there'll be a lot of head scratching as to what the job title should be as women start doing it, which is already happening.' Gussy left as Killy walked over to Arthur's office, knocked on his door and pushed it open. Arthur smiled at him.

'So what's the scoop, son, are we winning again?'

Killy took a couple of seconds to figure out his response. 'Yes, Arthur, I think we are.'

But he wasn't altogether convinced.

13

The scenes they were going to shoot at night, on what was now called the 'marine landing beach', were complicated, and involved a great deal of planning and preparation. Bunny and Pete, his best boy, were amongst the palms, measuring out the various distances they would have to run the power cables needed for the lighting. Killy was making notes on every aspect of the sequence and all the potential pitfalls. Pete pulled a thermos flask from his backpack and called out, 'Either of you want tea?'

Killy walked towards him. 'You got enough?'

Bunny, who was squatting against a tree rolling a cigarette, heard Killy's question and looked up. 'No, I'm alright, boys. I need a gasper first but if there's any left, I'll have one.' Pete poured Killy a cup and passed it to him.

'Cheers. I noticed your family name's Garcia, you got Spanish connections?'

'Yep, mum and dad. Proper Spanish cockney me, Killy.'

'Speak the lingo?'

'No choice. Neither of them have much English even now, so I was the family interpreter since I was a nipper. Still am.' He nodded towards Bunny. 'Why d'you think old grumpy nuts brought me out here?'

Bunny laughed. 'Well, certainly not cos you're the best

fuckin' electrician I ever worked with!' He finished his smoke and shoved the remains deep into the sand with his gnarled old fingers, 'Any of that Rosy still going?'

Pete poured him what was left of the tea. 'There you go. That's it.'

Colonel Kubitt walked into the clearing, looking as smart and crisp as always. 'You guys done? Rafa and I wanna check out who they hired in from the back streets of Nelson to play US marines. It should be interesting.'

As he turned towards the beach, Killy called after him, 'Regis, I'll come back to base with you two. I'd like to see the new recruits, myself. We're going to be spending a lot of time together over the next few weeks.'

Regis was sitting up front, so Killy took the opportunity to sit next to his newly-arrived assistant, ex-Master Sergeant Raphael Mendoza.

'How do things look, Raphael? Good spot to shoot?'

'Rafa please, Killy. Yes, very good location; plenty of beach to work on. Will you film the submarine sequence there, or fake it somewhere else?'

'Good question, Rafa. We're still talking that one over.'

'The sub will definitely make the landing much more realistic, Killy; seeing the marines coming out onto the deck at night, and loading their gear into the landing boats and then launching them. Regis and I did a lot of that type of work in the service.' They talked all the way back to the base, covering every aspect of what an amphibious military landing at night involved, and by the time they moored up to the jetty, Killy knew they were in very good hands.

He went directly to Marta's workshop, and stepping out

of the glaring sunlight into the big, high-ceilinged room was such a contrast. To the gentle intermittent whir of sewing machines, a dozen or so of Marta's team were working on piles of military uniforms laid in neat lines across the vast work tables. Another three or four of them were hurrying back and forth from an adjoining room, taking finished items through for fittings and carrying back more for alterations. The atmosphere was wonderful; there was lots of banter and laughter going on between the men and women, but everyone there was focused on getting the enormous job finished. The local extras who were to be wearing the uniforms might lack a trained military bearing, but they were definitely going to be dressed to look the part.

Marta burst in from the other room in a tailored set of military fatigues and a flowered bush hat that must have taken one of her milliners hours to create. She looked incredible.

'Hey, Killy, you sexy sonofabitch! Come give me a hug, I'm sick of uniforms. Except mine, of course. I love it! Where's Regis? Is Rafa with him, then? I hope so. My ladies are all crazy to see him. What a hunk!'

'You're not kidding. And you're not looking too shabby, yourself.'

She did a tiny mock curtsey. 'Why thank you, young sir.'

Killy nodded towards the room she'd come from. 'Fittings in there?'

'No, that's just the waiting room. I have Gussy hustling everyone along. Boy is he a good kid. And you found him on a plane?'

Regis and Rafa walked in at that moment and the whole room erupted in giggles and a lot of racy local Spanish, causing general hilarity. Marta waited until it began to calm down and then took over.

'OK, gentlemen, let's leave your adoring fans and go see how the guys you've got to work with look in uniform.'

She stood aside and let them through the door, then turned and whispered something in the local dialect that had all the ladies and Rafa in stitches. Killy didn't understand her.

'What did she say?'

Rafa could barely speak. 'I can't translate word-for-word, that was a Spanish you don't hear much anymore. But I certainly got the meaning; it was pretty raunchy stuff. Marta's some woman!'

'Certainly is, my friend, in any language! I'll leave you gentlemen here. Be carefil!'

Killy stepped outside into a gentle afternoon shower. There were umbrellas parked just inside, ready for protecting costumes once they were being worn, so he grabbed one and walked along to see the head of special effects, Tony Bird, or *the Prof*, as they called him. Wally was there with two of his stunt team, whilst the Prof's special effects technicians were unpacking the reinforced caskets that carried their kit wherever in the world they were working.

As he came through the door, Killy called out, 'Morning gents. Thought I'd give you a little courtesy call, Tony and make sure you're all sorted space-wise?' The Prof was scholarly-looking, even in the ancient blue overalls he always wore to work. Twinkly-eyed, neatly bearded, very tall and angular, he fit the nickname perfectly.

'Great thanks, Killy. Wally and I have been talking our way through the beach landing and the rescue, and we were about to get onto to the whole submarine scenario. Arthur assures me that it's from exactly the right period but he couldn't say what military class it was. The owner has made a lot of major changes internally at vast expense which, via computerised controls, supposedly make it possible to operate with a greatly reduced crew. However, I fear getting an antique submarine to surface and then dive on cue might prove quite interesting.'

'Well, it's scheduled to arrive at five this afternoon, so I'm sure once we actually see it and talk everything through with the owner, we'll have a much better idea of where we stand. So perhaps we should all rendezvous at the jetty for, let's say, quarter-to? Is that OK? Anyway, I'll see you later, I have to go and look at the dressing rooms. See you later, gents.'

Monika was waiting for him. 'Killy, I can't find a trailer big enough for Nathan anywhere on the island and it's too expensive to bring one in from the States, so Ali and I think we should take the space you've designated for the supporting artists changing areas, and convert them into two separate Star dressing rooms for Nathan and Serena. What do you think?'

'Nathan has a dressing room floor area specified in his contract and you can be sure he'll measure it down to the last centimetre, so let's do exactly that, OK? We've got the materials and the craftsmen, and there's still another area left we can divide up for the extras, and it's close to makeup and wardrobe, so nothing will change. When does Serena arrive?'

'Tuesday. Ali just finalised all her travel arrangements with her agent. She's evidently not keen on smaller aircraft, so Gussy is meeting her flight and then bringing her up here by boat. Other than that request she sounds very reasonable, so fingers crossed.'

As planned, by five pm Julian, Killy, the Prof, and Wally were gathered on the jetty watching the veteran vessel slowly making its way towards them. Killy was standing next to the Prof, who was looking it over through a small pair of binoculars while identifying it on a phone app.

'It's a US Navy Gato Class, Killy. According to this, it would have seen service in the Pacific against the Japanese. I'm astonished it's survived, I'd have thought it would have been scrapped years ago. Absolutely perfect for us, and this says a few of them were adapted for covert landings in the sixties! So, bingo. Well done, Arthur!'

By the time they'd all walked along to the end of the jetty, the deck crew had gone down below, leaving two crewmen securing a gangway. A tall, older man in a blue sailing cap beckoned them to join him, and his accent gave him away immediately as a Dutchman.

'Come aboard, gentlemen. I'm Lex, and this is Ilze, my wife, and our daughter Hannah.'

The two 'crewmen' now shedding their hard hats and work gear were, in fact, mother and daughter, neither one far short of six-feet tall and both with the same blonde hair and dazzling blue eyes as Lex. Killy did the intros.

'Good evening to you all, and welcome to Los Zapateros. I'm Killy Wilde, the first assistant director, and this is Julian, our director. This gentleman is Tony, the head of special effects, and Wally here is our stunt coordinator, both of whom you'll be seeing a lot of. She's a fine-looking vessel, Lex, does she have a name?'

'In her military days she was only ever known by a number, but that changed as she moved from navy to navy around the world serving a lot of countries after the US had finished with her. We bought her from the Brazilian government and christened her *Hondsbossch*, which is where our family comes from. Would you all like a little tour down below?'

'If that's OK with you, Lex?'

'Of course. I'll leave you in Ilze's very capable hands; she really runs the ship. Ilze, darling, I'll prepare cocktails on the forward deck, yes? Shall we say in half an hour?'

'Perfect, darling. Perhaps forty-five minutes?' She then led everyone down the steep steel ladder. 'Please follow me, gentlemen, and mind your heads; these boats were not designed for tall people. The steel is more than eighty years old but it's every bit as unforgiving as it was when they built her.'

Ilze couldn't have known to figure the Prof into her timing. He was absolutely in his element and questioned each one of the operating crew on every detail. His questions went on and on, but as they wouldn't be filming inside the sub all Killy wanted to do was hold the handles of the periscope the way he'd seen it done in so many war films, and then climb back up the ladder and breathe fresh air again.

Julian finally managed to ask a question, 'In terms of submerging and then resurfacing on cue, Ilze, is that going to present any difficulties?'

'From a static situation or in motion?'

'Static will be fine.'

'That won't be a problem at all, Julian. Whenever we're going to encounter bad weather, the crew take us down and on we go, untroubled by wind and waves. Now, shall we all go and have a drink up on the deck?'

Killy left everyone having cocktails, then walked to the area designated as the parade ground to check on how the military extras were coming along. He could hear Rafa's commands accompanied by the tramp of a lot of boots marching in time.

'Left, left, left-right, left!!'

Regis was watching the rehearsal as Killy came up behind him.

'They're looking pretty good, Regis.'

He turned and smiled. 'They should be, Killy, they're professional troops; the government has loaned them to us for a couple of weeks to show the supporting artists how it's all done. Our extras don't look quite so promising, but let's see how they shape up under Rafa.'

Just at that moment, Rafa roared out, '*Dismissed*!' and the men crossed to the armourer's workshop to hand over their guns, then piled into the changing rooms as Rafa, even out of uniform looking every bit the sergeant, marched over to join his boss who was explaining to Killy why the soldiers understood the English commands.

'There's always been a lot of US military input down here, Killy, and their commanding officer is a West Point graduate.'

'And are their insignia, guns, and packs all OK?'

'Yes, all exactly as they should be. And I hear you have a vintage US submarine joining the production. Would you mind if we go visit? Rafa and I both did submarine landings and we'd sure appreciate a little look-see.'

'Of course, I'm on my way back there right now. Follow me.'

Arthur was waving to them from up on the sub's bridge with a cocktail in his other hand and sporting yet another beach shirt, this one featuring a lot of iridescent yellow dragons that could probably have been spotted several miles out to sea. Lex saw the three of them approaching the gangway.

'Come aboard, gentlemen. We're having drinks on the deck and I shall be right down to join you.'

Regis and Rafa were more interested in looking round the sub than getting involved in an impromptu cocktail party, so as soon as they stepped aboard, Killy quickly introduced them to Hannah and Ilze and then explained to them and Lex what they would be doing on the film. Lex caught on right away.

'Delighted to have you aboard gentlemen. Perhaps you'd like a little tour below?' They accepted immediately and the three of them disappeared down the hatch.

Hannah was having a jolly time, with a mesmerised Wally and Julian hanging on her every word, as Ilze came and offered Killy another of her fearsomely strong cocktails.

'I'd prefer some sort of soft drink, Ilze, if that's possible? Big day tomorrow. By the way, I assume that you must have cleared customs out at sea this morning? No problems, I take it?'

'None at all, Killy. Of course, had we been going in the opposite direction we could have been held up for days, but nobody smuggles drugs *out* of Miami *into* Latin America, so they stopped us, stamped our passports and transit documents for the boat, and that was that. Without a doubt the return trip won't be as easy.'

'Excuse me?' They both looked up to see Arthur leaning over the rail of the bridge directly above them. 'Excuse me, Ilze. Killy, can you nip up here a minute?'

'Coming right up, Arthur.' Ilze watched him climb the steel ladder. 'I'll get you a glass of mineral water, Killy.'

'Hello, boy. Just been on the phone with Nathan's agent; they're saying Serena's profile is not big enough to be playing opposite him, and they want someone with more of a name.'

'So who the fuck do they think they'll get, Arthur? Bedford's gobbled up practically all the budget for talent, and we're lucky her agent's canny enough to let her do it for what you're paying.

These people are totally fucking bonkers. How did you leave it?'

'I said I'd signed her contract and I'm not going back on it. I had a quick chat with Nick in London, and he assures me Bedford has no casting approval anywhere in our agreement, so he either plays opposite her or he's breaking his contract, simple as that. The arrogance of some of these people. A reality TV star who gets a couple of big breaks, and now he reckons he's a new Tom Hanks! *Not a big enough name* to play opposite him? What a jumped-up schmuck! Serena is a proper, trained theatre actress. He should be so lucky!'

Then, just as Arthur was about to launch into another tirade, Ilze called up from the deck, 'Arthur, Killy, your drinks are here and I'm about to light the barbecue on the rear deck. We caught a lot of fish on the way here, can I tempt you?' The mention of food had Arthur smiling down at her like some benign old priest from his pulpit.

'You certainly can, Ilze. Grilled fresh fish? I should say so, eh, Killy? We'll be right down.' That was the beginning of the end of that evening.

14

He stood in front of the mirror getting ready to start the day and called Gloria, pleased he'd taken it easy on the drink.

'Hello, G, it's Killy—'

'Manjaro?' It was a little joke she'd made years before, and it had stuck. 'You want your hair sorted, don't you?'

'Well, it definitely looks like it needs it. Can you fit me in today?'

'Good timing. Say, ten'

'Perfect, G. Thanks, darling. See you then.'

He was working through paperwork when Sarah the script supervisor knocked and walked in through the open front door. Sarah's full-on cockney accent would be a bit of a giveaway but as most people said, she could actually double for Oprah Winfrey. She had a huge grin on her face.

'You bastard, Killy Wilde! Where were you on my first night here? You gone off me?' He walked across and wrapped his arms around her.

'Sorry, darling, I got tangled up with Arthur and the people who own the submarine we're using, and it all got a bit festive. I'm really sorry, darlin'. How you doing? Kids good?'

'Kids are great. Murray's got accepted for Cambridge!'

'That's wonderful! Good lad!'

127

'Yeah, can you believe it? My baby boy is going to be a doctor! Just in time to look after his poor old mum when she packs in all this nonsense.'

Killy smiled and hugged her again. 'Yeah, that'll be the day. And how's Elly?'

'Elly's ... well, you know. Elly's doing it the hard way, like her mum. She'll be tapping you up for a job this time next year, I reckon. So how's it all going?'

'This one is definitely not gonna be a pushover. Have you talked to Arthur?'

'Yeah, he said there'd been a few problems. Didn't really go much further, though. Anyway, I'm your next-door neighbour. Cushy digs, eh?'

He laughed at that. 'Up a notch from Mare Street.'

'Fucking big one, Killy. Anyway, I've got a meeting with His Majesty right now, so why don't you come for a beer when you're finished tonight? And give us a kiss, you sexy bastard.' She planted a big one on his lips and was gone. They'd had a thing going on for years. The kiss would stay with him for the rest of the day.

He'd allocated Gloria a big office in the old factory to house her hair and makeup department, and with help from Alain and his team of artists, she'd turned it into a swish-looking salon, with *Glamma by Gloria* on a hand-painted sign above the entrance, and a set of luxurious salon chairs and illuminated makeup mirrors that she now proudly gestured to as Killy walked in.

'My very first customer. Good morning, Mr Wilde.'

'Blimey, G, Arthur's really pushed the boat out for you, girl. And so much better than being six weeks stuck in a caravan, eh?'

'You're not kidding. Getting him to pop for it all took every ounce of my very limited negotiating skills, but boy was it worth it; we've even got our own little kitchen over in that corner room. So, any thoughts?'

'You tell me, beauty.'

'Let's have a look at you.' She stood beside him infront of a mirror and pushed his hair around with her right hand. 'I'm thinking a crew cut like Colonel Kubitt's? Your hair's good and thick and still not many grey ones going on. Yes, let's give it a go.' She nodded towards the twin shampooing basins.

'I just got out of the shower, G!'

'I don't care. You get over there and shut up. Beggars can't be choosers.' Top level hair care was another little perk of the business, so he did as he was told. She wrapped his shoulders in a towel and laid his head back in the basin. He looked up at her.

'Full treatment, eh, beauty?'

'Have to look after the landlord, Killy.'

She gave him a long, gentle shampooing and then a scalp massage so soothing that his mind drifted off the job and onto Sarah's invitation to come for a beer, and the soft, scented touch of her lips.

'You're thinking about Sarah, aren't you?'

Killy crashed back to reality. 'How did you know that?'

She was staring down into his now wide-open eyes. 'I know you two too well, and with you not turning up for dinner last night, we had a chance to chat.'

Killy was staring right back at her. 'About what?'

'Mmm, this and that; girlie talk. Anyway, let's get you sorted.' She rinsed his hair and wrapped the towel around his head.

'I could do with that every day, G.'

'Once a month is enough. Come on, follow me.'

She sat him down in her work chair and after a bit more flipping his damp hair around, she selected a pair of scissors and a comb from the tools of her trade set out in front of him, and went to work. Killy was looking at the photos of the cast blue-tacked all around her mirror; the standard makeup room rogue's gallery.

'Have you had a chat with our leading man yet?'

'Not him personally, no. He's evidently pissed off because Arthur refused to pay for him to bring his own makeup artist, so his PA called me and told me all the cans and can'ts and dos and don'ts. He's going to be a real pain, Kill. He insists on being made up in his dressing room, and he'll only be looked after by the HoD, which means my two assistants will be doing everyone else and I'll be stuck with him on-set and off. Lucky that we've got such a small cast of principals.' She pointed her scissors towards Serena Madura's photo. 'Our leading lady seems like a dream.'

'Yeah, she does, and this is a great shot of her. Arthur loves her.'

'He loves all his leading ladies, Killy, especially if they're classy, dark-blonde Latin Americans in their twenties.'

He smiled at her in the mirror. 'Yeah. Great taste in women; absolutely no taste in clothes. But at least he loves them like the daughters he never had.'

Gloria paused, nodding, and staring at the work she'd done. 'Yeah, you're right there, Killy, he does. God bless the dear old sod.' She started cutting again. 'I had a lovely chat with Serena and explained the situation with our leading man; I told her I would do her initial overall design so she's happy and all set up, and then Lotte and Hannibal can take care of her day-by-day. She loved it that they're Cubans; seems she's worked there a lot.'

Killy was looking at the photo of the actor playing the guerrilla leader, who kidnaps Serena's character 'Sandy' in the story. 'Ramon Batista, eh? Good looking fella. You heard of him?'

'I haven't heard of any of them darling, and that's weird; I always recognise at least one name.' She started clipping again. 'Monika told me they're trying to get Cutter Brown for the General.'

'Wouldn't he be great, G, eh? Did you see him in that HBO series as the old black Senator? Gets kidnapped by those rednecks? What's it called?'

Gloria was shaking her head. 'Can't think, but yes; amazing if they could get him.' She took one last tiny snip and stood back. 'So what do you think?'

He swivelled his head from side to side in the mirror. 'Fantastic, G, as always. Thank you, I love it! I'm seeing Arthur in a few minutes, and I bet you a tenner he'll want his done.'

'Well, if he does, tell him this afternoon will be best.'

'Thanks again, beauty.' Then he whispered, 'How's it going with Wally?'

Their eyes met and she nodded very slowly as a smile spread across her exquisitely made-up face. Killy winked and then they hugged each other without a word, and he walked out checking his phone. He had a text from Arthur: *Come to mine.*

He jogged the few minutes along the track to find the front door open and called out, 'Arthur, you decent?'

'Come in, Killy.' He was in another of his vintage silk dressing gowns; white polka dots on blue with matching slippers, which was pretty tame for him. He was making coffee, his hair still dripping wet from the shower. 'Here, I've made you a cuppa, son.'

'Thanks, I'm gasping.'

'Outside or in?'

'It's a lovely morning. Outside, eh? You OK, Arthur?'

'I could be better. Nathan is still breaking everyone's balls over the Serena thing, and if he keeps on about having to have someone with a bigger name, the distributor might cave in and I'll have no choice but to swallow it to keep the whole thing going. Anyway, I got in touch with the geezer who owns the LA agency she's with, a Mr Sieglovitz, who it turns out is quite influential in tinsel town, and he's stepped in and is going to make a few calls on our behalf … and on his behalf, too.' Killy was waiting for him to carry on but he just paused and took a deep breath, then a big slurp of coffee, but still said nothing. Finally, he sat back in his chair and stared at Killy. 'I had a meeting with Furio yesterday, and everything *vis-a-vis* customs is all kosher. But he knows somebody is following him and he's terrified. You had a haircut?'

'Yeah, just now. So who does he reckon it is?'

'Someone who knows it was him that the poor bugger they bumped off was going to meet, and that Furio was probably the last person he'd talked to. I suggested we bring him up here but he reckons if they can't find him, they'd go after his wife and kids; and that's what really panicked him. He's sure whoever it is thinks he's some sort of informer, and there's no way he can prove he isn't.'

Killy was staring at Arthur and imagining just how he would deal with a situation like Furio was in himself. He thought back to the way he'd greeted him when he and Julian had landed and it didn't make him feel good.

'So how did you leave it?'

Arthur looked at his watch. 'Right about now he should be

at the airport, meeting with two representatives of a company who organise close protection for diplomats and high-profile clients. They're going to be watching him round the clock from now on. It's costing an arm and a leg but we need him on the job and in one piece. He also reckons that this whole site is the key to what's causing all the uproar here; it's worth just shy of a billion dollars evidently, and the president who's getting his marching orders was all set to grab most of it. Where's Monika?'

Killy took out his phone and called her. 'I'm with Arthur. Any chance you can get over here, please, we need a chat? And if he's there, could you ask Julian to come as well? Great. Thanks, darlin'. And bring your laptop, will you?' He looked at Arthur. 'You want more coffee?'

'Yeah, make me another pot will you, son?' Arthur answered his phone as Killy went into the kitchen. 'Mister Sieglovitz, hello again.' He paused. 'OK. Hello, Mort. Thanks for getting back so quickly.' He went quiet again for a few minutes. 'That's really good news, Mort, thank you. Yes, you too. Nice to do business with you. Yes, I will. And to you.'

Killy put the coffee on the table. 'That sounded promising.'

Arthur was nodding to himself. 'Well, Killy boy, it would appear my new friend Mort Sieglovitz doesn't only own the agency that Serena's with, he owns several of them. He's also the executive producer of a massive new sci-fi film series, starring a very big name who just happens to be client of the same management company that looks after our star, Mister Nathan Bedford. Mort has assured me we'll hear no more complaints from Nathan about Serena being 'not big enough' to play opposite him. So that's one less pain in the arse to deal with.'

'Brilliant, Arthur. Can you give me a couple of minutes?

I'm just going to nip along to mine and pick up some notes.'

By the time he got back, Monika was there nattering with Julian at the kitchen table. Arthur came out of his bedroom dressed for work, actually all in khaki, which somehow suited him, although Killy thought the tasselled hippy sandals were a definite mistake. Arthur took charge immediately.

'We need to plan things to reduce our exposure in the event of what might well be a big upheaval if and when this current president is replaced. Equipment-wise, our insurance covers us but our first consideration is the cast and crew. We have to make sure the schedule will get as many of us on our way home as quickly as possible, so by the last day of shooting we're down to just Serena, Mr Bedford and a skeleton crew of the HoD's with a minimum of kit. Making sense?' It took nothing more than eye contact for them all to know they were in agreement, and that they were party to King Arthur showing exactly how he'd risen, as he put it himself, 'from flogging dodgy videos on Romford market', to become a successful and well-respected film producer. 'Right. I have a conference call in my office, so get a plan worked out in rough and when I'm back we can talk it through. See you later. Help yourselves to anything, but don't nick my biscuits. I know how many are left in the tin.'

The three of them spent the next hour adjusting the schedule, and then Arthur walked back in.

'Hello, boys and girls. How's everything going? Got it all mapped out, Killy?'

'I think we've pretty much cracked it, Arthur.' None of them were ready for the bombshell he was about to drop.

'Right. As I told Killy earlier, I had a conversation with Furio yesterday that gave me no option other than to organise some personal protection for him. He was due to meet with people from the security company out at the international airport this morning, but as yet he still hasn't shown up.'

Julian leaned across the table. 'Excuse me, Arthur, but as much as what you've just said is really a shock to us all, and particularly for you who know him personally ...' He was obviously searching for the right words. 'But I have so much to do to be ready to start, Arthur, I must ask you all to excuse me so I can process everything we agreed on and, well, get on with it.' Arthur had assumed a Buddha-like pose, his fingers crossed on his chest, listening, and nodding sagely.

'Quite right, there's nothing you can do, Julian. In fact, nothing any of us can do, really. So, on you go, and anything you need, just shout.'

Clearly relieved, Julian gathered up his notes and let himself out. It had gone quiet again, but of course the mental clock they were all working to had now started ticking just a little bit faster. Up until the moment Arthur had told them the news, Killy was trying to work out what Furio's absence was going to entail for the shoot. Now, he was hoping that Furio had decided to get himself out of danger and 'gone on the missing list', which was exactly what *he* would have done. He finally broke the silence.

'Arthur, what did the security company say?'

'They've already been into his flat. No sign of any disturbance, nothing saying he's made a move out himself, and his car's still in its parking place. Accessed all the CCTV on his block, called his wife in Florida but nobody's answering. His phone service, his wife's, and his kids', have all been disconnected, and emails are all bouncing back. Evidently, his wife's family are very big in the agricultural world in Brazil, at a level where they have a security company permanently on call in case of kidnapping, which is the big fear down there. My security guys reckon it's altogether possible that his in-law's people have gone ahead and lifted him and his wife and kids out, and have them hidden. Most likely back in Brazil. So, until we hear anything to the contrary, we have to hope their theory is right, that he and his family are all safe, and then move ahead without him.' There was a long silence again as they looked at each other wondering who would break it. It was Arthur.

'I think I'm going to get Gloria to do my Barnet. Monika, would you call her for me, please?' Monika looked at Killy, bemused.

'What is this *barnet*?'

He laughed. 'Old London rhyming slang; there was a massive annual horse fair up at Barnet in the north of London called Barnet Fair, and that rhymes with *hair.*' She seemed amused by this, and it had lifted the gloom slightly; but it was enough. She pressed a name on her phone.

'Hello, Gloria. Arthur would like to know if you can do his 'Barnet?' I have to say it needs some attention.' She looked back and forth between them, smiling as she listened to Gloria. 'OK, darling, he'll be along right away. She says any time is fine, Arthur, and to tell you that her assistants have arrived, and they'll be very happy to give you a manicure.'

King Arthur got up and put on his Panama, walked out across the porch, and down the steps as Killy got up to follow him.

'I'm going back to mine and get this all set out while it's fresh in my mind.'

Monika laughed. 'Your *Barnet* is looking very fair, Killy!'

Distracted though he was by the Furio scenario, the notes

he'd taken at the meeting made the rearranged schedule easy enough to organise and by nine o'clock, he was pretty much on top of things when there was a tap at the door. It was Sarah, looking wonderful in a dazzling red cotton sarong and holding two bottles of beer.

'Standing me up again, Killy?' He stopped himself telling her about what had been going on, deciding it would serve no purpose as they still didn't know for sure what had happened to Furio.

'Sorry, darlin'. Been reviewing the schedule and I completely forgot. I hope those beers are cold. Let's sit down outside, eh? I'll get us an opener. Glass?'

'Yeah, why not? I'm going to take the big chair.'

As he walked out, he opened both bottles, poured hers, and settled into another of the age-smoothed rattan armchairs and took a long swig. 'Cheers, beauty. Lovely to see you.'

She nodded and raised her glass to him, 'You too, babe. Have you got everything done?'

'Yup, and it all makes sense now. So tell me: what happened with the Clooney gig? It was all set to go, wasn't it?'

'What a disappointment that was; talk about a dream job for a single mum! Three months working from home, with the man of my dreams directing.'

'What went wrong, then? I never heard the full story.'

She sipped her beer. 'Script's based on a book, all political stuff. But someone was getting sued and the legal people got scared, so it's on hold until the case is settled. Simple as that. I was gutted. I love him.'

'More than me?'

'*So* much more than you, Killy. You're too young for me

now, and he's perfect. Anyway, here I am, back with the gang, and Arthur's just done a deal for Cutter Brown, who I'd dump anyone for in a heartbeat!'

'Slapper!'

'Hark who's talking! Killy Love-'Em-and-Leave-'Em Wilde!'

He was nodding ruefully. 'Very wild, some of them.'

'So how come we managed to stay mates? Both in the same boat, you reckon? You trying to find your mum, and me desperately trying to replace my dad?'

He was smiling. 'Yeah, and maybe it was just timing. Both of us starting to get a bit more clued up?'

'Well, at least you've not gone around spawning kids. Martin came with Susie and you stuck with him and finished up on good terms with her, so not bad going for a very wayward boy. And though I can't imagine myself without them, my life might have been a bit more straightforward without two kids by two different men, neither of whom even came close to replacing my dad. But I'm happy, and the kids both love me and their dads, so I got it nearly right, too.'

'You certainly did. And Murray going to Cambridge? That little boy, eh? He must be so proud of himself. And well done you, mum!'

'He is certainly proud of himself, but he's already panicking about Elly being in the flat alone when I'm away working.'

'Martin was the same when he went off to uni and left his mum at home on her own.'

'But you kept it all going with him, Killy. I remember us being away on jobs and you spending all your living expenses on hotel phone bills, talking to him for hours every night.'

'Yeah, but only because Susie was big enough to make sure he didn't lose contact with me. I was really lucky.'

'Well, she realised there was something special in you that was good for Martin to hang onto. How's he doing by the way? Still working in Geneva?'

'Really well and it sounds like he's finally thinking of settling down, which would be lovely. And you reckon Elly might want to come and work for me. How's she doing?'

'She's supposed to be taking her A levels, but she's just like I was at eighteen; parties and boys, and forget about the studying. I'm still paying for everything - and I thought teenage boys were expensive enough, but girls? I can't keep up.'

'Doesn't she have a Saturday job or something?'

'Are you joking? Work on the weekend? It'd ruin her social life. I tell you, these kids are on a different planet now, mate. She'd never get out of bed, anyway.'

'Well, if she can't get up in the morning, she's not going to last the first week in this game, is she?'

'That's exactly what I said. Have a chat with her could you, Kill? I'm wasting my breath. Just be dead straight and tell her, she listens to you.'

'Alright, I will. But if she screws it up, she's out. That's it.'

She raised her beer. 'Cheers, Kill, really appreciate it. You got any more?'

'Don't think I have.' He walked inside and opened the fridge. 'No, thought not, but I'll tell what I do have; local rum and fresh lime? You fancy that?'

She was standing next to him by the fridge. 'Remember the last time you and I were drinking rum? On that job in Iceland, hmm?'

'Yeah, but *that* rum was not *this* rum. This is the absolute, all time, numero uno. Have a sip; nothing like it.' He poured a little of it in a wine glass and offered it to her.

'Not neat, Killy, just squeeze a bit of that lime in it.' She took it and sipped it, and breathed in the fumes. 'Mmmm.' Then, dropping into her dad's old style Jamaican accent, 'Das a good drop a rom, Killy boy, jos a likkle bit more.' She held out her glass and that got them both giggling. He poured them a largish measure each, then squeezed the rest of the lime in hers, raised his glass, and took a little bit more than a sip himself.

'Cheers, beauty. Here's to old times.' They clinked glasses and leaned in towards each other, sharing a warm, rummy touch of the lips.

She stared right into his eyes and still in the same accent, whispered, 'So, Killy boy, weer do we go from here?'

Geographically speaking, not very far as it turned out, but they certainly went all the way. And, seemingly for both of them, for the first time in a long time.

15

Killy woke up alone, his hand stroking the still-warm sheet beside him. He swung out of bed to look at a note on the dresser and found that Sarah had answered his question.

Much better rum, and you too. See you later x

Ali waved as he walked into his office, and then followed him in. 'Morning, Mr Wilde, had your swim?'

'Certainly have, sweetheart. How're you today? Been a good girl?'

'Too good. I'm getting bored with my goodness. My goodness! Anyway, you and I have to go sometime today and look over the dressing rooms they're fitting out for the smaller part actors. Also, should I set up a bigger one for Cutter Brown? I mean, it seems a bit excessive for two days?'

'No need, darling. We can put Cutter in Ramon's one, he'll have those two days off. But definitely let's sort out the smaller units.'

'They're pretty basic, Kill, but they're practically identical, so hopefully no moans about who's got the biggest. Anyway, I thought we could have a wander over and talk to Gary?'

'Yeah, you go straight there now and I'll drop in and see how Wally's getting on with the stunt rehearsals.'

Stuntmen and women travel the world with all their

personal protective gear in massive holdalls, and as Killy walked into the area Wally had set up for his team, there were about thirty of the monsters lying open all along the back wall with kit spilling out of them. The hangar was a perfect place for them to train and rehearse, and even with the temperature outside in the eighties, this improvised gym was several degrees cooler. Julian was focussing on a fight that Wally was choreographing, involving three of the guys and one of the ladies, whilst the rest of the team practiced sequences he'd already set up with Julian.

The air was resounding with shouts and screams, and the whack of super-fit bodies slamming into the judo mats that covered their entire workspace. They were simulating hand-to-hand fights using imitation knives, guns, and machetes but apart from the fact that the weapons, the elbow and knee pads, and the personal body armour they all wore were unmistakably twenty-first century, it was like watching Roman gladiators training. Killy walked across and stood next to Julian. 'Good team, eh?'

Julian was videoing the action. 'Excellent, Killy. Wally's worked with several of them before on one of his films. Two of them speak good English, so it's all going perfectly.' He paused and made a quick note. 'Wally, I'd like to bring the lady into the fight a bit sooner and get her more physically involved?' There was nothing to be gained from Killy being there, so he left them to it.

Gary Molina, the construction manager, was six feet four, cockney born and bred, and rough as guts, with nothing but pure Spanish and Italian blood in his veins and fluent, thanks to his mum and dad, in both languages. Gary and his crew had been building sets for movies all over the world for years, and Arthur always liked to quote something he'd said that summed him up: 'Give me a week with the right gear and the right geezers, and

I'll build ya the fuckin' Taj Mahal, mate.' And everyone knew he wasn't joking. Gary was standing in front of one of the dressing rooms.

'Hello, Killy, Ali's worried these little rooms are a bit spartan? If you want, I can get one of my boys to fix some panels with makeup lights round the mirrors, get one of Bunny's boys to wire em up, and with a bit of paint they'll look like dressing rooms, instead of waiting rooms in a Mayfair knocking shop.'

'Well you'd know best about that Gaz. Anyway, sounds good to me; Hollywood all the way. Where's Ali?'

'Down the end. They're just finishing the wallpaper on wassername's room?'

'Serena Madura, do you mean?'

'Yeah. What a stunner she is! Saw her photo in Gloria's. I reckon I might stand a chance there, eh?'

'Yeah, I'm sure you're just the type of bloke she'd jump at, especially when she finds out about your missus and the four kids. Dream away, Gaz! Anyway, how's the superstar's swimming pool coming on?.' Gary shook his massive shaved head in disbelief.

'If you'd told me that there'd come a day when Arthur fucking Margolies would be paying me and a five-man crew to build a swimming pool for a so-called star no one's ever even heard of, I'd have said you were off your nut. However, to answer the question: it's all good and they're tiling it now. The surround has all dried out ready to take the slabs, filter system's in and ready to go, so it should be finished a week before he gets here. And the house itself! What a gaff that is! Wanna come and have a peep?'

'Not right now, Gaz, but definitely before we start. Gotta sort something out with the owner of the sub. See you later, mate.'

As Killy walked along the corridor, the whole place was

buzzing; painters, decorators, and chippies all working against the clock, exactly what he wanted this close to kick off. Ali stepped out of Serena's room.

'Have a peep at this, Killy, but please don't touch anything. They've done such a lovely job. Have a look at the bathroom — the tiling and the colour scheme Alain cooked up — it's perfect. I'm about to get it all decked out with flowers for her.'

'Lovely job, Al. Well done for pushing it along. Has she landed?'

'Yep, right on time and they're on their way now but no Ramon, his plane got delayed so he's going to have to overnight in the city. Gussy reckons he'll have Serena back here about nine. Monika and I will get her set up in her bungalow, all ready to start rehearsing with Julian straight after breakfast.'

'Great! I'm going to nip along to the sub. You coming?' As she turned to walk away, the look on her face was priceless.

'I'd rather have my eyes pierced, thank you. This is me on my way back to the office.'

Killy was walking up the jetty when Arthur phoned. 'Where are you, son? Chris has got a few queries on Julian's script changes.'

The 'few queries' took the rest of the day to get sorted, as even tiny script adjustments can result in cost increases of hundreds if not thousands of pounds. In this case, it was the addition of Cutter Brown to the cast; the budget had been based on the original script where the character that he would be playing hadn't existed, but after several phone conversations with the screenwriter in Los Angeles, Julian had persuaded her to create 'The General' to help strengthen the background story of Nathan's character. Now Chris had to find a way to adjust the finances to accommodate Cutter's fee for the two shooting days he would be with them. Killy left the meeting, his mind mangled with numbers and accountant-speak that gave him another sleepless night.

Breakfast sounded very jolly as Killy came into the garden. King Arthur was holding court, seated next to his newly arrived leading lady. He was decked out in a deep blue shirt with skeletons of giant tropical fish swimming all over it. He waved Killy across to them. 'Serena, this is Killy Wilde, our first assistant director.'

She put out her hand. 'Hello, Killy, lovely to meet you.'

He took it and noticed how delicate it felt in his. 'Good morning, Serena, a pleasure to meet you at last. Arthur doesn't stop talking about you. Welcome, and if there's anything you need, just ask and we'll do our best to help.' Julian was obviously keen to start working on the script.

'Killy, I think it might be a good idea if we had Gussy reading Ramon's lines until he gets here? And we've actually got Cutter Brown for the General, what a coup!'

'Certainly is, Julian, and now poor old Chris is pulling the last of his hair out trying to find the money to pay him. Anyway, I'll see you later.' As Killy went into the office, Ali was on her way out. 'Where are you off to, beauty?'

'Showing Serena her dressing room, then *reluctantly* taking a boat down to the house to make sure all the prep is on schedule. Is she still at breakfast?'

'Yeah. You'd better get over there and drag her away, or Arthur'll be chatting with her all day.'

It reminded Killy just how things were starting to move at a different pace now that there were actors arriving and rehearsing scenes with the director, having makeup and hair discussions and costume fittings, followed by tests on camera. Before too long, he'd be there on set; day one, first set up, first shot, first take. No matter how many times he'd kicked off a picture, just thinking about it gave him a buzz. He waved Gussy over. 'Morning, sunshine, you're about to do a bit of acting. Julian wants you to read Ramon's lines with Serena. Are you ready for that?' The very mention of reading lines with an actor would have a lot of crew members in bits, but not Gussy.

'Yes! I'll do my best Mexican accent.' Killy was about to tell him to simply say the lines but Julian wouldn't know a Mexican accent anyway.

He pointed at the door. 'As soon as you're finished, grab something for us both to eat from catering. You and I are going down to your house, so maybe give your mum a call? On you go, knock 'em dead.'

They met by the jetty and shared a salt-sprayed picnic as the boat bounced its way down the coast. 'So, how did it go with Serena? Were you nervous?'

'Not at all! I just did as Julian instructed me. It was interesting. I've been reading the script to get to know the story and Serena is amazing; she becomes that character of Sandy and speaks Spanish with an American accent! And Julian was asking her to try things in a lot of different ways, and she really likes to do that.'

'I'm sure she does, that's how proper actors work. How far did you get? Finish the jungle scenes?'

'We did, and she said I sounded like a Mexican gun runner.'

'And did you meet Ramon?'

'Briefly in Monika's office, they were discussing his

accommodation. I could hear them from out in the corridor and I don't think he's happy.'

'Yes, I'm afraid production managers spend a lot of time on those discussions. We don't have enough single occupancy bungalows, so he's only got half the floor space of Serena's, which I guess he's found out about and he's kicking off. But it won't be anything compared with how some of the big stars behave, believe me. Just watch, listen, and learn. Monika has a way of dealing with actors' unreasonable demands. Anyway, there's your mum.'

Lydia was sitting at the wheel of the pickup truck as they pulled alongside the jetty. On the drive up, Killy made a mental note regarding what would be entailed in getting a couple of hundred supporting artists off the big crew boats and up to the house, then bringing them all back down again at the end of what would be a long and trying day of filming. And having to repeat it all for the second day's shoot. As she slowed to go through the main gate, Killy turned to her.

'Excuse me, Lydia, could you stop for a second? How far is it from here out to the main highway?'

'Half a mile and the road is good all the way. The last section runs along the side of the army base, and they maintain the whole thing.'

She drove them on and then Killy asked her to stop by the two big generator trucks, 'Can you let me out here please, Lydia, I want a word with the gaffer.'

'Ah yes, the chief electrician! He's quite a character, isn't he, Killy? 'Bunny' you call him, yes?'

As he jumped out, he laughed to himself '*Good looking women of any age, eighteen to eighty, and Bunny'll be treating them to all his old lines.*'

147

Gussy leaned out the window. 'Shall I come with you?'

'No, have a bit of time together while you can. Ballroom in half an hour, OK?'

Bunny came over as they drove off. 'I hope you're not chatting up my new girlfriend, Killy. What a babe she is, eh? And how about this for a gaff? I could see myself as lord of the manor here.'

'Have a battle on your hands with Arthur, Bunny boy. Once Lydia had seen him tinkling on the ivories that was it: game set and match.'

Bunny laughed. 'Oh yeah? May the best man win.'

'So, Bun, moving swiftly on from your juvenile dreams, has everything made it up here in one piece?'

'We moan about potholes in London, Kill! I kept expecting to see a crocodile in some of the ones we had to get through. No wonder you're bringing all the extras in by boat. Anyway, we're well ahead of the game, mate; got the lighting rigs up in the ballroom ceiling so that's all ready to go, and Pete's sorting out the stuff round the garden, and the day-for-night blackouts are ready.'

'Great, Bun. See you in a bit.'

He walked across the lawns and round the side of the house, where Rosalia and some of her boys were working away in a kitchen set up under a big canopy, and as usual they were all singing and joking. He waved. 'Hola, Rosalia, que tal?'

She looked up and saluted him with her big chopping knife. 'Muy bien, señor Killy, muy bien. Mucho trabajo!' 'Lots of work indeed,' he thought. Location catering has to be the toughest job in the business.

Paddy the sound recordist was walking towards him with Ali and Gussy.

'All good with you, Paddy?'

'Yup. Gussy bagged me a lovely little room with no through traffic, so we're setting up in there now. Ali thinks we should bring the band up here tomorrow?'

She nodded. 'Marta could get their costumes sorted, Kill. She fitted them down in the capital but there's bound to be stuff that needs adjusting.'

Paddy caught his eye. 'Definitely be doing me a big favour, Killy; they've never done filming before and I could sort things out sound-wise in half a day.'

Gussy clearly had something to ask. 'Paddy, what happens if one of the band plays a wrong note when you're filming?'

'Good question. Musicians never play live on screen, they may have to do it thirty or forty times over the course of the day and exactly the same on every take, which is virtually impossible. So I record them before we start, obviously with no wrong notes, and that recording is known as the 'playback', which I play on speakers for each take, as the musicians mime to their own performance.'

Gussy was nodding. 'And the partygoers dance to the recording, so its identical on every take?'

'Got it in one, Gussy!'

Killy needed to move on. 'Bring the band up Al, good idea. Let's you and me go and see the ballroom.'

Alain was speaking to Lydia as they walked in. Killy was taking in the changes Alain had made. 'I love all the Impressionist paintings, Alain, where did they come from?'

'I took an afternoon off, Killy, and became a tourist. I walked around the excellent art museum in Nelson and took some photos. Then my brilliant colleagues blew them up, designed and made precisely the right frames to fit the spaces left by the ones we took down, and now Lydia would like to keep them.'

She was nodding. 'Do you think it might be possible to buy them, Killy? They look so much better than all that dull old Victorian stuff. The place feels alive.'

'I'll speak to Arthur, Lydia. I notice the grand piano is missing?'

She nodded towards Alain. 'My home in Paris, Killy, is worth less than that piano. If you knew who'd played it you'd understand. But the insurance even to have it in the room whilst we shoot was crazy, so it was crated up and stored safely away.'

Gussy was chatting quietly to Lydia, who asked them if they would like tea. Killy accepted for all of them and Lydia led them through the inner workings of the house, past areas only ever seen by family and staff, catching glimpses of the world Gussy had grown up in. Even in the purely functional parts, everything had obviously been built to last, with beautiful carpentry everywhere in the richest of woods. As they were about to pass what appeared to be the entrance to the kitchen, Killy whispered to Gussy that he wanted a quick look.

'Ma, I'm just going to show Killy the old kitchens. Where are we having tea?'

'In the library, darling. Take your time.'

He led Killy through the double doors that opened off the corridor and into the cavernous room, whose ceilings way above had enormous adjustable glass skylights. A massive cast iron coal-fired range, with countless ovens of different sizes, ran right across its entire width. Killy dreamed of having something like it.

'I'd love to see this place in operation, do they still prepare meals here?'

'I've never once seen it used. I'm sure ma must have, but

now we have a little family kitchen off to the side, built into what was a dining room for the staff. This is just a museum piece.' He was looking around at it all, uncharacteristically forlorn. 'To think one day it will all become my responsibility is too depressing, Killy. Let's go and have some tea.'

The kitchen was one thing but the library really did have to be seen to be believed. Lydia beckoned to them, as they walked in through the double crystal glass doors.

'Killy, do come and sit next to me. The library was my grandfather's creation. He built it when the house passed to him. He'd studied at the Sorbonne and then Oxford, and this was his pride and joy.' The walls were two storeys high, with thousands of exquisitely bound books, housed in endless mahogany shelves. Killy stood and took it all in.

'Lydia, I've always wanted to climb one of those sliding step ladders, would you mind?'

'Please do, Killy. Gustavo and his friends used to run up and down those steps and round and round the gallery for hours playing pirates. And he always had to be Captain Hook, didn't you darling?'

He didn't know where to put his face. 'Thanks, Ma.'

Killy stood at the top of the steps looking down at Ali slowly turning the huge antique globe, and running her fingers over its faded sepia surface.

'Planning your next holiday, Al?'

She looked up at him, smiling and shaking her head. 'I was just wondering how I could fit something like this in my flat. I'd have to move myself out.'

Lydia was pouring the tea. 'Gustavo would you offer Alison those little biscuits please? Alain your coffee is here, and I'll pour your tea, Killy, and please explain something to me: when I heard that a grand buffet would form part of the party scene, I'd assumed you'd need the kitchens. The poor old things haven't been used for years, I'm rather sad for them.' Killy came down and sat next to her.

'The buffet would be laid out for two days, Lydia, and under a lot of very hot lights. We never use real food as it goes off, and the actors and the supporting artists might be tempted to have a little nibble if it was real — and one tiny delicacy missing from a plate and projected up onto a forty-foot-wide cinema screen stands out like a missing tooth. So the buffet has been made by a specialist company in Miami and flown over here. In fact, it's been here a week and looks every bit as good as the real thing, I assure you — and no smell or mess or wastage.'

'So will people actually be eating anything, or do they just have to pretend?'

'The buffet will be set out in the background with waiters and waitresses moving amongst the partygoers, and there will be a few little edible appetisers, so the camera can pick out specific people in closeup nibbling them, but it's mainly drinking as that's much easier. The servers will top up the partygoers' glasses from champagne bottles filled with a special mix that looks just like the real thing.'

'No real drinks? People will be so disappointed.'

'We start filming the party first thing Monday morning, Lydia, and two hundred tipsy extras for an all-day shoot would be fatal. Real alcohol's never served on set.'

Thankfully Gussy butted in, 'Sorry, Ma, Killy still has to go and see Marta.'

'Ah yes! the American costume designer. She was funny.

Let me come through with you. I'd like to make sure that the guest suite we've set up for Serena to change in does the trick.'

Marta was using the old coach houses that ran off from the kitchen side of the house; they'd been lying empty for years, but they were perfect for changing room space. Her team were setting out numbered racks, together with rows of chairs for all the partygoers. Marta was there, wearing a well-cut set of dungarees with beautiful hand-stitched pockets and patches everywhere, and a great feather in her jungle hat.

'Hi, gang! Hello again, Lydia, how are you? Coping ok with movie madness? Beginning to regret getting involved? Don't worry, honey, it only gets worse!'

Lydia obviously liked the banter. 'Not in the least, Marta, I'm rather enjoying having you all here. And you've made Serena's room look delightful. Thank you.'

16

Killy was at Julian's for supper and they sat at the kitchen table drinking beers and chatting, until Julian finally came up with what he wanted to talk about.

'Ramon is turning out to be a bit of a liability, Killy, do you know why Kramer hired him?'

'He'd directed him in a drugs-bust movie a few years earlier and Ramon had been very good playing a cartel hitman. He was perfect for the guerilla leader role in our film and Karl offered it to him. So what's the problem?'

'Well, first off I wanted him bearded as he was in his publicity shot, but he turned up here clean-shaven. He hasn't said anything to me but he's taking it out on Gloria because she's told him he has to wear a false one, and she's pissed off as there's hardly enough time to get a beard made. Fortunately one of her assistants does facial hair but that cuts into her budget. Not a good start.

'And also … I feel difficult about, it but Ramon's English is not good at all. He speaks an American English gobbledegook that Victoria was having to translate for me as well as his Spanish! Really embarrassing all round. In the end I suppose he could just shout the occasional word in English? He insists he understands what I'm saying, but a lot of the time he's clearly bluffing.'

'Well you're not stuck with him, Julian. If you can't

communicate with him and he's been hired because he's bilingual, we'll have to think about recasting him before he gets in front of the camera.'

'From his show reel, Killy, I'd assumed he'd be great in the part but I just can't get through to him and, frankly, I don't know what I'm going to do. I think I'd better work with him and Serena again tomorrow, and then make a decision.' There was a tap on the door. 'That'll be our supper. Let's eat outside.' Julian jumped up and met Rosalia's boys and after a lot of chair-scraping out on the porch, he stuck his head around the door. 'They've set the whole thing up, Killy, plates, cutlery, everything. So grab our beers will you, and come and sit where you like. Glass of wine?'

Killy walked outside. 'I'll stick with the beer thanks, Julian. Can I ask who the extra place is for?'

'Nathan's double. There's so much he's got to do, I thought it would be good for us both to meet him and talk him through it all. Let's tuck in.'

'Hello there, gentlemen. I'm doubling for Nathan Bedford?' Neither of them had noticed him until he was walking up the porch steps, and he was not someone you could easily miss at six feet tall with white-blond hair, wearing a stylish tropical shirt and shorts. They both got up and shook hands with him.

'Evening, Lars, I'm Julian and this is Killy Wilde, the first assistant. Come and join us.'

Lars seemed completely at ease. 'It's very kind of you to invite me, Julian, and nice to meet you both.'

'Have a seat, Lars. Killy and I are drinking beer, but there is some rather mediocre white wine if you'd prefer.'

'Beer will be perfect. Should I serve myself? This looks delicious.'

'Please do, grab a plate.'

'So, Lars, you're certainly going to earn your money on this job; how's your dancing?'

'It's fine, Julian. I'm no Michael Jackson, but I pick things up pretty quickly. Will I get a little time with a choreographer?'

Killy answered him, 'You will. She'll be with us in the morning, so you and Serena can start working with her straight after breakfast.'

'Thank you. It's sixties rock and roll jiving sort of style, am I right Julian?'

'Yes. And Enzo, our cinematographer, is going to synchronise the camera moves to complement you and Serena dancing, so we make it seem natural that we never see Nathan's face, or actually *your* face. Serena has done a lot of dance work in the theatre, so we should be fine.'

At exactly that moment, the lady herself came walking up the steps wrapped in a white towelling robe, her hair fastened in a ponytail. 'Good evening, gentlemen. I had a little swim and then saw you all out here so I thought I'd come along and meet my dance partner. Hello there, Lars. I'm Serena.'

As the two of them greeted each other Julian walked across the porch and got her a chair. 'Serena, how lovely to see you. We were just discussing the dance. Have you eaten? I'm sure we can put something together for you.'

'If you would just pass me a plate, Julian, I can serve myself. So, Lars, we start dance rehearsal first thing in the morning, yes? I'm so excited to be working with Chita.'

Chita Cordero had been runner-up in the national finals of one of America's biggest TV dance shows and had subsequently built a very successful career choreographing Latin American, and all the various dance fads that came out of the sixties, for TV and films. With a bit of persuasion from Monika, who'd worked with her before, Arthur had splashed out 'a king's ransom' to fly her over from Miami to work on the party scenes.

Her voice was echoing over the top of a Bill Haley number all along the roadway that ran to her studio space in the old factory. 'That's good! That's good, Lars! Now, step change! That's it, Serena! Muy bien! Muy bien!' Killy stood in the half-open doorway, watching Chita watching the two of them jiving. She was in her late thirties, barefoot, tall and slim, and wearing a long dark blue silk skirt over a very flattering black full-body leotard. Her dark olive skin and beautiful frizzy black hair showed off her stunning good looks. As Killy walked in she was changing the music on her phone.

'Morning, everyone. Hello, Chita. I'm Killy Wilde, the first assistant. How are your students doing?'

She was about to reply as Serena called out, 'We're doing brilliantly, Killy! Lars is fantastic, isn't he Chita? And Chita is such a wonderful teacher! We're having so much fun!'

Chita laughed. 'They're both extremely good, Killy.' Her English was perfect, with a very strong and sultry Latin accent. She put out her hand, the dark-veined skin set off with a couple of subtle silver rings. 'Pleased to meet you, Killy. Are you going to join us? You can be my partner.'

He shook it, looking her straight in the eye. 'That's a recipe for disaster, Chita. I'm OK freeform, a few crafty moves, but when it comes to learning steps I have two left feet. You need to get Arthur on the floor, he loves to jive.'

'Yes, I met him last night at dinner. He's quite a character. It doesn't surprise me he's a dancer. So tell me: will I get some time with all the supporting artists before we start shooting the dance sequences, so I can pick out some who look like they can actually dance? In that way I can keep them closer to Serena and Lars and move the not-so-good ones out to the edges. Will that be possible?'

'Julian will need to work with Serena and Lars, so he and Enzo can figure out the camera moves. But I'll make sure while they're planning that we can let you find the good ones, OK?'

'Thank you. Anyway, excuse us, Killy, we have a lot to get through. Are you sure you don't want to join us?'

'No thanks, Chita, gotta get on. Work 'em hard and I'll see you all later.' As he walked away, listening to Buddy Holly belting out another of his mum's favourites that he'd grown up with, he was reflecting on just how much he'd changed. 'Time was, Killy, you'd have homed in on Chita like a laser. You must be growing up.' His thoughts ran really deep. 'One night with Sarah and you know not to go breaking more hearts all over again — your own in particular.'

Gloria's makeup department was just a little way along the dock. He tapped on the door and stuck his head in. 'Sorry to bother you, G, can you spare me a couple of minutes?'

'I was coming out for a smoke anyway.' She was lighting up as she came through the door to join him. 'Everything alright, Kill?'

'Depends how you look at it. Julian's got problems with Ramon, and I hear you had a bit of a run in with him?' She took a deep pull on her cigarette, and slowly shook her head as her eyes darkened.

'He's an arrogant little prick to tell you the truth, Killy, that's all there is to it. I get why he's annoyed about the beard but he was speaking to me as though I were a piece of dirt. It really upset me. And I certainly let him know it!'

'You should have told me, G, I'm sorry. But look; Julian has to decide today on whether to recast him, so can you hold off getting the beard started?'

'No problem. And I must say in complete contrast to Ramon, all these young, local supporting actors are delightful. Just let me know what Julian decides.'

'Cheers, G. See you later.'

Killy went straight along to check on special effects.

'How's it all looking for the submarine scenes, Tony?'

'Well, I have to say the family are certainly better hosts than submariners. Anyway, to answer the question: the crew have been rehearsing submerging and resurfacing in exactly the right spot on cue, with Ilze relaying the commands, and so far diving down is not too bad, but bringing it back up level is tricky. Anyway, they're all working at it between cocktails, and I'm sure come the day all will be fine.'

Killy walked along the dock to check on the costume department. Marta and two of her team were outside, down on their knees with brushes and various mixtures in pots, working on some of the guerrilla outfits they had laid out on the concrete, 'breaking them down' to look like they'd been lived in for months out in the jungle, and treating the sweat marks they'd stained into them to ensure that they didn't disappear down the drain when they were washed each night.

Marta looked up at him and pointed a rubber-gloved finger at her lips. 'Give me a little kiss, Killy,' So he did. 'Mmm, nice. You Irish boys are good kissers.'

'Even London Irish?'

'Yeah any Irish, even Boston; gotta be in the genes. So

what's happening, buster? I hear we have a little actor problem? I just fitted him this morning. Not very communicative.'

'Yeah, communication is the problem. Was he OK with you?'

She shrugged. 'With me, yeah, but a bit dismissive with my tailor who was helping me fit him. And very picky, wanted lots of adjustments. For living in the fucking jungle already?'

'OK, good to know. Have you met Lars yet?'

'The Swede? No, he's due here for a fitting. I hear he's a dish and my girls eat blonds alive.'

'Tell them to save some for Serena, they may have competition. See you later.'

He fixed himself a sandwich in his bungalow and worked through a pile of notes. At around four pm, Sarah Scripts tapped on the door and walked in.

'Any chance of a cuppa, Kill?'

'Of course. If you'll just stick the kettle on and come and sit down, I'll make it. Just one more little thing, then I'm done. So tell me: how's Julian getting along with Ramon?'

'Blimey, Kill. Victoria's doing her best but the more Julian asks her what Ramon is trying to say in English, the more Ramon resents it.'

Killy went into the kitchen. 'You want milk, darlin', or are you still drinking it black?'

'No, I finished with all that healthy stuff. Had me mum jumpin' all over me about me teeth getting grey. I'm forty-five and she still treats me like I'm ten!'

He passed her a cup. 'And how's it going between Ramon and Serena?'

'Like you said, Kill, she's such a charmer. And it's obviously embarrassing for her, cos it's taking so much time to work through even the short scenes, and they're not managing to get any sort of flow. Julian keeps trying to get Ramon to vary the pace and the intensity but he starts way up there, energy-wise, so he's got nowhere to go.'

'Does Julian know you're over here?'

'Yeah.'

'OK, so what's your take on it?'

'Oh, Killy, please don't ask me. I hate things like this, I really do. Work is so precious, and it's even worse for actors.' She took a very long pause, obviously troubled by the decision he was asking her to make. 'Well, I suppose … if you want my honest opinion, his English is definitely not up to it. That's it. I'm sure he's a good actor but I can't understand a word he says.' Killy found himself staring right into her eyes.

'So, Julian's rehearsing with them until six, yeah?'

She looked down at her notes. 'Yes. Then Ramon is scheduled for a second costume fitting, while Serena goes to Gloria to work out her hair styles for both of the party sequences.' She looked back at him. 'What do you think?'

He paused. 'Well, it's the director's call now, and if he can make it work then fine, but if we are letting him go, it has to be before he gets in front of the camera. Excuse me.' Monika was calling.

'Killy. Alberto loves the part and he's another big fan of Serena, but he's hot and there are a lot of people wanting him right now.'

'So what's the deadline?'

'His agent has to have the deal agreed by six our time here, Killy, or we're going to lose him.'

'And so Alberto's English is definitely good?'

'He's bilingual, half American.'

'OK leave it with me.'

Sarah was looking at him. 'Somebody lined up to replace him? Who is it?'

'He's called Alberto Curro. He really wants to do this but he's got another job on offer. I'm going over to Julian now.'

She blew him a kiss as he headed for the door. 'Good luck, babe, rather you than me.'

Overnight, Julian had looked at film clips of three actors who could potentially replace Ramon; Alberto's work had impressed him most but the fee his agent wanted was by far the highest, so Monika had haggled long and hard to get it down to a figure that Arthur would accept. Now having got that far they couldn't miss out on signing him, and so Julian had to decide. Killy stood in the shadows watching the rehearsal, but focusing on the director not the actors, then as Ramon turned face-to-face with Serena, Julian stared directly towards Killy then lowered his eyelids and very subtly shook his head. Of course that was the easy part; they were on their way to signing a new supporting actor. But now someone had to tell Ramon he was fired. Killy went directly to Arthur's office.

'So, what's the story, son? Does he stay or does he go?'

'He goes I'm afraid, Arthur.'

'Right, this mess is mine to clear up. Ana! Would you get me Ramon's agent on the line please? Tell him it's urgent.' He gave Killy a wry smile. 'You want to listen in on this?' Killy nodded. The phone on Arthur's desk rang and he picked it up, and signalled Killy to close the door. 'Just to be sure, Ana, it's actually the boss I'm talking to. Señor Saldo, yes? OK, put him on please.'

He looked at Killy then pressed the speaker button on the phone.

The agent spoke with only a slightly accented English, 'Arthur, good afternoon, how are you today?'

'Good question, Carlos.' He slipped effortlessly into his producer persona, eyeballing Killy throughout. 'In all honesty I could be better. It's Friday afternoon, we start principal photography on Monday morning, and obviously time is precious, so I shall get straight to the point. After careful consideration, primarily on the part of our director and in conjunction with the key members of my production team, I've decided to release your client from his contract. His English is not up to the standard we had been given to believe it was.' He made it clear that their letting Ramon go was nothing to do with his acting abilities.

There was a rather long pause and then finally Carlos responded, 'In all honesty, Arthur, I'm not surprised. Ramon had established a great rapport with Karl Kramer but he'd told me that he was finding it very difficult to understand your director's English pronunciation. Obviously he's learned American English, and I know myself he's not been well taught, so I think if we put the separation down to artistic differences, we can all move on. His English needs a lot of work.'

Arthur came in immediately, 'Unless there's anything else, I thank you for your understanding, Carlos, and your candour, and look forward to doing business with you again.'

'A pleasure as always, Arthur. and my best wishes for a successful shoot.'

Arthur sat the phone back in its cradle. 'He's a canny operator. He's probably got two or three more young guys like Ramon on his books and he's far more concerned with future deals with us, or just as importantly with people we talk to, so that's that! How's it all looking for Monday, son? All shipshape?'

'Yup, raring to go, boss, now that's all settled. I'll see you later.'

Killy stood in Monika's doorway as she was finishing the deal with Alberto's agent.

'And please tell Alberto one of our people will be waiting for him at the airport to bring him directly here, and also Julian asked if he could familiarise himself with the jungle encampment scenes following the kidnap? That's wonderful. A pleasure. I certainly shall. Goodbye!' There was no mistaking how Monika was feeling.

Killy was smiling at her. 'That obviously went well. When's he getting here?'

'Tonight, Killy! He's just finished a movie in Havana, and he'll be on his way to the airport as soon as his agent phones him.' This was a real stroke of luck, as they could have been held up badly by a cast change at this stage.

'Well done, guapa! I was expecting Monday at the earliest, so that gives us a whole day tomorrow for costume, hair and makeup, and then a day of rehearsal.'

She was nodding and looking very happy. 'How did it go with Ramon's Agent?'

'Smooth as silk. I listened in; he wasn't a bit surprised. Ramon had already told him he was having a problem with Julian's English.'

'I called an old girlfriend who'd worked with Alberto last year, and she said he's fantastic, everybody loved him. We're really lucky he was available, Killy.'

'Yes and that you beat his agent down, darlin', or Arthur would never have gone along with it — and who knows who we would have finished up with? Have you put Gloria and Marta in the picture?'

'Straight away. No tears from either of them.'

Julian arrived, looking exhausted. 'Hello, you two. All change, eh?'

17

It was seven o'clock on Saturday morning and with two more days to go before they started shooting, the day off on Sunday would be no day off at all. They were at the stage where for every department there weren't enough hours in the day. Killy was in the kitchen when he heard something he couldn't quite decipher. There was no real ambient sound where they were, except occasionally the waves slapping on the sand would filter through the trees, but this was altogether different. It sounded just like what it turned out to be.

He walked onto the porch and coming along the track was Rafa, looking magnificent in a military olive green tshirt and shorts, leading a troop of a hundred men, jogging in step in ranks of four and all dressed in the same kit as their leader. The sound he'd heard was a hundred and one pairs of rubber soled army boots hitting the hard sand track in perfect unison.

As they came level with Killy, Rafa called out, 'Eyes right!' and every man did just that at exactly the same moment, eyeballing Killy. He saluted them but it felt false, so he started clapping instead, so impressed with the way Rafa had turned these young civilians into a convincing military unit in such a short time, and he kept it up until they finally rounded the bend.

Killy spent the morning in his office finalising the first

day's shooting schedule. Ten minutes after he'd finished, Julian came and poked his head in the doorway.

'Serena and Alberto hit it off immediately and as we started to rehearse, it gradually dawned on me that to accommodate Ramon's poor English, they'd changed the script to have him speaking Spanish, and so now with Alberto playing the character as an educated, middle-class rebel who speaks good English, it changes the dynamic between the two characters completely. And they've both done their homework. They're all over it with neither of them faffing around trying to remember lines! I want to build up some more of their stuff, the chemistry between them is extraordinary. I'll see you later.'

Killy finished all his notes and headed along to the base. The area around the jetty had been turned into an outdoor café, with two big tented areas set up with large and small tables. Gloria and Marta were already nattering by the table laid out near the serving counter and sampling from the various appetisers, salads, bits of grilled fish, or meat on skewers, all before choosing from the main dishes of the day. Killy joined them.

'Hello, girls. Good spread, eh? Want to get served before the queue starts?'

Marta poked at her midriff. 'I'm gonna gain twenty pounds if it's like this every day, Killy. You should have done it American style; all-day chuck wagon, very basic. This is like a goddamn banquet every lunch time, and I can't resist it.'

Gloria had been served her main course early. 'Going to join us, Killy? Let's sit at that table over there. I've got to run back inside in a few minutes.'

'Yeah, great, I need a quick chat with you both anyway. Julian wants me to ask Lex and both the ladies to be extras in the party scenes, how would that work for you?'

Marta was up for it immediately. 'That's a great idea! Three tall blondes to dress for the party. They'll look great. Send them right over!'

One of Gloria's assistants was calling her, so she picked up her plate. 'Sorry, kids, gotta run, important hair decisions to take care of. Just get them to come and see me, Kill, and I'll sort them all out. Be a pleasure.'

'Thanks. I haven't asked them yet but they're bound to be up for it. If not, I'll call you.' He turned back to Marta. 'Are you sure you're going to be OK dressing them all?'

'Killy, you think I came from the garment capital of the Western Hemisphere to this fucking Caribbean boondocks with no back-up? With the fabric stock I packed, and my gang of cutters and seamstresses, I could dress the cast of a Broadway musical! Overnight, if necessary. So yeah, if they're going to get suckered into being extras, send 'em round, poor bastards.'

'I know, I know, darlin'. But don't put them off, Marta, they'll be living the dream.'

'Yeah, and such a dream, Killy. Shunted round like cattle in a pen, move here, move there, talk, don't talk, mime, walk this way, now that way. But don't worry, babe, my lips will be sealed I promise you, and who knows, they may get a kick out of it. You want dessert? They have ice cream!'

'No thanks, I'm heading down to the sub to ask them if they want to do it.'

Lex and family were lunching up on deck with Gary, Killy recognised his laugh from fifty yards down the jetty.

...

Twenty minutes later, and with three new supporting artists all delighted to have been asked, Killy and Gary were walking back to the base.

'That Lex geezer, Kill ... he does things like this for fun, he's one of the richest men in Holland, made it all in deep-sea salvage. He spent fortunes doing up that old sub! His dad was on them in the war and he decided he wanted one.'

'How d'you know?'

'I'm a nosey bastard. I looked him up online and just asked him all about it. What a great bloke, really down to earth. Talking of down to earth, d'you wanna have a butcher's at the superstar's gaff?'

'Yeah, let's go mate.'

They saw the villa through the trees.

'Whoever designed it knew what they were doing; look at it, it's stunning! And the carpentry; you couldn't even get wood like that these days.'

They walked up the half dozen steps onto the veranda that completely encircled the whole building, and outside each set of louvred double doors that opened onto it were perfectly matched suites of deck furniture.

'Has Arthur popped for all of this, Gaz?'

'No, the furniture was already here. Come on, let me show ya inside.'

Killy stood in the doorway taking it all in. 'What did you have to change Gaz? This is unbelievable, mate. It's beautiful.'

'Bedford's missus didn't like the colour scheme, so Alain had to deal with that. This is what we did, through here. Look.'

'No wonder Arthur was ready to explode; this must have cost thousands, just for the fittings.'

'And I tell you, Kill, squeezing in everything they wanted in this kitchen was a nightmare. Looks good though, eh? And come out here.' They stood in one of the double doorways and gazed at the pool as the sunlight flickered through the trees onto the surface of the water; it looked absolutely perfect.

'Well Gaz. When I win the lottery and build my dream home I know just who to come to; do you do mates' rates?'

'Not on your Nelly if you've won the lottery, mate! I'll stitch you right up!'

'Cheers, pal. I'll remember you in my will. Anyway, that's it for daydreams, I'm gonna get my head down for a real one. Have a good day off, mate.'

As Killy walked back along the track under the palms the whole six-week shoot, and the potential for things outside his control to go wrong, was weighing more and more on his mind. And he still had no update on Susie, he'd no idea where Furio was and now he was terrified he was falling in love with Sarah all over again. And he was desperate for a decent night's sleep.

He did in fact get one, but was woken by his phone ringing just as the sun was rising on the final day off. It was His Majesty.

'Hello son, were you still asleep?'

'Yeah, but I had a better night than I have for ages, Arthur. What's up?'

'We're getting a flying visit from the DEA.'

'What do they want?'

'Wouldn't say over the phone, son, they reckon they'll be here in fifteen minutes. I'm already in the office, so nip down here pronto.'

The prospect of a Sunday morning visit from the US Drug Enforcement Agency didn't exactly fill Killy with joy, but he showered and changed and jogged his way along to the base, intrigued as to what might be the reason for this little surprise. Something was telling him it could be about Furio. He heard the beat of a helicopter's rotors coming from out over the sea, and he made it to the parade ground just as it touched down.

Arthur and Monika were standing side by side as he came and stood behind them. No one said a word. The letters DEA were emblazoned along the tail section of the military helicopter, and as the rotors finally came to a halt, the side door slid open and two big men in flak jackets, worn over short-sleeved khaki shirts, stepped out and stood either side of the doorway. Each carried a small, stubby machine gun.

A short, fat man in a flak jacket but unarmed stepped out, said something to his companions, both of whom towered over him, then came walking across with one of them right behind him. He was grey and balding and sweating profusely, and bearing in mind the rather impressive entrance he'd made, seemed completely out of place.

Arthur whispered, 'Looks like my old mum's chiropodist.' Killy managed to keep a straight face, but Monika couldn't stop herself laughing out loud whilst doing her best to make it seem like a coughing fit.

'Good morning. Arlen Crozier, DEA. Which of you gentlemen is Arthur Margolies?'

Arthur stepped forward and put out his hand. 'That's me. And this is Monika Sanchez and Killian Wilde, my key personnel on the project.'

The man shook his hand. 'OK, Mr Margolies, what I have to tell you may take a little time. Is there somewhere we can sit out of the sun?'

'Of course, my office is just a couple of minutes' walk, and it's nice and cool and very private. We'll be the only people in the building. Can we offer you some coffee?'

'No thank you. Lead on, please.'

Arthur's wisecrack had set the tone and like three naughty kids on the way to the headmaster, they were all having a job controlling the giggles as they led him and his man along the corridor. That, however, all came to a halt as soon as they were settled in Arthur's office, the armed guard facing them with his back against the now locked door.

'Mr Margolies, what is your relationship with Furio Asante?'

'He's someone I've employed several times as a fixer. Due to the inherent vulnerability of a film production on location I have to do everything possible to ensure that all and any potential problems are pinpointed and smoothed out before they occur. His local knowledge and connections are indispensable to a film project such as this.'

'Do you know where he is right now?'

'No I don't, and I have to say I'm extremely concerned as he seems to have disappeared.'

'Mr Asante is currently being held in the capital by the local police.' The three of them exchanged sideways glances. Killy was pleased he'd been right but the general tone of things so far wasn't too promising regarding Furio.

Arthur took a breath.' Can you tell us why?'

'He's being questioned in connection with the recent assassination.'

Arthur moved onto the front foot. 'Mr Crozier, should I assume you've not flown up here just to tell us that?'

'Correct, sir. How well do you know Mr Asante?'

'Our connection is purely business. He lives with his family in Miami, and operates throughout South and Central America. We enjoy a very cordial relationship, but it doesn't extend into either of our personal lives.'

Crozier looked over their heads at the guard behind them. 'Eduardo, wait outside.' He left and closed the door behind him.

'OK. Everything I'm going to say to you is strictly off the record, and if asked I would deny having said anything you're about to hear, OK?' Arthur nodded. 'So let me tell you something about Furio Asante that you might find interesting. Mr Asante has a big problem. Gambling.

'His business interests, as you know, involve extended periods away from home and for several years he has been gambling way beyond his means, mostly on credit, and losing heavily in casinos throughout the region. Unfortunately for Mr Assante, members of a criminal organisation who operate these casinos arranged for all his gambling debts to be called in, knowing that he had no way to cover them. They duly informed Asante that unless he helped them with their business on the island it would lead to a very negative outcome for him.

'So your colleague, having no alternative, came and spoke to us. And so while smoothing the passage of goods and personnel in and out of San Tomás for clients like you, Mr Asante has been working for a very big illegal drug smuggler *and* the United States Government.

'He has been moving the proceeds of illegal drug sales. The people he's working for have an interest in the political situation here on the island, and to effect the changes they want to make takes a lot of money, and they have an almost infinite supply of that.

'But this is not the kind of money that you can transfer electronically. It moves in cash, in bills of very high denomination, the most favoured being the five-hundred-euro variety; and as he has a constant green light through customs here, Asante moves the cash for them and nobody knows anything about it. Except us at the DEA.'

He sat back, pulled a handkerchief out of his trouser pocket, and gave his forehead a good mop as he watched how the news was affecting them. Neither Killy nor Monika moved a muscle.

Finally Arthur spoke, 'Right, Mr Crozier, where do we go from here?'

'Clearly Asante's arrest has alarmed the people he's working for, and then hiring a security company to find him has drawn their attention to you. And that is not good for anybody, particularly you folks. Our plan was to let him continue operating, gradually building our case, but with him having been arrested and thus put in danger of being eliminated by agents of the people he was working for, who are actually inside the jail where he's held, about a half hour ago Mr Asante was put on a US Navy jet and flown out of the country.'

Arthur took a breath. 'Can you tell us where he's been taken?'

'I'm afraid nobody can, Mr Margolies, but for sure it will be somewhere safe. What he was doing put him in grave danger of losing his life, and even though his evacuation has forced us to go ahead and apprehend the people he worked for earlier than we intended, the assistance he rendered the US Government will ensure that he is suitably rewarded and, more importantly, protected.

'So now you can call off the search for him and save yourself a lot of money. Have a nice day. We'll find our way back to the helicopter.' With that he stood up and called out, 'Eduardo, let's go!' The door opened immediately.

Arthur went and stood in the doorway, watching them walk down the corridor. 'Blimey, no wonder Furio was losing the plot, I'm amazed he was able to do anything at all. Anyway, the main thing is we know that he's alive and most importantly that he's going to be safe, so we'd better get on and shoot this movie. If you'll excuse me, I'm going back to my bed. Far too much excitement at this time of the morning on our last day off.'

Monika stood up to follow him. 'Killy, can you tell me why none of this surprises me? I never trusted that man. I don't know how or what you feel about him but while I'm glad for the sake of his family that no harm has come to him, I'm equally glad I won't have to spend time around him ever again. Anyway, I need to get moving; I have a week of work to get through before tomorrow; I'll see you.'

As Killy walked back to his bungalow his phone buzzed in his pocket; it was Susie. 'Hello beauty, how are you?'

'Really good, Kill. I've been down with mum all weekend and there's a message on the house phone from the practice saying they've got me in for a scan first thing Monday. What a relief.'

He breathed deeply. 'Blimey darlin', that made me a bit tearful. I thought you'd be hanging around for weeks. Have they said when you'll get the results?'

'No, but the doctor told me last week she'll push them. I can't tell you how much better that's made me feel, Kill. Anyway, how's it going? You start tomorrow morning, don't you? Oh, mum's on the line. I left her a message to call, sorry.'

'No problem, say hello from me. Everything's good here thanks darling, especially now you've made my day. Text me how it all goes. Love ya!'

He sat on his porch enjoying the solitude and the cool morning air, knowing that for the coming six weeks there was unlikely to be a spare moment to reflect on anything other than the job. But now he felt calmed by the fact that Susie was being looked after and that they would soon know where they stood. It had lifted his spirits to a point where even the extraordinary episode with the DEA seemed far less important. No more hoping for the best but constantly terrified of the worst. They would soon know exactly what was going on inside Susie.

'But what if it is what you don't want to hear? What then? Eh, Killy boy?'

18

Phone, charger and iPad. One by one, Killy slipped them into his battered old work satchel. He was all ready to go at exactly a quarter to five. He slung it over his shoulder, stepped out onto the porch, and went across to Sarah's. Her door was already open.

'Morning, Killy boy. Off we go again, eh, mate? Sleep alright?'

'Like a baby. I feel fantastic. You?'

She picked up her big work bag and the folding camp chair, which together she called her office. 'Yeah, dropped right off.' Killy gave her a hug and they both let it turn into a deep kiss, and then they drew apart, smiling. 'Let's go, Kill. We don't want to miss the boat on the first day.'

Killy kissed her on the lips very lightly. 'Don't worry, I'm not missing the boat again.'

They exchanged a smile, Sarah with an inquisitive movement of her eyes. Then they went out to start the job.

The jetty was lit up and all hustle and bustle. Enzo and his team were passing dozens of reinforced aluminium cases, that carried their precious cameras, lenses, and all the associated gear down from the jetty and into the camera boat. Everyone shook hands and wished each other the best for a great shoot. Then out of the darkness loomed King Arthur, resplendent in a brand-new safari suit, with a bright blue-and-white silk scarf draped around his neck, and his Panama perched on his still-wet hair.

He lifted it and saluted the Italians, 'Buongiorno ragazzi!' And then again to Sarah and Killy, 'Morning, you two.'

'Morning, Arthur. You coming with us?'

'I'll join you there for breakfast, son, I got a lot riding on it. So no pressure!' He laughed out loud and grabbed Killy in his huge arms and gave him a rib-cracking hug. 'Monika, Alison; morning, ladies. And you too, Mr Burford-Brown; are you ready for this, Julian? You're looking rested, you sleep well?' Julian was clearly amused by Arthur's exuberance so early in the morning.

'Soundly thanks, Arthur. And yes, I certainly am ready. Couldn't be more so.'

Arthur stuck out his hand. 'Very best of luck, Julian, we all have great confidence in you. See you on set, everyone. Break a leg!'

The camera boat headed off with a big roar of its engines, Enzo and his crew all waving back and laughing as it ploughed out into the darkness. Monika and Ali waved them off, then gathered everyone else together for a big group hug. Monika kissed them one by one, mother hen as ever.

'You have a lovely first day, all of you. Good luck to us all, gang. Mucho suerte!'

They climbed down from the jetty and settled themselves into the boat, Julian and Killy on the back seat with Sarah between them, as the skipper swung them out into the darkness, steadily building up speed. It was a flat calm and as they raced over the surface, all three of them turned and waved back to Monika and

Ali as Julian shouted out over the roar of the engines what they were all thinking, 'Two great ladies! They really make you feel looked after, we're very lucky!'

Twenty-five minutes later, the skipper was edging them alongside the jetty. Gussy helped the three of them out then drove them up, and led them directly through the house and into the family kitchen. Two big pots of coffee were on the table, and a massive old-fashioned china teapot next to them. Killy picked it up and felt the weight.

'Couldn't you find a bigger one, Gus?'

'I dug it out specially. It belonged to Linda, my Scottish tutor, she brought it all the way from Dundee. There are paper cups so you can take them with you. I'm going to check up on the caterers.' Killy served himself and Julian, then they walked round the outside to the terrace and into the ballroom. Alain was there already, coffee and cigarette on the go.

'Bonjour messieurs. At last, we begin!'

Julian was taking in every detail. 'Fantastic job, Alain. It always looked magnificent but now — what can I say? When Enzo gets it all lit up, it's going to set the film off perfectly. Bravo!'

'You're very welcome, Julian. It's a pleasure to be working with a real gentleman, they are so rare.' They laughed and gave each other a brotherly hug. As Killy left them he picked up the strong scent of brewing coffee coming from the camera room, where Enzo and his crew were sipping from their tiny stainless-steel cups that travelled the world with them, together with a portable espresso machine, in its custom-made aluminium case. They knew not to offer Killy a drop of their elixir, as a tea-drinking Englishman, even witnessing their daily ritual was bordering on the sacrilegious. He nodded to them and followed the electric cables across the lawn to the main generator, where Bunny and Pete were sipping from mugs of steaming tea.

'Morning, boys! Alright Bun?'

'Yup. Here we go again, Killy boy. How many's this we've done?'

'Gotta be five, eh?'

'At least,' Bunny was rolling a cigarette and nodded towards Pete. 'Want tea, Kill? He's got a kettle on the go, so it's fresh.'

'No thanks, mate, just finished one. Has he been behaving himself, Pete?'

'Must have been; he's in the next room to me and I can hear every move. And anyway, there can't be any female in the world could put up with his snoring, 'cept maybe a hippo.'

Killy was laughing, 'Yeah, I'm sure they'd get on really well! All your local boys turned out alright, Bun?'

'All good. No complaints at all, mate. I can't understand them, and they don't have a fucking clue what I'm saying, so thank god we got the Dagenham Dago here. The wardrobe girls can't leave him alone; they're making him shirts, and everything. I don't reckon he'll ever go home.'

Pete rolled his eyes, and shook his head. 'He's an animal, Killy; he won't leave them alone. He's only got about three words of Spanish and he's chatting the ladies up all the time, and trying to get me to translate what he wants to say. I keep telling him my mum and dad are respectable people, so I never learned gutter Spanish, and anyway I'm sure half the time if I told them what he was actually saying they'd punch his fucking lights out. Or mine, more likely.'

At five minutes to eight, Julian, Enzo, and Killy stood by

a long, extended hoist known as a Telecrane, which would lift the remotely controlled camera right up to ceiling height and give the cinema-goer a bird's eye view of the entire party. But first, Julian had to set up the scene. The brand-new runners that Ali had chosen were already doing a good job, and by eight on the dot Serena and the four supporting actors playing her friends, together with two hundred party-going supporting artists and thirty-odd waiters and waitresses, were all assembled on set, breakfasted, made up, costumed, and ready. Killy sent Ali a text: *Your runners are working well.*

Everything was going to plan. There was a lot of nervous laughter, and Serena was great, chatting to everyone and not being at all stand-offish, as some actors can be with extras. Clearly a lot of people knew each other, which was good as it was a party, albeit a make-believe one. Everyone involved in the scene was dressed sixties-style, even down to the uniforms Marta had the waiting staff wearing. There was a real apprehensive but very positive energy in the room, exactly what was needed.

Killy stepped up onto the bandstand. 'Good morning, ladies and gentlemen. *Buenos días,* señoras y señores. My name is Killy, and I'm the first assistant director.' He extended his hand and nodded towards Julian. 'This gentleman is Julian Burford-Brown, our director.' Julian gave a polite nod to the room and went back to his notes as Killy continued. 'Now, please, if you speak English would you raise your hand? Thank you. Almost everyone, which is good because I've already exhausted my Spanish vocabulary. So could I ask you all to make sure everyone understands that we are now a team and we have a big job to do today, and then again tomorrow. Today's scene is the very opening of the movie, and every single one of you will be visible at all times. Please remember this is a joyous occasion, so plenty of energy, and please listen carefully to the instructions I and my assistants give you. If you have any questions, ask one of them and we will get you an answer. Our wonderful choreographer, Chita Cordero, is here and needs some good dancers for the final scene of the film, which we will be shooting tomorrow, when there will be a band up here where I am and a lot of dancing where you are now.'

He pointed over their heads at Chita, definitely the biggest name in the room, and everyone turned and, led by Serena, gave her a big round of applause. Killy put his hand up to still them. 'Chita, could you just tell everyone what you're looking for?'

Knowing they were pressed for time, she was very brief, explaining everything she needed in Spanish and English, and then she called out, 'Thank you, Killy!'

'Thank you, Chita. They look a very talented group of people, so I'm sure you'll find just what you want and maybe someone here is going to follow in your footsteps!' That definitely caused a stir. 'OK, everyone. This is going to be a long day, so don't use up all your energy this morning. Thank you.'

But of course quite a lot of them did, and by the time Killy was getting ready to call the lunch break, several of them were looking as though the sheer boredom induced by repeating the same sequence over and over again, even though it was just chatting and laughing in groups, requiring no large amount of energy, was taking its toll; and they would still have another five hours to go after the break. To their credit, they'd been dealing with the demands of the job very well, and the serving staff had made things easier as they'd been hired in via a catering company, and as professionals were used to being on their feet for hours. Once they'd been told which groups to serve, with what, and in which order, they clearly found the whole process much easier than doing it for real, and it was them following Julian's directions, weaving in and out amongst the various groups, serving trays of fake food and glasses of pretend champagne, that brought the whole glittering, jolly, panoramic opening scene to life.

With the 'establishing' shot complete, Killy let Chita and Serena start assessing the extras who considered themselves dancers in preparation for the following day's filming. Killy walked into the middle of the floor.

'Right, ladies and gentleman, that's a break for lunch. Everyone back here ready to go in one hour. All you party folk have done a wonderful job, but the real test will come this afternoon when we'll be going over exactly the same scene again but filming it all from different angles, so please don't forget what you were doing and where you were in relation to each other. Thank you.'

Filming party scenes is always hard, and especially coming back after lunch, having to recreate the morning's work with the same energy. Nothing must change — it has to be identical — and it's as relentless as the Chinese water torture. Enzo and Julian had decided to start the afternoon with the camera and the operator seated on a low, very heavy four wheeled trolley known as a dolly. The director sets the pace required for the shot and the grip pushes the dolly along the tracks that are laid out with great precision across the floor of the set. It's very simple and effective and is known as a tracking shot.

With that shot complete, Serena and the young, local actors playing her friends were being filmed chatting and laughing in medium closeup, using two static cameras, shooting from opposite directions. And then, when those shots were complete, Enzo set up the main camera for Serena's first closeup of the picture. Then they ran into a problem.

Good actors make screen acting look easy, but the camera takes the audience right inside an actor's soul and there is no fooling it. Even though she was much more used to acting on stage, Serena loved the camera and the camera really loved her. Her closeup was done in just a few takes. Sadly, it was not the case for the aspiring young actor playing her boyfriend when the camera was on him. He only had to smile at her and nod and then say, 'Yes, let's go,' in response to her line in closeup. He couldn't cope and kept forgetting his words, and then his throat dried up. Serena did everything she could to help him, but he kept on losing his nerve, take after take. Julian tried to put him at ease but after giving him three or four more attempts, it was obvious he was never going to get the better of his anxiety. Julian did his best not to make him feel even more foolish and had a quiet chat with Serena and then quickly did her closeup again but with her saying her line to the boy's back as he walked away from her. So he never got his closeup; his big chance and he'd blown it. It happens.

The rest of the day went smoothly, so Chita got more time with some of her recruits for the following day's dancing and Julian got all the shots he'd planned, and so, right on time, Killy ended the first day's shooting, 'That's a wrap! Supporting artists, you've done a great job. Thank you, everyone, and have a good evening. See you all bright and early tomorrow morning.'

...

But the 'bright and early' start the following day was a washout, and the crew travelling down to the location in the smaller boats had a very unpleasant ride, as the sea was heaving with a big swell, and the only way to deal with that was to take it at about half the normal speed, so their boats rolled up and down the whole way. Arthur had been busy all of day one and so he was determined, whatever the weather, to be on set for day two, but during the boat ride down he hardly spoke at all.

Killy helped him up onto the jetty. 'You're a little green around the gills, Arthur. You OK?'

'Blimey, son, I'd never make it as a fisherman. I feel as sick as a dog. Are we in this pickup?' Arthur climbed straight into the front. 'Morning, Gussy. Take it nice and slow, son, I'm feeling a bit queasy. Are you alright in the back there, Sarah?'

She and Killy had dealt with the trip better than the boss. She leaned forward. 'We're OK thanks, Arthur. Did you take a seasickness pill?'

Arthur shook his head. 'Like a bloody fool, I thought I'd be alright. But I certainly will before we go back. Have you got one you can spare, love?' She was already rooting in her bag and handed him a pack.

'Here you go. Keep them, I brought plenty.'

Killy's phone rang; it was Wally. 'Morning, Kill. Bit of a problem with the kidnap escape stunt mate; the duplicate police vehicle didn't make it to the docks. We could take a chance and go ahead tomorrow with the one we do have, but if anything goes wrong and we can't fix it, we'll need to wait on the backup one coming in anyway.'

This was a hiccup that Killy had to deal with immediately. 'You'll need up to forty-eight hours to rig it, right Wal?'

'Yep, deffo.'

'How would it work for you if we switched the whole sequence to Monday?'

'Actually, Kill, Monday's better. Then if there are any mechanical issues, and bearing in mind how old these vehicles are there could well be, I'd have the whole weekend to get things sorted.' Killy had calculated that the change would give Julian Wednesday, Thursday, Friday, and Saturday with Serena and Alberto, so they'd have a good, clear, unbroken run at the jungle scenes.

'OK, Wal, Monday it is, mate. Let the Prof know will you?'

'He's right here, Kill, and he's nodding.'

'Give him my best. See you soon.' His phone was buzzing again, it was Monika.

'The boat dispatcher just spoke with both the captains, Killy. They agree it's too risky with a hundred of the partygoers on each vessel, and they think it might be midday before the sea calms down sufficiently to bring everyone to the location.'

But it didn't calm down. And to make things even worse, Killy had to make the decision to call it a day and send the crew back through it all again. Arthur was so overdosed on the seasickness pills everyone had given him, that he slept all the way and had to be helped out and led to his bungalow.

The lost day's filming of the dancing at the house had to be moved forward to the following day, and on the boat back from having finally completed it all, Gussy was full of questions but Killy for once had to put him off.

'Tell you what: you phone Rosalia now and order us some supper on my bill, and get it sent over to mine so we can eat and have a post-mortem. I just need to clear my brain; what a fucker of a day that was!' Killy closed his eyes and as they bounced over the water, he let the wind and the spray blast his head clear.

Their food was set out on the kitchen table and after Gussy brought beers from the fridge, they sat down to eat.

'OK. Ask away, Mister Santini'

'Everything takes so long, Killy! We lost day two, but adding day one and today's filming together, we have only six or seven minutes of screen time! Twenty hours of work for just seven minutes!'

He nodded.' Yup, three to five minutes a day of usable film is what we need to get for a job like this. Some days we get more, but at times you struggle to complete even less.'

'OK, Killy. My next question is why did we have to do the big dance sequence so many times? The dancers Chita chose were great, so what was wrong?'

'For amateurs, I was really impressed with how they managed to keep going the way they did for, what was it, sixteen takes?'

'Seventeen, Killy. They did it *seventeen times!* They were soaking with sweat, and the poor costume ladies, all trying to dry the shirts and dresses with hair dryers so the sweat didn't show! And Gloria and her team with all the sweaty hair to keep in place, and makeup running down everyone's faces!'

Killy was nodding, 'Yes, well, to make Lars doubling for Nathan work, it meant Enzo keeping the camera on Serena with Lars's back to the camera while they reversed their positions as they jived. Lars is not a trained dancer and no matter how hard he worked, the poor bugger kept getting the timing wrong so the camera was catching his face as they turned. And then when he finally did get it right on take thirteen, we still needed another one for safety, which was why we had to do four more takes to get a good one and were in such a rush to finish.'

'And it got so hot in there, Killy, with all the windows blacked out and no air?'

'That's what happens shooting day-for-night; the lights Enzo was using to give the room a basic indoor level generate a lot of heat, and it just boiled the whole place up. You can't have fans on while you're shooting because it gets picked up on the soundtrack. And I've known it get far worse. It's torture for everyone, and especially those poor supporting artists who thought they'd be having fun. I'd be surprised if any of them ever want to be in a picture again. But people do, you know; they can't resist it.'

'And so, Killy, why did we do it day for night? Couldn't we have filmed on through an evening, which would have been much cooler?'

'You can't ask a crew to work all day and an evening, and then start at four the next morning; people can get really disoriented. Anyway, in the end we got it done. Let's eat. I need to get to bed.'

19

At just after six pm on Saturday, the last day of their first shooting week, the entire crew was clapping as Serena and Alberto stood in the midst of them on the jungle camp set, looking very happy and slightly embarrassed as Arthur, all in crimson and yellow, raised his right hand for silence.

'Right, boys and girls. I've been in this business a long time but I have rarely, if ever, been so impressed. The way you, Serena, and you, Alberto, and of course you, Julian, have worked together to win us back the day we lost to the weather, has been a privilege to watch.' He paused and looked around at everyone, 'And I want to thank every single one of you for getting us four days' work completed in three brilliant days. So have a nice restful day off tomorrow. Thank you all.' He put his arm around Killy. 'Moving the stunt to Monday was a great call, son, well done. It's what won us that day. Make sure you get plenty of rest tomorrow; I'm proud of you, boy.'

Killy slept most of the day but then, as rapidly as it always does after a day off on location, week two came around, and at eight on the Monday morning, Wally and the Prof were about to talk Killy and Julian through the kidnap escape stunt they'd been preparing all week. Wally was pointing along the broad red-dirt road through the section of forest they were using.

'OK. So the guerrillas' kidnap vehicle with Serena's stunt double, hooded and locked in the boot, comes tearing round that big bend, crosses over the river here, and pulls in behind those bushes, luring the police vehicle into following them over the bridge, which they will blow up as it crosses it. They get nervous and detonate the explosives too soon and the police driver manages to skid to a halt. The guerrillas then start firing incendiary bullets at the police vehicle's fuel tank and the whole thing explodes in a fireball. Then they drag Serena's character, Sandy, out of the boot of their vehicle, push her into the back seat, and take off. That's the setup, Guv.'

Julian walked to the end of the bridge and leaned over what was in reality a very wide, water-filled trench designed to look like a bend in a river, with bushes, rocks and trees growing up both banks. He turned to the Prof. 'So Tony, can we make it all look a bit more threatening?'

'Give me a second please, Julian.' He then spoke into his radio mic, 'Jimmy, go on turbulence please.' As they looked down, the whole thing gradually turned into a raging torrent. 'How's that, Guv? Wild enough for you?'

'Really impressive, Tony. How does it work?'

He was on the mic again, 'Power off, please, Jim. It was a bit of a tricky one, Julian, as there are no rivers anywhere on this end of the island, so we made a bend of one right here. The local soil is basically sand, so once we'd dug the ditch it all had to be lined with concrete and sculpted to look the way it does by Alain's team, who then did a brilliant job of dressing it with those big fibreglass rocks and all the bushes and trees. We built the bridge first, then dug out underneath it, and I managed to salvage ten twenty-thousand-gallon water storage tanks from the cannery to give us enough of a reservoir to hold the contents of our river. Then we hired in six big floodwater pumps from the local fire department and there you go, Guv: raging torrent at the flick of a switch.'

Julian was laughing. 'Bloody brilliant, Tony. Thank you everyone, it's going to look fantastic on screen.'

A second camera unit, with Wally directing, had been shooting the lead up to the stunt with a drone, filming the car chase all along the jungle tracks from high up over the tree canopy. Second units are used to save time and make it possible to film scenes that don't absolutely require the director to be present. So with the car chase and the build-up to the stunt all shot from the drone, Julian could go ahead and direct the main stunt sequence. With Enzo on the camera, they shot the kidnap car, driven by one of Wally's stunt drivers, coming racing around the bend, mud flying everywhere, and looking as if it could take off at any moment. It crossed the bridge and then ten seconds later Killy called over the radio for the police car to come racing after it, with another stunt driver at the wheel, and at precisely the right moment, the Prof pressed a button on his phone and blew the bridge literally to pieces as the stunt driver brilliantly skidded the police vehicle to a halt, finishing up exactly as planned with its front wheels dangling over the rushing torrent, as Killy shouted, 'Cut!'

Next they shot the rebels firing across the river at the police car as the Prof, hidden in the bushes, exploded the vehicle's fuel tank and two stuntmen dressed as policemen, both wearing fire-proof kit, burst out of the front doors covered in flames from head to foot. Then, once Killy called 'cut', the rest of the stunt team rushed out of the bushes and doused their flaming colleagues with fire extinguishers. The final shot of the day was filming the hooded stunt lady standing in for Serena being dragged from the boot of the kidnap car, and brutally rammed into the back seat as the car roared off along the jungle track and disappeared in the distance. Once it was complete and they gathered around Julian's monitor to watch the day's work, it was clear that everything had gone exactly as planned, without a hitch, and looked fantastic.

The following day, Wally and the Prof were preparing the jungle combat scenes, and getting the special effects and all the stunt crew ready for close-up shots of hand-to-hand fighting, explosions, and men being killed and wounded. This was all to be shot with Lars standing in for Nathan, who in reality would be two thousand miles away filming a commercial on a street in Chicago. No business like show business.

The stuntmen playing the twenty or so marines were wearing jungle-camouflage face paint, and Regis and Rafa had shown Gloria and her team exactly how this had to be applied. Marta's wardrobe team had made up netted covers for all their helmets, and artificial leaves and bits of real undergrowth had been woven into them by the art department. Julian now stood in front of all the camouflaged marines, with Lars as Nathan in the middle, as he viewed them through the camera. He nodded his approval.

'Regis, Rafa; thank you. With Lars' face painted like that there's no way you'd ever think he isn't Nathan. I'm happy, so let's start setting up for the first shot.'

With the same meticulous attention to detail that they'd applied to the appearance of the marines, the military men had also planned out the attack on the guerilla camp. This involved deciding precisely where Nathan as the commander would place himself, and how the whole assault would evolve, step by step.

They then began to choreograph for Julian, together with Enzo and the camera crew, exactly how the whole advance towards the guerilla camp would proceed. Wally and the Prof followed every detail, ready to set up the different stunts and explosions involved in the action. There were a dozen interconnecting scenes to be filmed, so as well as everyone having to learn their positions for each sequence, they had to know exactly where to finish up in readiness for the next shot. It was all worked out like a chess game, and then deconstructed so it could be filmed section by section.

While they were walking everyone through the whole of the first series of moves, Paddy the sound recordist drew Killy aside. 'Take these headphones, Killy.'

He put them on and stood listening, obviously none the wiser, then took them off. 'It's just a lot of static to me, Paddy?'

'No, mate. It's not good — that's military for certain, Killy, on that frequency. A lot of ground-to-air chat. If those planes are going to be anywhere near here, we're bolloxed.'

Killy spoke into his walkie talkie. 'Gussy, Paddy's picking up military radio traffic and he's worried about aircraft sound interference once we start shooting. See what you can find out.'

Julian waved Killy back to him. 'I think we should keep working out all the action through the rest of the morning and then shoot it after lunch. Killy?'

'Definitely. Just fixing all the camera positions will need at least another hour, so yeah let's do that.' As Julian got on with his preparations, Killy started to wonder whether the military radio traffic could have something to do with the current political situation, and whether this might be the thin end of a wedge.

Lunch over, Killy was watching a final rehearsal of two stuntmen marines dragging a wounded comrade to safety, and then miming the effect of the explosion that would throw them all headlong into a ditch. Gussy was walking towards the set and Killy met him on the pathway.

'Evidently, a big arms shipment was intercepted during the early hours of this morning and the military are on full alert around the capital. It was their radio traffic that Paddy was picking up. But in terms of actual aeroplane noise, it's too far away to affect us.' He took a bit of a pause. 'However, my friend at the airport is asking herself the same question as I am: why would anyone be shipping arms here?'

'And did either of you come up with a possible answer?'

'No. She only knows about it because her friends in air traffic control had to be informed, and her take on it is to wait and see if the arms seizure is reported by the media and if it is, it's genuine, and there's nothing to be concerned about.'

'And if it isn't, what then?'

'Well then, Killy, it means it's being covered up and so the changeover of the president might not go quite as smoothly as my uncle predicted.'

Killy was trying to keep Julian out of it and fortunately he was on the other side of the set with Wally and the Prof. 'So presumably it would be on the local news feeds first, and pretty quickly?'

'Yes, Killy, and so far there's nothing.'

As they started the first scene, there was no plane noise and Paddy was picking up no military chatter at all. They were filming a sequence that involved Lars as Nathan leading a group of six stuntmen marines crawling through the undergrowth towards one of the guerrilla group's machine gun positions, as Enzo with the camera on the dolly was being pushed slowly along the tracks, surrounded by the marines, and filming their point of view as the machine gun blasted off hundreds of harmless blank bullets to give the cinema audience the sensation of being under fire.

At a prearranged moment, Julian shouted out, 'Action, Lars!'

He instantly jumped up and ran, zig-zagging towards the machine gun, then threw a dummy explosive directly into the bushes concealing it and dived to the ground as the Prof triggered a compressed air blast that blew a shower of dirt and general small debris right over him. The real Nathan would then repeat the scene with the camera filming his face at the moment he threw the explosive. Julian turned to Killy. 'Well I think we've all bought that one, so shall we go over to the Prof and get started on today's big bang?'

Killy saw Gussy walking across the set. 'Definitely, Julian. Just give me a minute, I'll be right with you.'

'By the look on your face, Gus, something good's happened?'

'Really good. It's certainly not being suppressed; it's all over the media.'

'Are they saying who's involved?'

'No, just that customs received a tip-off about drugs but found several container-loads of weapons that were on their way across the Atlantic.'

'If you had to bet on it, would you go for that explanation being the truth?'

'The more I think about it, the more doubtful I am.'

'So you don't believe it then?'

'Knowing of the change that's going to happen, Killy, it seems too much of a coincidence. But of course there is one way to be sure.'

'And how's that?'

'Speak to Uncle Philip. But in person.' With Furio gone, Gussy was their only access to official information.

'Of course. Get on your way.'

'Are you sure?'

'Yup, go on. See you tomorrow.'

20

The following morning they were scheduled to start filming a very early sequence in the story, where Nathan was training troops in jungle warfare tactics back in the US. He was being lifted out by helicopter and flown to his headquarters, where 'The General' would interview him and assess whether he was the right man to lead the marines on the rescue mission. Lars standing in for Nathan was ready to be hoisted out, but the helicopter pilot had called through to advise production there was a storm going on over the capital and he would have to wait until it cleared. Killy walked back from the set to find Ana standing in the doorway of his office, holding one of the phones as if it might explode in her hand.

'Señor Killy. Monika and Ali are not here and I have señor Cutter Brown on the line.' Baseball is huge in that part of the world, and Cutter Brown had been a legend there long before he'd retired from the game and started his acting career.

Killy smiled at her. 'I'll take it, Ana.'

She just about managed to say to the caller what she was doing, 'señor Brown, I will pass you to señor Wilde, the first assistant director. Thank you, sir.'

Killy whispered to her, 'Something to tell your family, eh?' She crossed the office in a state of near collapse. 'Good morning,

197

Mr Brown. Killy Wilde here, First AD. What can I do for you?' His rich, deep-southern accent was familiar to Killy immediately.

'Good morning. Call me Cutter please, Killy. As you know, I'm down here a week early with my wife for a little vacation and I wanted to bring you guys up to speed with our arrangements. One of my dearest old teammates has invited us to stay at his beach house, so I'm not going to need accommodation.'

'That's all great, Cutter, thanks for letting us know. Could you send us the address where you're staying, and one of our boats will come and pick you up for your uniform fitting and hair and makeup discussions on Saturday morning? We'll be coming off a week of nights, so if possible it would be really helpful if you could stay on for a working lunch with Julian, which would give him the morning to sleep and be ready to chat with you about the script? Just to make sure you're happy with everything?'

'Be a pleasure, Killy. Please send Julian my best wishes and tell him I'm looking forward to meeting him.'

'Of course. Have a restful week, Cutter.' Killy was tempted to add that he might need it but decided not to.

'Thank you, Killy. See you Saturday. Goodbye.'

The helicopter they were waiting on finally arrived. Julian decided that as they were pushed for time and that the sequence was part of a flashback, he could keep it as simple as possible. He shot the helicopter arriving over the clearing and winching down the stunt crewman who put Nathan into a harness and signalled for them both to be winched back up. The camera stayed on the hovering helicopter as they were pulled inside, then as it flew off over the treetops, Killy shouted cut. That was all they needed and he broke them for lunch exactly on schedule.

The afternoon plan was to work on the indoor set and

film the big build up to the final confrontation, involving Lars as Nathan following Alberto through the escape tunnel. It all went to plan, and filming through the sides of the false tunnel that Alain's team had built worked perfectly as the two men crawled through the semi dark, both intent on finishing the other off. By six o'clock the two actors were exhausted and Julian was happy with it all,

'That's a perfect point to pick it back up with the real Nathan coming out of the tunnel. So thanks, Alberto and Lars. Really good work, guys. Over to you, Killy.'

'OK, everyone, that's a wrap on today. And tomorrow we're indoors again, for flashback sequences in the prison cell and the torture chamber. Have a nice evening.'

An hour later, Killy was out on the porch eating the light supper Rosalia had sent over, and sipping on a cold beer, when Gussy walked up the steps.

'Good evening boss. Did you manage OK without me?'

'Yeah, a good day. Have you eaten yet?'

'Yes thanks. Can I help myself to a beer?'

Killy waved him into the kitchen. 'So how were things in the big city? Did you see Uncle Philip?'

'I certainly did, and he'd like to bring my mother to the set next week.'

'Don't forget we're on nights; it might not be the best time for a set visit.'

'I told him that and it's fine, they'll come directly to the beach by boat. I suggested they have a bite to eat with us before we start shooting and then stay and watch, if that's OK with you?'

'Of course, they'll be very welcome. Did you get more news on where the weapons are?'

Gussy became a bit more businesslike. 'Yes, they're back

in the state armoury where they came from.'

Killy put down his knife and fork. 'And so what did Uncle Philip have to say about that?'

'The arms were a ruse. designed to scare our president and remind him that his time in office is coming very close to an end.'

'So who could have organised all that? And how?'

'This is Latin America, Killy, anything and everything is possible. Uncle Philip thinks it might have been Washington but knows there are other interested groups who have the capability.'

'So will your president go quietly?'

'Well according to Uncle Philip, whether he does or not he has some powerful supporters who don't want to see him go at all.'

'Did Uncle Philip indicate how that might change things?'

'No, but by the way he spoke I know he's concerned.'

'Did you say anything to your ma about it?'

'We tiptoed around the subject of the arms being discovered. She's definitely a little on edge. Her generation have been through a lot of upheaval over the years, and she speaks to Uncle Philip daily.'

'So they'll just wait and see what happens? Is that their plan?'

'The first part of it, Killy. Then they will do what a lot of people here do at times like this; they'll fly to Miami directly after their visit to the set.'

...

At seven on the dot the next morning, Killy walked into

Monika's office. She was waiting for him with a very disapproving look on her face.

'So, Killian, Cutter Brown phones me and *you* take the call? Poor Ana can still barely speak.'

He laughed. 'What's the big deal? You're never impressed by actors.'

'We don't think of him as an actor. He's a father figure, Killy. He's the man we all want to be our daddy. And *you* got to speak to him! That's why we were all so excited when he signed to do it.' She dropped the angry performance, and became a little girl, a side of her rarely seen. 'What was he like, was he nice?'

'Very warm and friendly, and absolutely genuine. What impressed me most was the fact he was calling us himself, and not doing it all through his agent.'

'Yes, that's why I was so annoyed that I wasn't here. Every woman on the crew loves him.'

They laughed over Ana's handling of the call. Evidently, her elder brother had been a successful baseball player in the local semi-professional leagues, and she and all her family had been fans of Cutter forever, so it really had been like a call from above.

Ten minutes later, Killy walked onto the torture chamber set. He wanted some time to himself and just sat and thought about being inside a dank, scary, underground dungeon, the creation of an American screenwriter and a French designer, in what had been for years a deserted hangar on the edge of a tropical forest and how, despite all its crazy ups and downs, just how much he loved his job. Julian and Enzo were the first to arrive, discussing the level of lighting Julian wanted.

Killy nodded to them. 'Morning, gents. Lovely day for a torture scene. Shall I call Alberto and Lars, or do you want to talk things through first?'

Julian looked to Enzo, who was actually more interested in his coffee and shrugged in a typically Italian way that it was fine by him whatever Julian wanted. 'I think if you call them in, say, five minutes, Enzo and I should have the shots sorted out; then we can rehearse while Bunny gets it lit.'

The whole place was coming to life. Bunny's boys were setting lights and carrying in all the equipment needed for Enzo to enhance the already sinister atmosphere, that Alain's team had created, with the magic of cinematic lighting. Paddy was setting up his sound recording equipment at the back of the hangar as Gussy helped organise a group of the local extras, all chosen for their threatening appearance, who were playing the torturers. Gussy then translated into Spanish Julian's explanation of what he wanted them all to do with the array of grisly-looking items designed to coax an answer out of Nathan. Alberto and Lars came to the set and Julian told them his thoughts on how far the torture could go before Nathan's hood would finally be taken off, but obviously the longer it stayed on during the scene, the more he could do using Lars. Alberto asked Julian if he might make a suggestion, something not always welcomed by directors, but he was all for it.

'Over to you, Alberto.'

'Thank you, Julian. OK, let's suppose the torturers drag Lars out of his cell, along the corridor and into the torture chamber, and then hang him upside down from one of those hooks up in the ceiling? Then I can spin him and walk around him as I question him, which would be terrifying enough but hooded, absolutely unbearable. And then finally when he refuses to respond we unhook him, drag him to the steel table and fasten him down.'

Julian took over. 'Yes Alberto! Then when we have the real Nathan, we start with him on the table, pull the hood off him and carry on with the fun! Brilliant, that is exactly what we'll do. Thank you.'

Lars was looking a bit unsure about the whole idea. 'Excuse me, Julian, but I'm not convinced I can cope with spinning like that upside down with my head covered. There's a very good chance I'll be vomiting?'

Julian had obviously been thinking along the same lines and he looked across to Killy. 'If we weighted one of those false bodies Alain's team made for the aftermath of the big battle scene, and hooded it and dressed it as Nathan, I think we could do Lars a big favour and save ourselves a lot of nasty mess. I felt like throwing up at the very thought of it myself.'

And so they started filming the torture scene with a hooded Lars standing in for Nathan, and ended it with a man-made body standing in for Lars. It worked perfectly and was a great way to end the week; not too stressful, and allowing them to finish the final shot just before the scheduled wrap time, and not needing everyone rushing around in a panic to complete the day's work with a week of night shoots looming ahead of them. It meant everyone could have a two-day weekend and sleep late on Monday morning ready for the first night shift, which would start as the sun would be going down. It meant breakfast would be served at four-thirty pm on set and, just to complete the total bodily confusion, the lunch break would start at midnight. And they would be doing that right through the week.

Killy slept well on Saturday night, but on Sunday night, his mind kept running through all the possible ways the political situation might affect them. At dead-on four am Monday morning, with a whole day to go before they would actually start their first night's work, he was wide awake wondering how things had gone with Susie's scan on the other side of the Atlantic. He went and sat out on the porch, waiting for the sun to come up through the palms. Usually something he loved to do, but not with twelve hours to go before he started an overnight shift. Then Susie texted him:

Had scan, lovely people, let you know as soon as I get any news, fingers crossed xxx. He texted her back: *So pleased! Keep me up to speed. All good here. Lotsa love xxx*

The lights came on over at Sarah's, and after a few minutes she came out onto her porch and waved. He held his cup up and pointed to it and beckoned her over. She got the message, and by the time she walked up onto his porch, he was pouring two cups.

'Morning, Kill. Just what I need. How come you're up so early? You OK?'

'Yeah. You?'

'I'm fine. This tea's great. Is everything alright at home?' It flashed through his mind to tell her about Susie's medical situation, but it could wait until they'd had the final report.

'Certainly is. Susie loves being at mine without me. How about you? Kids OK? Tell you what, why don't I call Ellie, eh? Good time for me to have that chat with her, you reckon?'

'What is it, middle of the day at home? Yeah she's probably up. Give it a try.'

Killy spent an hour talking to her. Eighteen, or just about to be, a young woman he'd known since she was a little girl, now really troubled by the fact that unlike her academically gifted brother, who knew exactly how and where he wanted his life to go, she didn't have a clue and felt completely adrift. They finally came to an agreement that as soon as he'd fixed his next job, and was starting to crew up, she could come and work for him as a runner.

Sarah had gone back to hers for a shower and as he finished the call, she opened her side window and called across, 'I've made us a bacon sarnie.' She was standing in her doorway as he walked up onto her porch. 'So how was that, Uncle Killy? Did she listen to you?'

'We had a really good chat and I'm giving her a start as a runner on the next job. She actually sounded keen.' They sat and ate and nattered, and then, as he started to clear their plates, she put a hand on his to stop him.

'What did you mean the first morning, when you said about not missing the boat again? Put the plates down, Killy, what did you mean?' He stood looking at her, clearly with something to say. 'What's up, Killy Wilde? Come on, tell me.'

There was so much going on in his mind; what he wanted to say was how being with her again had made him realise how he missed her company, but it wouldn't come. He wanted to be with her but simply couldn't let himself say it, and she knew him too well to try and drag anything out of him. She smiled at him.

'Right, I'm ready to go back to bed now. I think I might sleep, wanna join me?'

He nodded a bit sheepishly. 'I think that could be just the answer.'

They missed the first crew boat, scrambled out of bed, and just managed to jump on the following one to be greeted with knowing smiles from several of the crew. But neither of them really cared; they were both free to do what they wanted, and a lot of what Killy hadn't been able to say had been said during the course of a wonderful few hours.

Over the weekend, Rosalia and her team had set up a temporary catering operation back through the trees from the landing beach location, right next to the clearing for the generators and general transport. Everything was ready to go for a week of nights and by the time Killy and Sarah, certainly not side by side, walked up the beach, the whole crew and all the extras were lining up for their teatime breakfast.

They'd had an old barge towed up from the capital, fitted it with a small generator for work lighting, and anchored it about a hundred yards out from the beach, where it would serve as a floating camera platform and mooring for the submarine. Just as the empty crew boats were heading back to base, the red speedboat came roaring across the bay with Lydia at the wheel wearing a black leather jacket with a white silk scarf streaming in the wind. Uncle Philip was sitting next to her dressed in immaculate boating gear, topped off with a very sharp-looking sailing cap. Gussy helped them both ashore as Killy walked down to meet them.

'Uncle Philip, this is my boss, Killian Wilde. Killian, my godfather Don Felipé. And ma, of course; no need for introductions.'

Lydia put out her hand to him. 'Hello, Killy. Thank you for inviting us.'

'Lovely to see you again, Lydia. Welcome to our little world, in your backyard. Don Felipé, pleased to meet you, and welcome. In about an hour and a half we'll be filming a sequence where a troop of US marines comes ashore on a rescue mission, paddling small boats, so I'm afraid it won't be that interesting; not much acting but hopefully a lot of action. In the meantime, the caterers are serving breakfast up there through the trees, and you're very welcome to join us.'

'Thank you so much, Killian. Shall we just follow you?' Killy smiled to himself as Gussy had been right, his English was certainly a relic from a bygone age.

The guests were intrigued to see what was entailed in setting up a film shoot and after breakfast, which they both seemed to enjoy, Uncle Philip asked Gussy endless questions, whilst Lydia was more intent on watching Enzo and his team setting up for the first shot of the night. It was, as the scene description on the call sheet put it, *'landing boats loaded with marines being paddled towards the dark and threatening shoreline.'* The wind had come up and the sea was a lot livelier than it had been on the ride from base, and with thirty heavily armed men paddling little boats, it was going to be a long night. Uncle Philip and Lydia watched for a couple of hours then said their farewells and zoomed off back to the capital.

Getting the men and their little landing boats into the water from the barge was tricky so after a couple of near-capsizes, Killy and Julian agreed it would be better to start from the beach and tow the boats loaded with the men and all their gear out into the darkness, then position them as Julian wanted to film them from the barge paddling towards the shore. They worked on through until the midnight lunch break, and then afterwards on into the early hours, until Enzo, now shooting individual close-ups, looked up at the sky, shook his head and signalled to Killy they had to stop right there. Day was dawning and the first night shoot was over. After the long previous day and it's exertions, and then the long shift through the night, Killy was on his knees, and quite a few of the stuntmen were looking seasick.

He bellowed through his little electric loudspeaker, 'Thanks, everyone, great night's work. That's a wrap! See you all back here for breakfast at tea time tomorrow. Have a good rest.

Lars, well done and thank you; day off for you. Lucky man!'

Gussy and the runners were helping everyone onto the crew boats and by six am, in almost full daylight, what had been a hive of activity all night was now an empty beach. Killy and Sarah travelled back in the same boat but knowing they had to sleep, with nothing more than a peck on the cheek and a smile, they walked to their own bungalows. Killy dragged himself up the steps vowing as he always did that he'd never do another night shoot as long as he lived. There was no point stopping to make tea or to eat, as Rosalia's boys had kept them well supplied with hot drinks and snacks throughout the night. So he brushed his teeth, closed all the shutters, turned his phone off and, after putting stoppers in his ears, climbed into bed and pulled on the mask he'd saved from the flight over. And crashed out completely.

In the relentless way film shoots progress, they were all back on the beach and finished with breakfast by six o'clock the following evening, and ready for the second night's shoot. Killy was watching Enzo check the light for the umpteenth time, when he finally nodded.

Then he finally nodded. 'Andiamo, Killy! Let's shoot!'

Killy switched on his megaphone. 'OK, girls and boys. Another jolly night of fun and games so, everyone, let's clear the beach please and get all the gear up behind the treeline.' They were going to film the reverse of what they'd done the night before, jumping forward in the story, with the marines returning to the submarine after the rescue. Julian wanted two stuntmen marines made up and bandaged, as though badly wounded in the fighting, being carried through the trees to the beach on stretchers and then taken out to the sub by boat. Fortunately, although now they had no moon, the weather had changed in their favour and the sea was calmer. Regis and Rafa were organising the marines and making them look as though they'd just fought their way back through several miles of enemy-held jungle, helping Marta and her team spray their uniforms with water to ensure they looked sweat-stained, and generally roughing them up with dirt and lots of blood-soaked bandages.

Julian called across to Rafa, 'What about the two stretcher cases? How would they manage them in the boats?'

'Only one thing you could do, Julian: lash two boats together, side by side, and set the stretchers front to back, lying next to each other where the boats are joined. With two men paddling at the sides in each boat it will be slow, but it should be relatively safe, and with all their guns and equipment in the bottom of the two boats it will give additional stability. Shall we lash the boats together in the bushes, Julian, that way the boys can pull them across the sand on camera and then load the wounded on the stretchers down by the water line?'

'Great stuff, Rafa. Could you be getting that organised now for me please?'

'OK, Julian!'

It was clear he'd formed a strong relationship with the stuntmen, and within a couple of minutes they were about to begin rigging up the makeshift floating ambulance when Julian called out, 'Rafa! Just hold on one second, we should get this on camera. Enzo, how difficult would it be to put a camera on this? We just need to show the audience a closeup glimpse of them lashing the boats together to build the tension.'

Enzo was nodding approvingly. 'I agree, Julian.' He and Bunny had a quick discussion as to what gear would be needed to light it and in about fifteen minutes, Enzo was ready. And another fifteen minutes got Julian the little scene he'd invented.

The night was going to be moonless and so, before the evening's work had started, Bunny's sparks had mounted a big, filtered light on a scaffold tower they'd erected high up in the treetops. It gave just enough silvery moonlight flickering through the treetops to enable the audience to see the marines drag the boats across the beach from the treeline. Even without the power that music would add to the scene, it was easy to understand what Julian envisioned; watching the stuntmen marines gently loading their wounded comrades onto the boats was really moving. Killy had been right; this director certainly knew his stuff. The night's shoot had been a great success all round, and Killy wrapped it up before dawn started to break.

21

The following morning, whilst Killy and all the crew would be sleeping, the submarine was scheduled to leave the base and sail down to the landing beach, and moor up alongside the barge to be ready for the third night's filming. However, at around nine am Lex had been so alarmed by the way the wind was increasing in strength, he'd phoned Monika to say that tying up to an anchored barge in those conditions wouldn't be safe. So they agreed to wait and see how the weather would be by midday; but by then it had become a full-blown storm.

Killy woke up just after noon and turned on his phone to find a message from Monika to call as soon as possible, and listening to the wind lashing the trees outside was enough to tell him what she wanted to talk about.

He called her, 'Hola, guapa! It's the weather, yeah?'

'And it's going to get worse, Killy. Arthur called me; he wants to speak to you as soon as you're awake.'

Killy walked up onto Arthur's porch and found him in the kitchen, dressed soberly in a khaki top and shorts, with his hair looking very neat, not chewed. 'Morning, Arthur. Or afternoon. Whatever it is. We missed you. No titfer?'

'Blew off, it's probably halfway to Miami by now. I've had to comb the old barnet. How's it all going, son?'

'Well thanks to our plan to get on and shoot everything we could do with Lars, there's nothing we can switch to today that doesn't need Nathan.'

Arthur bestowed Killy with one of his fatherly faces. 'We're doing fine, son. There's two day's weather contingency built into the budget and we've already made back the first day we lost, so if we lose tonight that's still one in the bag. And who knows, we might even be able to nick this one back.'

'Yes, Arthur, we might. But then again, we might not. And it's like with your driving licence; better with six points to spare than three.'

'Yeah well, give yourself a break, son. We're well and truly on top of it, alright? We're halfway through week four of a six-week shoot, bang on schedule. Stop worrying. You're worse than my old lady. You were due to be doing the sub stuff tonight?'

'Yeah. It was supposed to moor up this morning, ready for two nights of shooting, and now this.'

'Right. Well if there's nothing else you can get on with, tonight has to be a write-off cos this weather's forecast to last through till the morning.'

'OK we'll reschedule and finish the week on the sub. Anyway, how was Miami? Did your trip go well?'

'Really well, son. Remember me talking to Mr Sieglovitz, who owns the agency Serena's with? By sheer coincidence, we were introduced to each other at an industry networking breakfast and we finished up talking all morning, and then having lunch together. The science-fiction stuff he's doing that I told you about ... I did, didn't I? Yes, of course I did. Anyway, that's already under starter's orders, and it's way too big for us at the moment, but he's got three scripts he's looking at with medium-sized budgets, action with a bit of romance thrown in, like this one. He wants to see a rough cut of this as soon as we can get it to him and if he likes it, he's going to put one of them our way.'

'Would it be over this side of the pond?'

'Definitely. He likes to work from Miami as it's central to all the Americas, and he's got his own jet, so he does a couple of days in LA every week then goes back to Florida, plays golf, and does deals over the phone. And he's a lot older than he sounded; he's gotta be eighty if he's a day, and fit as a fucking fiddle. Puts me to shame. For us, he'd be looking at pictures he could market in the states, where there's evidently a big Spanish speaking audience for stuff with a mix of Spanish and English-speaking actors, which is what he likes about this one. He's also got a big investor in Canada, so could be something there as well.' Killy nodded and smiled.

...

They did lose the night, but at a few minutes to five the following evening, the crew boats were skimming across the water for the penultimate nights work. Once breakfast was over, Julian and Killy agreed that they'd be better off practicing getting the boats up out of the water and onto the deck of the sub. In that way they could solve any problems that would doubtless crop up, and it proved to be a good move. Hauling the boats out of the water and onto the sub was not easy, but the stuntmen marines were all very strong and fit and with Rafa and Wally instructing them step by step, after a couple of run throughs, they'd got it all shot.

The real problem was the two stretchers with the wounded men strapped to them. On the first attempt with the two lashed-together boats, as the first stretchered man was lifted out, it upset

213

the balance completely and they dropped him into the sea between the boat and the side of the sub. Fortunately two of the stuntmen immediately dived in and rescued him, but it shook everyone up — particularly the man strapped to his stretcher.

It took almost the whole night to get to the point where Julian felt things were safe enough to have a first go at a shot, so that meant they were really up against the clock and only just managed to finish filming all the boarding sequence before Enzo called the night to an end.

Killy wrapped it up over his megaphone, 'Right everyone, thanks for tonight. Tomorrow night is going to be a big one, so try and get a good rest as it could well finish up a bit of a kick, bollock and scramble.'

And just as Killy had predicted, the fifth and final night gradually got more and more hectic, but it served to show how cool Julian could be under extreme pressure. In those sort of situations, Killy had dealt with directors exploding and hurling the blame for problems in every direction, expletives definitely included, people fired, others terrified and reduced to tears. But Julian just kept doggedly plugging on, never even raising his voice.

Killy was blaming himself for not having thought it through more thoroughly. Next, they were shooting the marines setting off on the rescue mission, then filming them actually launching their boats in the moonlight and starting to paddle towards the shore. Regis and Rafa had realised that the structural changes Lex had made to the sub was going to cost them an hour, but in the end they cheated things and made it look militarily correct, and got everything finished with no mishaps. They broke for their midnight lunch greatly relieved, and probably nobody more so than Killy.

As they sat chatting about the shots they had yet to finish, Killy noticed Lex seemed less at ease than usual. A non-performer having first night nerves. Ilze and Hannah were sitting with Marta and Gloria, and judging by the laughter the nerves were all very steady at that table.

It took the first two hours after the break to get everything ready to complete the landing sequence. Filming from the beach, the marines paddled towards the cameras, as, in the background, the sub slipped beneath the sea exactly as planned. Killy then had to keep the cameras running to get the shots they needed of the sub surfacing at the beginning of the sequence. However, when it finally appeared, its bow was pointing right up in the air and it took at least five minutes to get it levelled out. Lex then took several minutes to come through on the walkie talkie.

'Apologies, Killy, not so good and my fault entirely.'

'Killy here, Lex. The submerging was perfect but we need the surfacing to be level, so get the crew to go through the same action but dive down to periscope depth, then raise the periscope and swivel it around very slowly through three-sixty degrees while we film it from the camera boat, and then resurface.' Killy called, 'action on submarine,' and it dropped slowly beneath the surface. The periscope came up and surveyed all around it, then disappeared. They all waited by the camera with fingers crossed, but this time it reappeared rear end first, with propellers still slowly clunking round in the night air and not at all the dramatic image they needed. Killy whispered to Julian, 'Like a duck with its arse in the air.'

Once again there was more precious time lost, as Lex got up onto the bridge. Julian was finally getting a little bit uptight. He took Killy's walkie-talkie. 'Julian here, Lex. What went wrong that time?'

'Apologies once again. I think I'm not passing on your commands promptly enough. Ilze will do it this time.'

Julian looked at Killy and shook his head. 'Great, Lex. Thank you.' Then he lowered his voice. 'Fucking hell, Killy, we still haven't got a surfacing shot we can use. This could go on all night.' Killy's instincts were seeking an alternative but they were stuck, so once everybody was ready he called *action* again, down went the sub and then, finally, perfectly level and just where they needed it to be for the cameras, the sub broke the surface.

Everyone breathed a huge sigh of relief and as Killy shouted, 'Action on boats!' the stuntmen paddled steadily towards the sub. That was one good surfacing sequence, and shot from two cameras, so now they could go on to complete the boats landing on the beach as the sub slowly dived in the background.

This shot was a bit more complicated to set up; Julian wanted two of the stuntmen marines in the boats to turn and look back towards the sub as it disappeared beneath the surface, so that in the edit he could cut from them looking back at it, to a close-up of it going down. They decided to rehearse it one time and to film the rehearsal so that if it all went according to plan, the take might be usable.

Killy called, 'Rehearsal action on the sub and boats.' But the sub didn't move and the stuntmen paddling the boats were getting too far away from it for the shot to work, so there was nothing else Killy could do but to call out, 'Cut!'

Julian was shaking his head slowly. 'Obviously a communication problem, Killy.'

Ilze popped up on the bridge waving her walkie-talkie, so they passed a spare to the skipper of the camera boat, who powered directly out to the sub. Hannah was up on deck holding one of their long fishing poles, and having fixed a plastic bag to the end of it with gaffer tape, she put the defective walkie-talkie into it and swung it out, so the skipper of the camera boat could swap it with the replacement. They were running far too close to the wire.

Killy called as soon as the handover was complete, 'Are you ready to go again, Ilze?'

'Yes, sorry about that. It just went dead. Everything ready here, Killy.'

He called out again, 'Rehearsal action on sub and boats!' Right on cue the stuntmen started paddling.

He nodded to Julian, who spoke into the walkie-talkie, 'Ilze, that's rehearsal action on the sub, thank you.'

Enzo took his eye from the viewfinder, scanning the last of the night sky; they had to get it this time. On Julian's monitor the shot was working perfectly; the paddling marines looked great, the submarine was positioned right behind them and the ones who'd been chosen to look back timed it immaculately, not holding onto it for a second too long. Slowly and evenly, Ilze took the dear old *Hondssbosch* steadily down into the deep. Enzo looked upwards and then to Killy, and drew a finger across his throat; the night and the week over. They'd made it by the skin of their teeth.

Killy woke the next day to find a text from Arthur:

Well done sunshine, I told you not to worry. Having a little welcome lunch for Cutter Brown in the garden at 1pm, dress optional, see you there.

The thought of Arthur following any dress code made him smile. He walked into the garden a couple of minutes early. Arthur, resplendent in lurid green tropicals and hair slicked right down, stood up from the table and did the introductions.

'Cutter, this is Killy Wilde. I think you two spoke on the

phone.'

Cutter Brown was even more impressive in the flesh than on screen, at just about six feet tall, solidly built, and with close-cropped, greying hair, he stood up and put out a massive right hand. 'Killy, good to meet you. I've been hearing a lot about you.' They were looking at each other directly eye to eye.

'Good things I hope, Cutter — but not from Arthur, surely?'

'No, I just spent the morning with Marta and Gloria. I told them I'd spoken to you, and man they were singing your praises.' Julian came walking across the garden.

'Cutter, this is Julian Burford-Brown, our director.'

'Hello there, Julian. Brown meets Brown, eh? Let's just can the Burfords, shall we?'

That was exactly Julian's style. 'Good for me, Cutter, I never liked that side anyway.'

They shook hands warmly and there was obviously positive chemistry between them; Cutter had to be early sixties, Julian young enough to be his son, and with no male-to male competition going on. The lunch was to get director and actor together, so Killy wandered over to the bar just as Monika and Ali arrived, looking very smart for a Saturday lunchtime on location.'

Hello, girls, something special going on? Possibly lunch with Mr B?'

Ali was straight back at him. 'We're off duty now, Killy, so order us a beer each will you? Please! And actually, we've already been introduced, but as we were in work gear we decided as Arthur was kind enough to invite us, we'd make an effort.' Killy called through to the kitchen for three beers as Monika turned to him.

'Killy, Gussy is right now having a phone conversation

with his uncle. I think we need to have him tell us exactly what's been said.'

'Definitely. Get him to come to mine after lunch, if that's good for you? This is all cooking up into a nice little devil's brew; a regime change, plus Nathan and co arriving tomorrow afternoon. Shall we go and join the party?'

Cutter was a joy to be around, and when there was a little lull in the conversation, Killy finally got an opportunity to ask him about his nickname.

'Is Cutter just a short form of Cuthbert, or was it something to do with the way you used a baseball bat?'

He was amused by the question. 'Both I guess, Killy. My kid brother couldn't pronounce Cuthbert, so he always called me *Cudber*. Then it became *Cudder*, and it stayed with me. But it actually goes deeper; my maternal great-grandparents were slaves, and I was raised in the little cabin they'd lived in on what had been the plantation. My daddy still grew a small field of sugarcane and I was big for my age, so I got to cut the cane with him, and because I'd been blessed with a strong right arm and a quick eye, I got to be very good at it. That combination turned out to be just what I needed to play baseball, so *cane-cuttin' cudder* became Cutter Brown. And you better believe Cutter's a whole lot better a name than Cuthbert, when you're playing in the Major Leagues!'

Monika got a call at four o'clock, and the fact that she took it meant it had to be work. She stood up and announced to everyone, 'Sorry to say that Mr Brown's boat is ready to take him away from us. If you're ready to go, Cutter, Ali and I will walk you down to the jetty.'

He immediately stood up and started shaking hands. 'I guess I'd better get back to my wife and our hosts. They're having a dinner for us tonight, and tomorrow I need to work on my lines. So Arthur, Julian, Killy, Monika, and Alison; thank you all for your hospitality and good company, and I'll see you Monday morning. Lead on please, ladies.'

Julian excused himself almost immediately, 'I need to get on top of the scenes between Cutter and Nathan, so please excuse me, I'm going back to mine. Thanks for lunch, Arthur, and more to the point, thank you for hiring Cutter. He's going to lift the picture to another level. What a lovely man. Let's hope we're going to feel the same way about our hero. And on that subject, I'd like to do a bit of work with him tomorrow. What time does he arrive, Killy?'

Arthur answered, 'Early afternoon. I'm going to meet him at the strip with Monika, then take him and his family to the villa. What would suit you best: invite them to an early supper in the garden?'

'Yes ... In fact no, Arthur, just in case he brings his family; could you perhaps suggest a working supper for him and I at eight? That would be so much better for me.'

'Certainly shall, Julian, good idea. Americans eat early anyway. I'll get Monika to sort it out, and let you know.'

As soon as Julian left the garden, Arthur looked Killy straight in the eye. 'Got something to tell me?'

'Gussy's been talking with his uncle regarding the political situation, so we arranged to have him meet with you, me and Monika.'

'When?'

'After lunch, so now if you like?'

'Get hold of Monika and tell her to bring him to mine ASAP. We need to keep right on top of this, son; we're far enough along to plan for people and equipment to start being shipped out.'

'As a courtesy, Arthur, do we include Julian in this?'

'No, he's got far too much on his plate already. If it turns out he feels he should have been asked, I'll deal with it. Executive decision. Just the three of us and the kid. See you soon.'

22

According to Uncle Philip, the president had been given a date by which he had to leave, but he'd also pointed out that there were definitely two or three high-ranking military men working very hard to make sure their leader didn't go without a fight. Once Gussy had left, they started to work out the order in which the different departments could be released.

Once all the jungle action sequences involving Nathan were complete, the stunt team, special effects, and the armourers could be signed off. Regis was moving on to another project, leaving Rafa to supervise everything military that remained, and Alain's art department personnel would have packed up and moved on to their next job several days before the shoot finished. Marta would be ready to ship out the costumes and her team as soon as all the extras were released, and she would personally take care of anything costume-wise, along with Gloria doing hair and makeup for Serena and Nathan's final scene. Enzo had already arranged to finish the shoot with one of his crew and a lightweight camera. Paddy could cover sound on the last couple of days on his own, so that would get his assistants on their way, and Pete was travelling with the generators and all the associated gear back to Miami, leaving Bunny to light the final shots for Enzo. Gary and his construction crew had already moved on.

The plan was to have as many personnel as possible safely on their way home by the middle of the final week. For the closing scene of the movie, with Serena and Nathan in the garden, it would be just heads of department as the crew. This was all dependent on everything going according to schedule but the one big unknown, their 'Star' Nathan Bedford, wasn't even going to be on the island until the following day. He was carrying the movie in terms of its prospective audience, and they were totally dependent on him coming up with the goods right from day one.

It wasn't necessary for Killy to be part of Nathan's welcoming party, but when Arthur suggested that he come with him and Monika to the airstrip, curiosity got the better of him. It was blazing hot out on the runway, the sun on the roasting tarmac having a mirage effect and making it look like a sheet of silvery, shimmering water. As the three of them stood in the shadow of one of the three brand-new people carriers Monika had scoured the island to find, Nathan's jet flew over them, made a big turn, and then dropped down for a perfect landing. Everyone onboard had been cleared through customs at the international airport, so there were no more formalities to be dealt with and as soon as the pilot had switched off the engines, the side door to the plane opened and a set of steps automatically dropped down, and out stepped a smartly-uniformed young woman officer.

The local ground crew were already by the side of the plane, with two big, very old and beaten up four-wheeled trolleys, and when the young officer opened up the rear compartment, it was clearly packed full of baggage. Next down the steps were two young boys around six or seven and they ran off immediately into the shade of the control tower as a very thin, blonde, and frazzled-looking young woman, dressed in a white top and matching jeans, appeared in the doorway and shouted at the boys, 'Marlon, Averil, would you please come back here now!' They didn't budge, so she shrugged and walked over to join them.

The bigger boy stood and stared at her defiantly. 'Mommy, where's the limos at?' Monika looked at Killy, shook her head and rolled her eyes at the thought. Then down the steps came Nathan Bedford, the man himself, as the bigger boy yelled again, 'Daddy! There's no limo here. Where's our limo at? You promised us we'd get our own limo?'

The little boy joined in, 'Where's our limo? We want our limo. You promised us, Daddy!'

Nathan stood at the bottom of the steps with his hand on the rail, as if he were posing for the camera. With the wrap-around sunglasses, white safari suit, and matching baseball cap, he looked pretty much like his photo, but definitely, whilst almost identical physically, he had a more handsome face than Lars. He stared at Arthur as he walked towards him, with a look of disdain not even the shades could disguise. 'Are y'all here to meet us? Cos if y'are, the boys are asking the question I want answered: where's the goddamn limos at?'

Arthur put out his hand. 'Good afternoon, Nathan. I'm Arthur Margolies, the producer, this is Monika Sanchez, our production manager, and Killian Wilde, the First AD. Welcome to you all. Did you have a good flight?'

With certainly no warmth intended, barely looking at Killy or Monika, he took Arthur's hand. 'Call me Nate. And no, we didn't have a good flight. There was turbulence pretty much the whole fuckin' way, and now you're here with a bunch of vans for me and my family, when it clearly states in my contract there will be two limousines assigned to us from the moment we arrive, right through to our departure?'

The 'vans', as he described them, were all in mint condition, and with their uniformed drivers had cost Arthur a great deal of money to hire for two weeks. Ever ready to defend her boss, Monika stepped into the fray.

'Good afternoon, Nathan. Unfortunately, there are no limousines anywhere on the island, and if you read your contract carefully you will see there is provision for the 'top level of deluxe transport subject to local availability'. I'm afraid this is the very best.'

Nathan clearly didn't appreciate Monika's no-nonsense style. 'Right, Ms Sanchez. Would you please take us to our villa? We need to check it out.'

The three of them sat speechless in Monika's little four-wheel drive, listening to the air conditioning whilst the drivers and ground crew loaded all the luggage into one van while Nathan and his wife sat themselves in one of the others and the boys sat side by side next to the driver in the remaining one.

Killy couldn't stop himself saying something, 'Classy, eh?'

King Arthur almost exploded, 'Classy? I've got more class in my arse. Fifty thousand dollars a day? I wouldn't give you a fucking fiver for the lot of them. Excuse me, Monika.' The drivers were ready to follow them to the villa, and as they moved off Arthur started again, 'I've had as much of this as I can take, Monika. What is it they call 'em in the states, 'trailer trash'? Well whatever it is, I don't ever want to set eyes on them again. Let me out as we go past mine please, I need a shower.'

They dropped Arthur off, and a few minutes later Monika led the family up the steps of the villa. As she opened the front door, Killy stood like a rather pointless doorman while the whole

225

family filed past him as though he didn't exist. Nathan stopped in the middle of the hallway and looked all around him and then back at his wife.

'It's a lot smaller than it was in the video. What ya think, honey?'

She was shaking her head. 'I still don't like this colour, Nate. I told you it should have been a lighter blue and that's what makes it feel small. Let's go take a look at the kitchen. Come on, boys, go check out the 'fridgerator.' The two of them followed the boys who, by this time, were standing in front of the wardrobe-sized, double-door fridge freezer, looking amongst the dozens of items Victoria and Ali had stocked it with. The bigger boy stood back staring into it.

'There's no root beer! I told you to tell 'em I wanted it. There's only dumb old coke.'

The little one then chimed in, 'And no Dr Pepper neither, Ma. This place is shit. I hate it.'

The woman looked straight at Monika. 'Watch your dirty mouth, boy! I'm sure they'll fix it. Let's go look at the bedrooms. Are they through here, Ms Sanchez?' She pointed towards the corridor to the right, and then led the boys and Nathan away with her, leaving Monika and Killy staring at each other in shock. Monika shook her head and mouthed, *It's as though they're buying it!*

After a few minutes of doors opening and banging shut, they all came walking back along the corridor. Monika held out the keys.

'Are the bedrooms to your liking, Mrs Bedford?'

She took them from her. 'For two weeks they'll do, Ms Sanchez. And we're not married. Yet.' She glared at Nathan. 'Are we, honey?'

He turned away and walked out onto the veranda. 'Don't start that bullshit again, Charlene. C'mon boys, let's go check out the pool!' They grabbed a hand each and went with him. Charlene was looking daggers at his back as he walked away, and it wasn't difficult to read her lips mouthing: *fucking shit head.*' Then she realised they were both staring at her.

'OK so we need to feed these boys. How do we get room service, Ms Sanchez?'

'Just pick up any phone, dial one hundred, and someone will take your order. Do you speak Spanish?'

'I don't but he's Texan, so half of what he says is Spanish.'

'Well, Charlene, all the staff here are local people and they do their best in English, but better if you have some Spanish. Both of the third assistants are bilingual, so I'll give you their numbers to call if you have a problem.'

The younger boy came racing back shouting, 'There was a big fat fucking frog in the pool ma! Daddy killed it with the net! Smashed it right on the head! We're hungry, can we get room service?'

'Not if you don't watch your mouth, kid, there's people here. What you want anyways?'

The elder boy arrived and they both yelled in unison, 'Pizza!'

She yelled back, 'You wannit now, or when you're finished in the pool?'

As they ran off, the bigger one bellowed down the corridor, 'Now! And Root Beer and Dr Pepper!'

Nathan shouted out, 'The pool needs a fence round it, the young'un cain't barely swim!'

Charlene looked at Killy and started towards the

bedrooms. 'Are our bags in yet?' He suddenly realised she was asking him.

'They should be outside the bedrooms on the veranda.' Nathan walked back in and took the keys as Charlene made her way down the corridor.

'The boys want pizza, Nate. I'm gonna freshen up.'

Killy and Monika stood by the main doorway waiting to be dismissed, until Nathan finally spoke. 'OK so we decided not to bring the nanny or the chef. Only two weeks here, it didn't seem worth it, but Charlene ain't too big on cookin', so we'll do room service. And just keep the icebox loaded with snacks for the kids. What was the room service number?'

Monika took a deep breath, 'It's one hundred and Charlene says you speak Spanish. The staff are all locals, so it's good that you do.'

He half-smiled. 'Not a problem. Back home we deal with those people all the time.'

Monika was visibly seething at the mention of 'those people', but obviously decided to gloss over it, 'Nathan—'

'—I asked you to call me Nate, Ms Sanchez.'

She forced a smile. 'Fine, Mr Bedford, Nate it is. Julian, our director, would like to have a working supper with you to discuss tomorrow's scenes, and he suggested at around eight this evening in the garden restaurant? Would that work for you?'

He nodded rather grudgingly. 'Yeah, OK, I'll be there. You better send someone to fetch me.'

She nodded. 'One of our third assistants will be outside your door at five minutes to eight. It's very close.' There was obviously nothing more to say, certainly not from him, so they left. Monika was speechless, but soon had Julian on the phone.

'Everything's set for supper at eight, Julian, and it's just you and Nathan, or Nate as he likes to be called.' She listened for quite a while, then said, 'Well he's not really, as you Brits might put it, *my cup of tea*, but I'm sure you'll be able to find the best in him.'

From what Julian told Killy over breakfast the following morning, his working supper with Nathan had been a complete waste of time and now, after an hour on set, it was obvious why. They didn't have a single shot completed, and were standing behind the camera watching two actors rehearse a scene which only one of them knew the words to.

Killy leaned over to Julian and whispered, 'He hasn't a clue, has he?

Cutter was on top of all his lines and doing his best to keep the dialogue flowing whilst Nathan clutched his script as though his life depended on it, stumbling his way through from line to line, constantly misreading.

Bunny whispered to Killy, 'Couldn't act his way out of a fucking paper bag.'

Julian led Nathan away from the camera where they couldn't be overheard, and told him he was going to have the lines written up on big sheets of card. These are affectionately known as Idiot Boards but he didn't tell Nathan that. The fact that the two actors were facing each other across the general's desk made it much easier. Once the cards had all been written out by Sarah Scripts, and the task of holding them up directly in Nathan's eyeline behind the camera had been assigned to a very nervous Victoria, clearly terrified she might get them in the wrong order, they finally managed to complete the scene. However, it became clear when they started rehearsing the next one that Nathan didn't know his lines for that one either. Thanks to more idiot boards and Cutter's patience, they managed to finish the whole office sequence and only ran over the scheduled finish time by twenty minutes. Nathan left the set as soon as Killy called the wrap, without a word of apology to anyone.

Cutter was sitting at the general's desk whilst one of Gloria's assistants took photos of his hair and makeup from all angles; a precaution taken with actors after every scene to ensure that if for any reason the scene or a part of it has to be repeated at a later date, it can be perfectly reproduced. He really looked the part in his General's uniform, as one of Marta's ladies took pictures of every detail; West Point ring, tie knot, military insignia, and so on for the same reason. As she finished, Julian walked across to him.

'Great work today, Cutter, thank you. The scene is really going to anchor the story. I'm sorry about Nathan.'

'Pretty poor behaviour all round, Julian. I'm afraid if this goes on tomorrow, I shall have to say something to him. That boy has no manners, and he's certainly no actor.' It was a bad position for Julian to be in, as the director has to be the means of communication whenever there is any form of negative energy between actors, but Cutter couldn't keep it all bottled up any longer. 'It's a fucking disgrace, Julian! Guy has no respect. Not even an apology. And he's a racist, I can read it in his eyes. His name says it all; his parents would never have called him that if they weren't die-hard white supremacists.'

Julian looked puzzled. 'Sorry, Cutter, you've lost me there.'

'Nathan Bedford Forrest was a rich, southern slave trader, who raised his own regiment of cavalry in the civil war. Renowned as a great rebel general, famous for fighting behind the lines, and putting fear into the hearts of the Union soldiers. He was also the original leader of the Ku Klux Klan. There's no way that fucking little pissant was named Nathan Bedford by accident.'

23

Killy woke in the middle of the night from a really bizarre dream featuring Nathan all kitted out in Klan regalia, brandishing a burning cross, about to face off with Cutter wearing his baseball kit and wielding a huge bat. That wasn't an easy one to shake off and he barely slept from then on, his mind taken up with attempting to stop things going too far. He popped Julian a text as soon as he was fully awake …

Need a quick chat re Cutter asap.

Julian called back soon after, and obviously worried, himself, they met up and walked to the base together.

'What do you think, Killy? I've been going over it all night.'

'I suggest you two to have breakfast together in his dressing room once he's ready. He'll be in makeup now, so I'll send a runner to ask him to join you. He has most of the lines today, Nathan just responds, so I think it would be better all round if you can persuade him to bite his tongue and get the day over with.'

'Yes. All we need is an on-set fight, Killy, and young and fit though our hero might be and thirty years his junior, I think I'd have my money on Cutter if it came to it. Just one punch from that right hand of his would finish it. Don't worry about the runner, I'll go and see him now. I'll do my best.'

His best worked. The two actors were called to the parade ground set, shook hands, and nodded to each other, seemingly ready to work. Rafa had spent days rehearsing the military extras for the scenes they were about to shoot and now he was going to see how well they performed in front of the camera. He assembled them in ranks all standing to attention, ready to listen when the general made his speech to them. Rafa and Regis walked up and down between the lines ensuring everything was in order, and checking that the spaces between the men were identical, that every weapon was being held correctly, and that Nathan was standing in exactly the right spot.

Cutter took his place on the small, raised reviewing platform and waited patiently for Julian and Enzo to sort out the first big wide shot with the camera shooting from behind the men, over their heads and directly at him. Once that was done there would be multiple versions from various angles, with Cutter going through his speech on every take.

After another ten minutes, Julian called out, 'Can we set up for a rehearsal please? And, Rafa, would you start with all the marines standing at attention, and when Killy calls *'rehearsal action'*, order them to stand at ease. Cutter, if you could take your own cue from them, that would be great. Thank you.' Rafa explained everything to the men in Spanish and then walked along to Nathan and showed him exactly how to come to attention and then to stand at ease. Killy noticed Nathan wasn't too pleased at being instructed, but he got it right after a couple of attempts and Rafa walked to the side off camera. The rehearsal went without a hitch and Cutter gave the speech perfectly, so they moved right on for the first take. Cutter then delivered his lines faultlessly on every following take, and within a couple of hours they were ready to do a reverse of the whole thing.

For the next shot the camera would be positioned up on the platform behind Cutter, to give the cinema audience his point of view as the troops listened to him.

Killy called to Enzo, 'How long?'

'Fifteen minutes please, Killy.'

Killy gave him the thumbs up. 'Let the men know they can relax for ten please, Rafa.' Nathan left the set and walked directly back to his dressing room, while Cutter sat off to the side in his canvas-backed chair, which was placed next to Nathan's empty one. Under normal circumstances the little breaks between shots are when actors can chat and maybe run lines and get to know each other. Killy called everyone back and they quickly worked their way on, with the camera picking out various individuals Julian wanted to feature as well as Nathan, all listening to Cutter. Within an hour he was happy with what he'd got, and ready to set up for a tracking shot with the camera focussed on Cutter and moving along in front of the men to give their view of the general; after every few feet the camera would stop to focus on Cutter saying parts of his speech that Julian would feature in close up.

Killy called out, 'OK, everyone, take twenty minutes. Thanks, Rafa!'

Nathan once again headed directly for his dressing room, whereas Cutter picked up his chair and carried it across to where Sarah was chatting with Regis and Rafa, who both immediately jumped up and saluted him, as Rafa shouted, 'Attention!' It amused Cutter but caused a lot of confusion among the military extras, who were gathering in groups having just been dismissed. When they realised what had happened they all joined in the joke. It took about twenty minutes to set the tracks and get the camera mounted, then Enzo gave Killy the nod.

He was standing with Julian and called out, 'OK, everyone, let's do a camera rehearsal. Get the guys in position please, Rafa, and please tell them as before they should be listening to the general.'

Gussy went to collect Nathan for the rehearsal, but came back alone. 'He says he won't be seen in this shot as it's all on the general, so he's taken his uniform off and he's staying in his dressing room and doing a workout. This put Julian on the spot.

'Fucking hell, Killy. Cutter is addressing this speech to Nathan and his troops, he has to be here.' He paused. 'OK, let's run the rehearsal without him and I'll go and speak to him over lunch.'

Killy took over. 'Right, everyone. Positions for a camera rehearsal, please.' Cutter was up on the platform ready to go, but had obviously noticed Nathan was missing.

He stepped down, walked across to Julian and in a very controlled whisper said, 'Excuse me, Julian, does that arrogant sonofabitch think I'm going to do this speech without him here? Because with all due respect to you, sir, I am not happy to do that.'

Contractually, an actor is obliged to work to a director's requirements, so unhappy though Cutter might be about doing the speech without his co-actor being there, Julian could have insisted Cutter go ahead without Nathan and reluctantly or otherwise, he would be legally bound to comply. Julian had obviously come to the conclusion he had to do something there and then.

'Killy, just give me a couple of minutes. Excuse me, Cutter.' He walked off in the direction of the dressing rooms.

It was up to Killy not to allow this interruption to become a drama in itself, so he called across to Enzo who was actually ready to start. 'Julian will be right back, Enzo. Do you want to run through it again if I get Cutter to take his position on the stand?' Enzo was canny enough to know Killy was stalling, and went right along with it and gave him a nod. Cutter was not quite so keen to play the game, but he'd obviously realised it would be better to take as much heat out of the situation as possible. Whatever happened next needed to be contained and not allowed to become a spectacle. He nodded and made his way back up to his position.

The grip was pulling the dolly back along the tracks to his start position just as Julian walked onto the parade ground, followed by a very obviously pissed off Nathan tucking his shirt into his trousers.

Killy took over. 'OK, everyone. Positions for a camera rehearsal, please. Cutter, I'll call rehearsal action for you, then Julian will give Enzo a visual.' Julian momentarily took his eyes off the monitor, glanced at Killy sideways and shook his head in disbelief.

Killy whispered, 'Welcome to Hollywood, Guvnor.'

Cutter finished the speech and Julian, still staring at the final image of him on his monitor, nodded. 'That's it. Rehearsal over. Thanks Killy.'

Killy called out, 'OK, we'll shoot this after lunch, so back here ready to go in one hour. Pass that on to the guys please, Rafa.' Yet again Nathan took off immediately. The troops followed Rafa's instruction and raced away to get in the line for food. Julian and Killy stood looking at one another as Cutter and Sarah walked towards the catering tents. Within a couple of minutes of work stopping, the set was deserted apart from a troubled-looking director and a very inquisitive First AD.

'So what happened in his dressing room, Julian?'

'I told him it's not the way I like to work, Killy, and that even though he would not be seen in the shot, Cutter's speech was definitely directed to him and his men and I wanted him there.'

'Well played, Guv, if I may say, keeping Cutter out of it. Let's go and get something to eat. We've got a big afternoon in front of us.'

...

Things after lunch ran exactly to schedule. The tracking shot worked perfectly, and Julian was delighted with the whole scene up to that point. However, when they started to rehearse the section where Cutter was face-to-face with Nathan, congratulating him in front of the men, it became clear yet again that Nathan hadn't bothered to learn the simple but very logical responses to the General's lines, but after three failed attempts to run through the scene the skies opened up and Killy sent everyone inside.

Gussy grabbed one of the big cast umbrellas, opened it up over Nathan, and walked him back to his dressing room. One of Marta's ladies meanwhile was attempting to do the same for Cutter, the problem being she was less than five feet tall and couldn't actually hold it over his head, so in the end he thanked her, took her by the arm under the umbrella and hurried both of them giggling towards the dressing rooms. Killy was staring out at the rain, trying to guess how long it would go on for, when Paddy came and stood next to him, obviously listening to something on his headset.

He spoke into Killy's ear, 'Cutter and Nathan have still got body mics on from the wide shots and neither of them gave me a chance to turn them off when they legged it just now. Cutter must have followed him into his dressing room and he's reading him the riot act, so you'd better have a listen Kill, if it turns ugly you might have to step in.'

Killy took the set of cans Paddy offered him just as Nathan was speaking, 'Why do I need to stand there listening to you doing the speech for the ninety-ninth fucking time, man? And what difference does it make? The fucking camera's on you, not me!'

'I'll tell you why it matters, Mr Bedford; it's because we are *acting*, and acting depends upon mutual respect between performers and it doesn't matter that the camera isn't on you. You may be the star of this movie, but the sequence we're doing right now is there to build up the strength of your character in the story, so the better I do my job the better it makes your character look. And all that apart, you still don't know your fucking lines! If a contractor showed up to work on your home without his tools, you'd fire his sorry ass wouldn't you? Learn your fucking lines, man, and learn to have respect for your fellow actors.'

The door slammed and Killy took off the headset as Paddy pulled out his little ear bud, a big grin on his face. 'Good stuff, eh?'

'Priceless, mate.'

'Sound department's little perks, Killy. Have that one on me!'

There was an icy sense of distance between them as Nathan and Cutter stood face-to-face on the very last take of the day. Eyeballing each other, the two characters shook hands and Nathan snapped a very smart salute to end the scene.

Julian looked away from his monitor. 'Thanks, Killy, that's good for me.'

'And thank you, Julian. Right everyone, scene complete and a wrap for today, and a release on the fantastic Mister Cutter

Brown!' Everyone stopped what they were doing and gave him a big round of applause, but Nathan stalked off the set without a word to anyone, followed by the poor lady who was responsible for dressing him and who from her expression was obviously not enjoying the job. Killy called out that as Cutter had to be on his way as soon as possible, anyone who wanted to should go to the jetty and wave him off. He and Julian walked directly there and quite soon afterwards Cutter arrived, completely surrounded. The place had emptied out to see him off: Marta and her whole team, Gloria with her two assistants following Monika, Ali, Victoria, and Gussy walking along the dock. He was obviously very moved, as they were all clearly sorry to see him go. He was running late and finally he managed to climb down into his waiting boat. He held up a hand.

'Friends, I can't tell you what a pleasure this has been for me. Let's hope we all get to work together again. Julian, thank you so much for everything. Until the next time.' Cutter sat beside the skipper and they were on their way. He turned and waved as the boat made a big curve out across the bay, and for everyone waving back it was like saying goodbye to a close member of their little family, even though he'd only been with them for two days.

The following morning Rafa's troops were going to be filmed marching up and down the parade ground in the build up to the general's speech they'd just shot the day before. There was a lot of nervous banter going back and forth, as this was the moment where the hours of drill practice had to pay off. The cameras rolled and they got it perfect every time. Not a step out of place anywhere. When Killy called *cut*, scene complete, the entire crew spontaneously cheered them.

Over lunch, Julian decided to make a change to the

afternoon's work. 'I'm going to cut the scene we were going to shoot, Killy; it's too long and I can do without it. Is there something we could move onto instead?'

'What about the guerrilla camp close-ups to match with the ones you shot in the ballroom?'

'Perfect, Killy. Great idea.'

Julian and Enzo had spent a lot of time during the party scenes picking out the details they wanted to highlight; shooting very tight close-up shots of lips sipping from crystal glasses, and daintily prepared little tidbits being slipped into exquisitely made-up mouths, and focusing on tiny details of jewellery and various trinkets sparkling in Enzo's lighting. Now Rafa started organising the guerrilla camp with old tin cups and plates full of rice and beans, and rough home-made bread being cooked on smoky campfires by battered and bearded jungle fighters. Mixing the detailed shots from the two scenes when the film was edited would give the perfect contrast between First and Third World Julian wanted. Shots like that take a lot of time and a great deal of patience, as it only works if the detail is correctly enhanced with exactly the right level of light and shadow. It's like filming a commercial, where small details carry big messages. For Julian, who'd done a lot of them, an afternoon to lavish attention on it was a gift.

The problem Julian had found difficult to deal with in the detailed close-ups they'd shot in the ballroom was the extras' inexperience. Getting one of the partygoers to pop a tiny morsel of food into their mouth in exactly the same way over and over again had proved frustrating. Now a shot where a hand was stirring a pot of food over a fire and then lifting the spoon to taste from it, ten, twenty, maybe thirty times was demanding a lot of patience too. After a few takes, a trained actor will be able to keep on repeating whatever the action is at exactly the same speed and in exactly the same way *ad infinitum*, but it's not always so easy with nervous amateurs. As in the ballroom, Julian's patience paid off; he gradually worked through the list of shots he wanted, and five minutes before they were due to finish he smiled and nodded.

'Job done, Killy, these will all work perfectly. And Rafa, thank you so much for your patience, and please pass on my thanks to everyone. Tell them I thought they worked like professionals.'

'Actors, or guerrillas, Julian?' Rafa's joke went down really well when he translated it to the men.

To enable them to shoot exterior scenes with Nathan during both daylight and darkness on the same day, Killy scheduled two so-called 'extended days'. It meant a late start for everyone with breakfast on set at 12 noon, lunch at 6pm, and the wrap at midnight. The star was going to be busy, with scenes of him leading his men from the landing beach inland to find the guerrilla camp then, after the ensuing battle to rescue Serena's character Sandy, getting her back out of the jungle to the submarine. They had four days to get everything finished. So the pressure was on.

24

Arthur was flying to LA on business and then coming back to be with them for the end of shooting, and as they had the morning free, Monika arranged for Killy and her to meet him for breakfast. He'd toned down his travelling outfit, presumably because his tropical style wouldn't quite cut it in Hollywood, and he was looking very smart in a well-tailored linen suit and, for him, a rather subdued light blue shirt. He was laying waste to a plate of pastries as Killy walked across the garden.

'You're looking primed to take on Lala Land, Arthur. Like the suit.'

'Had it made where Furio gets his done; or did. Cheap as chips, and really well put together. Good bit of schmutter, as my old mum would have said, may god bless her.'

'Buenos dias, señores.' Monika came in and gave them both a kiss on the cheek and sat down with them. 'Movie mogul in the making, Arthur. Pass me the coffee will you, please?'

He poured her a cup and handed it across the table to her. 'Pastry?'

'No thanks, I'm going to have some eggs. You, Killy?'

'Please, Monika. Scrambled with some toast?'

She called out their orders to the kitchen. 'Anything for you, Arthur?'

'I'm fine with the pastries, thanks. They'll be the death of me, and a week in the States as well. Gotta get back on the diet.' Monika exchanged a quizzical glance with Killy as neither of them had ever known him make any effort to control his intake.

Killy smiled. 'Another week, and you'll be back to home cooking, Arthur.'

'I should be so lucky! From the freezer to the microwave, and she doesn't have a clue what it is! That's why I'm always eating out and putting on weight. Anyway, I've just been going through all the daily reports and, barring real bad luck with the weather, I reckon you're going to finish early, son.'

'Definitely a good chance, Arthur. When you back?'

'I'm due here on Thursday night, then once we're all done we'll get down to the capital, and as the wrap party's going to be back in London, I've organised a dinner for us at the restaurant Gussy sent you to, Killy. Casa Salvador? So we'll have a good night out, then a midday flight to Miami, and then an overnighter back to London.'

'Well let's hope you're right, Arthur. I'm going over to talk through today's work with Julian. Our leading man has a tough one in front of him, so we want to be sure the shooting order for this afternoon doesn't leave him with no energy for tonight. Have a safe journey and see you on Thursday.'

For an actor who has not been fortunate enough to work alongside a real one, it's not easy to appreciate exactly what the term 'star' means, especially now that it's become overused and undervalued. Nathan Bedford sadly fell into that category. He'd clearly learned his lines but instead of fully embracing Cutter's advice and appreciating its value, he'd responded like a spoiled child who still regarded himself as special. Dealing with someone like that is difficult, but the camaraderie that develops between crew members during the course of a shoot, particularly a difficult one, shields them all. They look after each other, and an overblown ego becomes just another hurdle to get over. And they do.

The two extended days got off to a bad start, as the first afternoon was scorching hot and humid. The scene they were starting with involved Nathan and his troops waking up in their jungle encampment, eating their field rations, and beginning their search for the guerrilla hideout. It was torture for everyone involved and by the time they broke for their six pm 'lunch', Nathan looked as though he'd run two marathons. After the break, when the sun had finally set, they started with the close-up shots of him coming out of a boat and onto the landing beach, which would be edited into the versions they'd filmed with Lars doubling for him. Unfortunately on the night they'd shot it with Lars the sea had been calm, and so after going through the whole exhausting process for a rehearsal, and then again for a first take, Sarah was shaking her head as she stared at the monitor.

'Sorry, Julian, but the stuff we shot with Lars is not going to cut with this. The waves are definitely bigger tonight.'

They were in a real jam. Nathan was sitting slumped on one of the upturned boats, his helmet off and the sweat pouring from his matted blond hair over the camouflage face paint, doing nothing for his looks or humour. Julian went and crouched down in front of him.

'I'm sorry, Nate, but we have to reset that sequence and do it again I'm afraid.'

He looked at Julian with complete disgust. 'What is your fucking problem, Julian?'

'Nathan, it's *our* 'fucking' problem; when we shot the scene with your double the sea conditions were different.'

'You mean I gotta do the whole thing again?' He lowered his head and spat in the sand.

Julian was now speaking very quietly and straining to contain his anger, 'not just you, Nathan, none of us wants to repeat it.'

Enzo saved the situation. By deftly adjusting the lighting and the camera angles, he managed to accommodate the changed state of the sea and quickly got everything moving again. Meanwhile the stuntmen, by now sick of both the scene and Nathan, the man they were all bigging up, worked their hearts out and got everything finished on time. The final scene to shoot was a shot of Nathan's face as he defused an explosive planted near the guerrilla's camp, but his expressions in close-up looked ridiculous and Julian had to keep him repeating it until he finally got two takes he was satisfied with. He nodded to Killy to wrap it up as Nathan stalked off.

For the first scene the following afternoon, Rafa and Regis were teaching Nathan the hand signals that enabled orders to pass silently between him and his troops as they were closing in on the guerrilla camp. The signals had to be clear and precise and militarily correct, but he kept on mixing them up, so yet again he cost them a lot of time. The next shot was Nathan and his radio operator stretched out side by side on the jungle floor as a snake came out of the undergrowth and sank its fangs into the false hand that was substituted for the radio man's real one. Nathan then had to signal to his men to halt while he took care of the man, who was desperately biting on his helmet strap to stop himself screaming.

The animal trainer in charge of the rather large reptile got it to do exactly what was needed for the camera rehearsal.

Having worked with animals a lot, Killy told Enzo to actually run the camera during the rehearsal in case it happened to be an off day for the performer in question. His decision saved them, as the snake only ever did it right the one time. They worked on more of the scenes where Nathan had to repeat individual sequences already shot with Lars doubling for him, and Killy called an end to the day just after midnight.

With the prospect of a day off in front of him, Killy was enjoying a beer as Monika walked up the steps of his porch and from her expression, he knew there was bad news.

'Gussy just had a call from his friend at the airport to say that the president has been secretly flown out of the country, and the capital is now under a dusk till dawn curfew.'

Killy swigged at his beer then put the bottle back on the table, took a deep breath and sat for a few seconds reflecting on what she'd said. 'OK, first question: is Serena still down in the capital?' The way that Monika was thinking her way through her response was enough to make Killy give her a really inquisitive look.

'Well, Killy, Serena in fact ... is in a hotel out at the international airport ... waiting to say farewell to Chita.'

'Sorry, love, don't quite get that. Chita left weeks ago?'

'Yes she did, but she ... returned.'

'What for?'

'Well, it seems ...'

The penny finally dropped and Killy sat right back in his chair. 'Monika Sanchez, you have to be kidding me!' He paused and stared as she shook her head, half smiling.

'I'm afraid not, Killy.'

'How the fuck didn't I hear about that?'

'Nobody knew, Killy. Evidently they clicked doing the dance scenes. After we'd finished shooting the party, the three of them went down to the capital to go clubbing? We all assumed she was having a thing with Lars but he had to come back here to work, and so the two of them spent a week together before Chita went home to Miami. She came back here a couple of days ago so they could spend some time together once we're finished.'

Killy was smiling and shaking his head in disbelief. 'And now the capital is under curfew. Just what we need. Can you get her on the phone for me?' Monika called her and passed the phone to Killy.

Serena spoke immediately, 'It's such a mess, Killy. Chita is still here with no information as to when her flight will leave.'

'Yes it is a mess, Serena, but we have to get you back here. Immediately. Julian has persuaded Nathan to spend tomorrow morning rehearsing with you, and it wasn't easy as he has a designated day off tomorrow in his contract.'

She went quiet, 'Couldn't we please rehearse on Sunday, Killy?'

'I'm afraid not, Serena; due to what's going on in the capital, I'm pulling everything forward so we can finish as soon as possible.' She knew there was no arguing with that. 'I'm really sorry, Serena. I'll get you on a boat at dawn tomorrow, so at least you'll have the night together.'

She sounded really dejected but there was no alternative. 'That's very kind. Thank you, Killy.'

'You're welcome, Serena. Say hello to Chita for me. I'll see you at breakfast.' He ended the call and had a flashback to his first sight of Chita, and his thoughts on her. He looked at Monika. 'How the fuck did they ever manage, on location, to keep a story like that under wraps? That is definitely one for the record books! I can just imagine Arthur's face when he finds out! Talk about the old world meets the new!' He was still smiling to himself as Monika took back her phone.

'Right, Killy. There's something I have to tell you and Arthur; let's get him on so I don't have to say it twice.' She called him and put her phone on speaker.

Arthur answered immediately, 'Hello sweetheart. I got your text about what's happened with the president and all the flight problems, so let's hope they get things back to normal soon.'

'I'm not so sure they will, Arthur, but I'm with Killy and there's something else you both need to know; Nathan's wife, or partner, or whatever she calls herself, has had enough of living at the villa. Their boys are frightened of the forest noises at night, the food is not good enough, and frogs and lizards keep invading the pool. So Nathan wants two suites at the Hilton and he's going to commute to the set each morning. He wants his own boat and won't travel with anyone else.' There was a very long silence. 'Are you still there, Arthur?' He said nothing, and she was looking at Killy as if to say *what's going on*? Killy just grinned, having a pretty good idea of what was about to come blasting down the line from LA. He was right.

'That fucking jumped-up wannabe and his pack of fucking ungrateful inbreds! Who the fuck do they think they are? They're *frightened of the fucking forest noises*? They're not that long out of the fucking trees themselves!' It went quiet again, and then obviously having calmed down, he came back on. 'Excuse my French, Monika. Anyway all we can do is learn from this and not get caught in another trap like it, ever again. So moving on, I'm flying to Miami tomorrow so I'm close enough to hop over to you once all the restrictions are lifted. Keep me in the picture. Love to you both and give Julian my best wishes.' The line went dead.

Monika turned to Killy. 'Will it cause you any problems if Nathan commutes? The Hilton sits just outside the city limits, so the curfew doesn't apply, and it's right on the seafront, with its own dock.'

'That's fine then. And anyway, he can pretty much do what he likes as long as he's at work on time. So yes, it will be OK.' Julian's name flashed up on Killy's phone and he answered. 'Hello, Guv. Just had Arthur on, he sends you his best. Are you still planning to treat us all to lunch tomorrow?'

'Thanks, Killy. And yes I certainly am, but let's say as soon as I'm finished rehearsing with Nathan and Serena. Also, I'm sure you'll be pleased to hear I'm going to dump the two scenes where our blessed hero performs life-saving surgery on his wounded sergeant; it's all too far-fetched, and god knows how long it will take Nathan to do it properly. I'm sure dropping all that should gain us the best part of a day, as I understand the clouds of war are gathering. See you in the morning.' Killy looked at Monika. 'He's dumping Nathan's surgery scenes!' Monika laughed, blew him a kiss, and left as his phone buzzed again. 'Wally. Everything alright, mate?'

'Yeah except for that jumped-up amateur who fancies himself as a star! My team are working their arses off to turn him into a fucking hero and he barely looks at them, let alone says anything. He needs to show some appreciation or one of them is going to accidentally give him a bit of a clump. And if it doesn't happen, I'm getting to the point where I will.'

'Yeah, he's upsetting everyone, mate. Julian needs to have a little word in his ear about lead actors having to lead and what that actually means. He's obviously worked around a lot of the wrong people, but thanks for telling me anyway.'

'I had to say something, sorry, Kill.'

'Glad you did mate. I'll see you tomorrow. Sleep tight.'

At seven the next morning, his phone woke him. It was Monika. 'Due to the current situation, Nathan won't be available to rehearse with Serena this morning, Killy, as he's decided to get his family off the island. His jet will be landing at the international airport around midday today and he is taking them there himself.'

'Have you told Julian?'

'Yes I phoned him immediately, he's on his way to meet Serena at the dock.'

Julian was at that moment helping her out of her boat. 'Good morning, Serena. Was it a good ride up?'

'Very good thank you, Julian. Do I have time for a coffee?'

He took a breath. 'Serena, there's a bit of a problem. Nathan isn't going to join us, as he's dealing with his family. He's concerned for their safety and he's sending them home. I'm really sorry.'

'He's what, Julian? Can't you insist on him rehearsing?' She was close to tears, and nothing Julian said or tried to say could console her. 'Chita is on her way back home to tell her wife that she's leaving her, and now you tell me Mister Bedford is refusing to be here? I don't know what to say.'

The lunch was fun, and with Serena not being there it turned into a 'Difficult Actors I've Worked With' symposium, and whilst everyone agreed they were saddled with a nasty piece of work as their leading actor, by the time they were all thanking Julian for his hospitality it was pretty obvious that Nathan was by no means the worst of his kind.

Everyone had the same idea and headed back to their beds, hoping to get enough sleep to carry them through what was doubtless going to be an eventful final few days of shooting.

25

The next morning they were scheduled to do the scenes where Nathan and his men rescued Serena's character Sandy from the guerrilla camp. It was Alberto's final day, which meant it might well be the last time he and Serena would ever work together, and possibly ever even see each other again. They were being made up by Gloria's assistants and there was a lot of laughing and general Spanish ribaldry, and a really emotional end-of-show atmosphere in the makeup room. Nathan, completely unannounced, stuck his head around the door, then came in and stood between their chairs, and stared at both actors' mirrors, completely ignoring the two makeup artists.

'Buenos dias y'all. Hi Alberto, good to see you. Serena, I'm Nate, pleased to meet you. See you on set.' He turned and walked out, leaving all of them speechless.

Within half an hour, made up and ready to work, Serena was watching Julian direct a rehearsal with her stunt double being dragged out of the bamboo cage she'd been held captive in. The lady had been told to put up a lot of resistance and, hooded as she was, hadn't realised that Nathan was right alongside her as she swung her right arm out, hitting him in the face with her elbow. An accident involving any actor can totally disrupt a movie shoot, and with the pressure they were under this was potentially disastrous. As everyone ran towards Nathan, who was clearly shaken up, Serena hissed through her clenched teeth, 'Yessss!' It got lost in the hubbub, but not on him.

The medic checked Nathan for concussion as the blow had landed full on his chin, but to almost everyone's relief he was declared fit to continue. Whilst Gloria worked her magic with camouflage paint on his already reddening skin, he stood glaring at his leading lady. The next shot was Nathan dragging Serena away from her captors but this time not using her double. Everything went well with the rehearsal, but Serena wasn't happy with the way Nathan had grabbed her, and quite correctly communicated that to the director.

'Julian, would you ask Nathan to be a little more gentle, please? He's so strong I'm afraid that if we have to do it many more times, my right arm might be really damaged.'

Julian was standing between the two of them. 'Of course, Serena. Nate, a little less energy please. We'll be on your face in close-up by then anyway and we've had one accident, so let's keep it relaxed. Thank you.' They rehearsed it again but Nathan did exactly as he'd done before. This time, Serena let out a stream of Spanish curses and pulled her arm away from him and stood rubbing it, staring directly at him.

At the lunch break Nathan went directly to his dressing room and Serena joined the rest of the crew in saying goodbye to Alberto. Julian made a little speech congratulating him and thanking him for coming in at the last minute and giving a great performance, as Killy thought back to Ramon being released from his contract and slipping quietly away in the night, having never played the character at all.

Serena and Gussy escorted Alberto down to the jetty, where Serena said her last goodbyes to a man she'd obviously had a great time working with at what was doubtless an important stage in both their careers. Killy had sent Gussy to ride in the boat with him to ensure he got away with no hitches, and more importantly to try and get a feel for how things were going in the capital.

Julian needed to complete a lot more detailed close-ups of an increasingly resentful Nathan copying exactly the positions that Lars had finished up in; made more difficult because he still failed to grasp that it was for his benefit.

As Julian approved the final shot, Killy announced more goodbyes. 'Right, boys and girls, that is a wrap for today. And I'd like to say thank you to Wally and everyone on the stunt team, and to the Prof and his brilliant special effects crew, and of course Colonel Kubitt and our armourers for keeping us all safe.' A lot of back slapping, kissing, and hugging took over the whole set, as for all those leaving, another picture had come to an end.

Nathan disappeared, not stopping to say anything to anyone, but every single person there noticed it. The Prof and his team said their goodbyes. Regis had a plane to catch, so he said his farewells immediately and Rafa drove him to the airstrip. Then, completely out of character, Wally gave Julian and Killy both a hug.

'Gotta get a move on fellas. Luckily the missus decided not to come and sit around here while I was working but now I've got seven straight days in Havana with her and her mother, while Gloria goes off gallivanting around New York; talk about getting it wrong. Mind you, that's definitely better than spending any more of my life around our so-called hero. Anyway, it's been great, Julian, and thanks for bringing me in on this, Killy. They were a terrific team to inherit. And by the way, I just spoke to Richie and he's already up and starting to walk, and sends his best. And thanks for getting me and Gloria back together; not going to be easy but it's definitely already a life changer for both of us.'

As they watched him jog off to the jetty, Julian turned to Killy. 'Great guy. I'd certainly like to work with him again. He's done a really first-class job.'

'He certainly has, Julian. Glad I got the chance to be back around him after all those years. I really enjoyed his company. Fancy a beer?'

'Good scheme, Killy. Let's go back to mine. There's a dozen great, big bottles of ice-cold Heineken that Lex gave me, and I want to have a little chat about the last scenes with our two lovers. It's going to be a fascinating end to the shoot.'

The plan was to start where Serena and Nathan had lost contact with the main body of the marines as the Guerrillas chased them through the jungle. Julian had changed the script to allow more screen time for the two of them to be hiding overnight, lost and starting to fall in love. Unfortunately he hadn't foreseen that the two actors had come to loathe each other. Fascinating it certainly did turn out to be.

The following two days showed that whilst Nathan now knew his lines, Serena had obviously never worked opposite someone with such limited ability. She soldiered on, scene after scene, knowing it was far too late to do anything to improve his wooden performance. Julian tried everything to get Nathan to vary the way he spoke the lines, but coming into the business the way he had, he was now involved at a level he'd never been prepared for. Their two characters were being pursued by a murderous band of guerrillas intent on avenging the death of their leader, but Nathan's delivery never conveyed anything but a sense of annoyance, or as Sarah Scripts whispered to Killy at one point, 'It's as though his wife has come back from the corner shop and she's forgotten his chewing gum.'

Towards the end of the second day, he got into an argument with Sarah over his wanting to smoke a cigarette as he and Serena sat by the campfire talking about their lives. Sarah had foreseen problems and advised Julian to try and talk him out of it, but Nathan had insisted. Julian planned to start the scene with a tracking shot of them from about twenty feet away to establish them by the campfire, and then cross-shoot their closeups with a camera on each of them. Nathan got the lines out but he kept taking puffs at the cigarette whenever he felt like it, and was arguing with Sarah about when he'd actually done it in the wide shot, as his closeup had to match it exactly, which was just what she'd seen coming. Continuity is an absolutely crucial job on any production, and the script supervisor notes every time an actor touches anything and with which hand. After Sarah's years doing the job, arguing with an inexperienced performer about something as basic as taking a puff on a cigarette at precisely the same point in each take was really trying her patience. In the end they did eight takes in close-up and Nathan was still getting it wrong, so there was no alternative but to go back and do the whole sequence again but with no cigarette.

That put him even more on edge and he started forgetting his lines. Julian tried to calm him down, but he wasn't listening.

'Nate, look; just try to relax. You know the words. Don't be so hard on yourself.'

Nathan started taking deep breaths, obviously in an

attempt to do as Julian had suggested, but never once did he even glance at Serena as his performance got further and further away from where it had been before the cigarette smoking was dumped. At one point it looked as though Serena was about to say something, but it would doubtless have made it even worse between them. They lost another hour, but they finally moved on to the last scene to be shot, with both of them sitting out in the dark in one of the little landing boats, waiting to be rescued by the submarine. There was quite a steady swell but no waves to contend with, and so it was simply a case of them staring into the night as Nathan kept checking the illuminated second hand of his watch ticking towards the hour the sub should surface.

All very simple, except for the fact that Serena had no stomach for the steady rise and fall of the sea, and during the first camera rehearsal she started throwing up over the side. Instead of being in any way supportive, Nathan was complaining about wanting to get finished and back to his hotel. Every time the nausea overcame her, Serena would put her hand up and call out politely for Julian to excuse her, then lean over the side to vomit. Gloria and Marta had to keep going back and forth on a crew boat to make sure she was looking the same for each close-up, despite the obvious discomfort she was in, but finally Julian got the shot of them pretending to see the sub come to the surface that they both faked really well, and they wrapped on schedule. Serena had definitely saved the day. Nathan disappeared.

Julian and Killy had planned to talk Monika through the final scene of the picture.

She was waiting for them in her office. 'Well gentlemen, this entire site is being taken over by government forces as of midnight tonight. The army are dispatching troops who will be stationed here until the current situation is brought under control. When I asked how long they anticipated this might take, I was told there was nobody available who could answer that question. We have to evacuate the facility at first light tomorrow, as it could potentially come under fire from forces hostile to the government.'

Julian was nodding to himself in a resigned way. 'Well I suppose bearing in mind the way everything else has been going, why am I not surprised?'

Killy looked at Monika. 'We'd better get things moving, eh, beauty? Thank Christ it didn't happen last week.'

She nodded. 'As you would say, 'let's look on the bright side'.'

At just before eleven pm, Killy stood with Monika, Ali, Gussy, and Victoria watching three big naval vessels being moored alongside the dock. Leaving Gussy to represent them, they walked back to the office to prepare for the final day, as gangways were lowered and squads of heavily armed troops filed down and formed up in ranks right outside what had been their unit base.

Killy was clearing his desk as Ali called across the office, 'If the international airport is back open, Arthur's planning to fly in from Miami tomorrow. And he's putting us all up at the Hilton as a treat, which will be a nice change from the charms of The Royale and that creepy old perv of a night porter.'

Killy shouted back, 'Right, Al; make sure everyone's ready to go, and it doesn't matter how early you get everyone down to the location. I'll feel much more at ease when I know we're all at the house together, alright?'

She stuck her head round his door. 'Don't worry about that, Kill. After all our lovely pretend soldiers, these ninjas on the dock with real guns and real bullets make me nervous. They all look about twelve. Anyway I'm going off to bed. Goodnight and bless us all.'

Things went to plan in the morning. Everyone gathered in the garden for a special goodbye breakfast before dawn and then, as they trundled their bags along the track on the last walk to the production office, Rosalia and all her staff stood waving them off and looking as sad as they all felt, saying yet another goodbye to one more branch of their ever-expanding family.

At the now sad and empty office, everyone who could helped Enzo, Cinzia, and Bunny with what seemed a great deal of gear for one small camera. Serena helped Paddy with his sound equipment, and together they all tramped off to the dock.

There were sentries at the foot of each gangway, but no other sign of military presence. They loaded all the bags and gear onto the boat, and then settled themselves in for the ride as Monika, Ali, and Gussy walked back to the office.

Killy was sitting next to the skipper as he powered them down the coast and when they were about to pass the submarine, he asked him to stop so they could say their farewells. Lex, Ilze, and Hannah were having breakfast on deck, and the shouted goodbyes and blown kisses clearly meant a lot to them. Everyone waved until their boat finally rounded the end of the bay. There were pickups waiting at the jetty with plenty of room for everyone and their baggage and the gear, and as they were driven up the slope to the house their skipper waved a last goodbye as he headed the boat down the coast to the capital. Othello, looking as immaculate as ever, was waiting to meet them under the portico with two of his assistants, who helped them unload, and then he escorted them through to the dining room where a spectacular brunch had been laid out. He waited for everyone and then, with a very gracious bow, made a short speech.

'Good day to you all. Señora Santini sends you her compliments and apologises for not being here, and hopes you all enjoy your last day at Casa Santini.' He stopped to have a word with Enzo, Cinzia, and Serena, and the four of them nattered away in Italian while everyone else gathered around the feast.

Killy and Julian walked out onto the lawn. 'Alain said he's getting two of the garden staff to shift some of those trees in the big planters, Julian. He said he'll need a couple of hours, and then you can come and let him know what you think.'

'All fine, Killy, but what the fuck are we going to do if this whole situation turns ugly? Considering the circumstances, shouldn't we just get everyone and all the gear back in the boat and find somewhere safe? It wouldn't be the most difficult thing in the world to mock the final scene up on a soundstage somewhere back in the UK? Arthur could surely claim the costs, no?'

Killy definitely sensed nervousness in Julian's voice, and was trying to think why his suggestion was not a good idea when his phone rang. 'It's Monika.' He put it on speaker and led Julian to the far edge of the garden as they both listened to her, obviously alarmed.

'Killy, we're standing at the dock with everything ready to go, but the military won't let our boat come in to pick us up, and they've ordered the skipper to take it back to the capital as this entire site is now strictly for military use. They say it's too dangerous to try moving us out by road as there are armed groups all over the place, so Gussy is doing his best to persuade the officer in charge to change his mind and allow us onto the boat. I'm sure you can hear there's a lot of heavy gunfire that we're told is one of their patrols under attack. I have to say I'm worried. And Ali is getting really panicked as we've just had to watch a whole line of wounded men being carried up onto a ship. I'll call you back, as soon as Gussy gets a response, and perhaps you can think what we'll do if it's a 'no'?'

She ended the call but was back on the line to Killy immediately. 'Right, so Gussy has got them to allow us to come to the house, but they insist we leave right now as the gunfire is getting closer. See you soon.'

Out on the terrace, everyone was in anything but an end-of-shoot mood, especially knowing that sitting around in such luxurious surroundings and sipping exquisite locally grown coffee was far removed from the reality of their current situation. Killy and Julian were looking across the lawn towards them, both trying to come up with a solution.

'Julian, I get what you say about abandoning the last scene but it looks like we're stuck here, and trying to escape by road might be a big mistake. I'm going to have a chat with everyone.' He walked across and as quickly and concisely as he could, put the crew in the picture as to what Monika had told them and that there really wasn't much they could do other than get on and complete the picture. He assured them that Monika and the others would be arriving shortly and very quickly a consensus formed that he was right, and rather than just sitting around waiting to see what happened next, they would all be happier to get on and finish the job. He gave the thumbs up to Julian.

Paddy was setting out his sound equipment at the end of the terrace, and one of Othello's assistants was plugging him into the power system as Killy joined him.

'Paddy, it won't be dark for at least three hours. Is everything alright, mate?'

'It's fine, but as we're so close to that army base, Rafa and I are going to listen in to what's flying around on the airwaves. He's been with Marta, trying on his uniform. Here he comes.' Rafa stepped out from the ballroom in his normal work clothes, not yet in the ceremonial US Marines uniform that Julian had persuaded him to wear in the background of the closing scene. He was not happy at all about appearing on screen, but Julian had begged and cajoled and finally managed to convince him that whoever would be wearing that uniform in the closing moments of the film had to look the part.

'Bad enough I have to be in front of the camera, but now Marta is pissed with me cos I've put on a couple of pounds with all the location food, and she has to let the pants out. It's those goddamn English breakfasts every day. I can't resist them.'

Paddy nodded. 'Fatal Rafa. Lucky it's only a couple of pounds; I'm sure I've put on a lot more than that. Anyway take these cans, it's very lively out there.' Rafa stood listening intently for a good five minutes, barely moving a muscle, then finally he took them off.

'I don't completely understand what's going on, they're using a lot of coded references, but something is building up for sure. How long before everyone else gets here, Killy?'

'Already here, they're in the ballroom.'

'Good. I need to have Gussy listen in.'

Monika and Ali came out through the French windows just as Nathan came striding towards them across the lawn. 'OK, Ms Sanchez, what the fuck is going on with my boat? I got out and the guy driving it took off! How the fuck do I get back to my hotel?'

Monika nearly lost it. 'Mister Bedford. Would you first of all stop using profanities? If you calm down, perhaps we can have a civilised conversation and I can answer your questions without an audience.' He followed her off the terrace and onto the lawn. 'The boat-chartering company is in a very difficult position, Mr Bedford; they have been ordered to send all their vessels back to the capital, and it was only because the owner knew who to call that they allowed your boat to bring you here on condition that the captain should return directly to the company base.'

'You still didn't answer my question. How do I get back to my hotel?'

'We're all overnighting at your hotel. I'm afraid you'll have to travel back there in the crew boat with us, as it's the only vessel we've been allowed to keep here. These are difficult times, Mr Bedford, and we have to work together. I will personally ensure that you have a section of the boat to yourself, but that's the best I can do. I hope it answers your questions satisfactorily?' With that she turned and walked away, leaving him stranded and speechless on the lawn.

Chris turned to Bunny. 'That's the way to do it, Monika.'

Bunny smiled, 'Yeah, boxed him up like a kipper.'

Monika went and sat down on the terrace wall next to Killy and Ali, as Nathan strutted off into the house. She whispered, 'How I detest that man.'

Gussy brought them coffees on a silver tray and then, slipping it under his arm, he made a low bow. 'Is there anything else I can get you, Ms Sanchez? An axe maybe?'

She nodded. 'Well-honed please, Gussy, the night is just beginning. OK, Ali, let's go into the ballroom and see how Serena's getting on.'

Paddy offered a set of headphones to Gussy. 'Rafa's been listening in on the military. He thinks it's coming from the base up the road. Perhaps you can pick out something he's missing.'

'Yes, and then I'll call the commander there, he's an old family friend.'

Julian and Killy were looking at the adjustments Alain had been making. He was sitting on the stone wall at the edge of the garden, smoking a cigarette with his back to the view of the sea, as Julian called across to him, 'As ever Alain, perfect. Has Enzo seen what you've done?'

'Yes, and he's going to use some big old church candles and some oil lanterns Othello is giving us to light it, so if the sky stays clear, it will look good I think.' Killy went back to see if Paddy had any news while Gussy was on the phone in the garden, clearly having problems getting through to the family friend on the base. In the end he gave up, but then his phone rang and seeing who it was, he took the call and spoke for a few minutes.

'That was Uncle Philip, calling from Miami; the reason I can't get through to the base commander is because he's being held captive there and used as a bargaining chip.

Rafa came straight in. 'Did he say anything else?'

'Yes. There is an operation being mounted right now to rescue him. But that was it, except to say that we should be prepared for the whole island being shut down, and that will extend to the international airport as well.'

Killy wasn't thrilled with the news, but at least he understood what was going on. 'OK, I'm sure we'll be well looked after at the Hilton until everything opens up again, so let's get ready to start as soon as Enzo gives us the nod. I want finish this fucker and be on our way. I'm in the mood for a party!'

Everyone had the same thought in mind and after a couple of camera rehearsals, they all waited for Enzo to decide that daylight had finally come to an end. He checked the light with his meter and nodded to Killy, who smiled and said, 'OK Enzo, let's just have another little rehearsal and then we'll shoot one, OK?'

The scene started with Nathan and Sandy walking across the terrace away from the ballroom, while behind them Rafa closed the French windows and then turned towards the garden and stood to attention. The camera was filming all this from a point out on the lawn, and with the way Enzo had lit the house with the lanterns and flickering candlelight reflected in the windows, and the ceremonially costumed Rafa closing the doors and standing sentinel, it really did look magical. As the two actors moved slowly towards the camera, they stopped at a pre-arranged point and looked into each other's eyes, and finally upwards in the direction Julian had given them as though staring at the moon. The moon wasn't actually where it needed to be, but in the final edit several weeks later, by way of movie magic in a studio thousands of miles away, it would be there in all its glory.

Julian nodded and Killy called out, 'Right that's a cut on rehearsal, thank you. Final checks please, and we'll shoot one.'

Normally at that point the set would suddenly turn from being inhabited only by the actors into a busy workspace, for everyone on the crew to make sure that their department was ready for the camera to cast its penetrating eye over their work. But now they were really down to a bare minimum crew, as Marta and Gloria checked both the actors against the folders of continuity photos taken, of Serena and Lars, after the party scenes all those weeks before. Sarah was casting her eagle eye over everything that would be in the shot, right down to the fittings on the French windows. Situations where there is no going back to a location mean that one wrong tiny detail can finish up at best costing a fortune, and possibly mean a whole scene having to be dumped with both calamitous artistic and financial consequences.

Julian was keeping the shot as simple as possible with Rafa closing the doors, turning, and standing to attention; watching the two actors walking to their stop position, then holding hands and looking at each other and finally gazing up at the moon. Then they would do a close-up on each of them as they looked into one other's eyes and that would finish it. Julian smiled and gave Killy a nod.

'Thanks Julian. OK, everyone, let's stand by to shoot. Final checks please?' Gloria and Marta both nodded. 'Thank you, ladies. Right, very still and quiet. OK camera?' Enzo had his eye in the viewfinder and slowly put a thumb up. Killy called out, 'OK, roll camera. Sound?'

Paddy called out, 'Sound speed!'

Then Enzo called, 'Camera set, put the board in please, Cinzia.'

She held the clapper board up in front of the camera and in her lovely Italian accent called out, 'Scene one hundred and fifty-two. Take one.' She closed the clapper with an assured click, then it was back to Killy again.

'All good, Enzo?'

'Ready, Killy!' He looked at Julian, who gave him a slow steady nod. Killy left it a couple of seconds to let the actors take a breath, then called, 'And ... Action!'

Right on cue, Rafa closed the doors and turned out towards the garden and stood smartly to attention.

When the two lovers stared up at the imaginary moon, Julian called out, 'Cut! Thank you. I'd like to get one more just for safety's sake …' then, with a head splitting roar, a military jet came screaming directly over them. The sound was absolutely deafening and a few seconds later, four massive explosions lit up the sky. Great bursts of gunfire and several more terrifying explosions that seemed to be even closer followed, and then almost immediately the jet flew back over again, lower and louder than before.

26

The electricity had cut out, leaving no light but the candles and lanterns around the garden. Rafa was yelling over the din in Spanish and English as he ran towards two terrified ladies from the kitchen who'd been watching the filming, standing panic stricken on the lawn; he scooped them up, one under each arm and carried them screaming into the house.

Killy, Enzo, and Cinzia were running with the camera gear towards the ballroom. Nathan and Serena were still out on the lawn but she was now holding his hand with both of hers, screaming at him and pulling him back towards the house, clearly determined not to let go, until he finally shook her off and raced away into the darkness as she stood still yelling after him with tears rolling down her cheeks. Killy grabbed her and guided her towards Monika, who was waving one of the lanterns. She led them both through to the kitchen and then took Serena down a wooden stairway to the cellars. They passed Gussy coming up and shouting to Killy, that he was putting an antenna in the kitchen so that Paddy could continue to monitor everything from the cellar. With his phone's light on Killy found his way to the ballroom, where Enzo and Cinzia were packing up their gear.

'Where's Bunny?' Cinzia shouted, 'He was in the garden ready to adjust the lanterns for the next shot, Killy.'

Killy was already on his way. By the garden wall where the first lantern was still flickering, Killy threw himself down on the grass as the force of another explosion blew out the windows on the first floor of the house, sending a shower of shattered panes all over the terrace, but fortunately nowhere near him. The garden had been momentarily lit up but with still no sign of Bunny. Then, as he was planning his next move, Killy saw a vertical shaft of light coming from behind the garden wall.

He stood up and ran towards it, yelling at the top of his voice, 'Bunny? *Bunny!* Is that your light, mate?'

He looked over as Bunny shouted up from the darkness, 'Yeah I'm down here behind the wall, I was just having a jimmy when that fucking plane flew over, so I jumped off the top of it to get cover and finished up in the bushes down here. I've only just found me phone. Can you give me a pull up? I can get a foothold, but I can't reach the top.' Killy leant over and managed to grab his hand as another bomb went off and both of them let go, leaving Bunny scrabbling around in the undergrowth,

'Talk about Humpty fucking Dumpty.' Killy finally got him up and into the garden and they both ran towards the house. 'Come on Bun, everyone's down in the cellar.'

'Be alright for a glass of vino then, eh, Kill?'

'Yeah, I'll get Othello to come and serve you, I'm sure he'll be delighted. Better grab one of the lanterns, it's pretty dark in there.' They ran into the kitchen and down the stairs as another explosion rocked the whole house, followed by another great smashing of glass all over the terrace. The flash lit up Marta.

'Killy, that lousy chicken-shit Bedford ran off in my fucking three-thousand-dollar costume!'

The sound of a generator starting came from the other

end of the cellar, and then a very dim overhead light flickered into life. Everyone was sitting along the wall. Serena was crying and shaking her head.

'That coward just ran away like a frightened animal! I told him how he had made everybody's lives here unbearable, but I didn't have the time to tell him how much I despised him.'

Clearly upset herself, and feeling the same way about their now missing hero, Gloria put her arm around Serena and the two of them comforted each other in the half light, as bombs and the gunfire shook the whole house over and over again. Gussy and Rafa were side by side, listening in on the radio traffic.

Rafa looked up and shook his head, 'We have to get away, Killy. We're safe down here at the moment but it's too close to the army base, and from what I'm picking up, things are going to get more intense.'

Othello came down the stairs, followed by two of his team carrying blankets for everyone, as the cellar's stone walls were like ice to them after six weeks of thirty-degrees-plus temperatures. In a quiet moment, Killy looked at Julian.

'I'm afraid that's got to be it, Guv; no way we can carry on now.'

'That's fine, Killy. I always hated that final scene and I'm sure what we've already shot can work perfectly. So yes, that's it, I suppose. A bit of an anti-climax but yes, we've finished the picture.'

Rafa and Gussy were laughing at something they were both listening to. Gussy pulled his cans off and shouted out, 'According to the military headquarters, an "officer of the US marines has been apprehended"; he'd forced the captain of a boat to take him to the capital. He has no ID, so they've arrested him and he's currently under guard!' A huge cheer went up from everyone but then Gussy held his hand up for silence. 'Sadly, the boat was our one.'

Killy butted in. 'So now is a perfect moment for me to announce that our incredible director has told me to wrap the show up. Congratulations to us all, and let's hope our Texan hero has a great time in the capital!'

Everyone clapped and cheered and then, after another explosion, Monika walked up the stairs calling back, 'Now the picture is finished, I'm going to call the Hilton Hotel and pay the bill for Mr Bedford, up until breakfast tomorrow. By leaving the shoot before he was released, he's broken his contract and his accommodation is no longer our responsibility, and hopefully they keep the cretin here for a year.'

That brought another cheer, then Marta chimed in, 'Yeah, and the reason the sonofabitch has no ID is because his wallet is in his own pants in care of the costume department, and that's where it stays until I get my goddam costume back! And if I ever see him again, I'm gonna hit him so fucking hard he's gonna have to roll down his socks to take a piss.'

Everyone's spirits had been lifted, despite the realisation that now they had no means of getting to their hotel and the battle was getting hotter. Killy started to dial a number but as he ran up the stairs to get a signal, Susie's name rolled across his screen. He hesitated, but had to take the call.

She shouted down the line, 'Killy! I'm clear! It was a false alarm, she just phoned me!' A huge explosion shook the house again. 'What the bloody hell was that, Killy? Are you OK, darlin'?'

Killy was too overjoyed to spoil her happiness with the truth. 'Just shooting the last battle scene, love, special effects. We're nearly done. You've made my day, darlin'. What a relief. I'll phone you later when we've wrapped, alright? Loadsa love.'

'And you too, love, speak soon.'

Killy took a couple of deep breaths and gave himself a moment to let his relief at the news flood over him. Then after a couple of tries, he finally got through to Lex.

'Killy Wilde here, Lex, I need your help. Can you talk?'

'Sure, Killy, what can I do for you?'

'We're stuck in the middle of a battle at the army base next to Casa Santini, and we've just lost our boat. There's sixteen of us with our personal baggage and a bit of camera and sound equipment. Is there any chance you could pick us up and take us to Miami with you?'

Lex paused. 'I'm really sorry, Killy, but we have been ordered by the military to leave here before daybreak and go directly to our home port in Florida. There are naval patrols all around, so unfortunately we have to comply. But if you could get here before dawn, we'll happily take you with us.' That set Killy's mind whirring.

'OK, Lex. Let me see what I can do. But you can definitely take us all to Florida?'

'With the greatest of pleasure, Killy. But we must leave before daybreak.'

'I'll be right back to you, Lex, Arthur's calling me.'

'Killy, where are you, son? What's going on?'

'Long story, Arthur, but it's all turned very bold. We're down in the wine cellar at the house but the base along the road is being bombarded, so we have to make a move. I just spoke to Lex and if we can get to him tonight, he's happy to take us all to Florida.' He heard Arthur muttering in the background.

'Killy, I'm staying with Mr Sieglovitz, I've just told him

what's going on and he wants to speak to you, I'll pass you over.'

The man's accent was classic New York, but very calm and businesslike. 'Hello, Killian, Mort here. Let me see if I can help. Are you still there?'

'Yes, I'm here Mort, the line faded.'

'Right. I keep a boat at my home in the US Virgin Islands, and what I'm proposing is that we get it on its way to pick you all up and bring you back to safety. From what I heard of the conversation you're able to get off the island?'

'Yes, the submarine we've been filming with is heading back to Florida and they've offered to take us.'

'Send me a contact number for the captain of the submarine, and we'll fix a rendezvous out in international waters.'

'Mort, there are sixteen of us, and all our personal baggage and some film and sound equipment; are you sure there'll be enough room?'

'There's room Killian, send that number now and I'll get things moving. Good luck and *Bon voyage*, my friend.'

Killy sat under the kitchen table, the floor all around him covered with shattered crockery and glass. He was listening to the blasts and the machine-gun fire as he felt another tingle of joy that the news from Susie sent through him. He smiled to himself as he texted Lex's number to Arthur, thinking how crazy the whole situation was and trying to work out a way to get them to the sub, when Gussy ran up the stairs.

'Hello, mate, how are things down there?'

'Very cold, Killy. Nobody is panicking now but we have to get away from here.'

'Right, let me put you in the picture; Lex can get us off the island in the sub but he can only go directly to Miami, and he has to leave before dawn. Any thoughts?'

'Yes, I've had a lot of thoughts, Killy, but I have to say they were more about getting us all somewhere safe on the island. Your plan is a little more complex.' He took a long pause. 'OK, in the boathouse down by the jetty there are a couple of big inflatables we used to fish and dive from as kids that would take everyone and all the gear. I could tow them with the speed boat, and that way I think we could do it. How does that sound?'

'Good, but can you get us all, with the bags and the gear, down to the jetty safely?'

He was nodding. 'We can use the old pack-horse track they laid when they built the house. I'll organise Othello to get everything loaded into the gardening carts and get them down there, then I can come and—' The rest was lost in a great long burst of gunfire as he darted out of the kitchen.

Killy got through to Lex and explained the plan, then went back down into the cellar, where everyone was draped in their blankets and jumping up and down trying to get warm. It had gone quiet again as Killy stood in the doorway.

'Gussy and his guys are taking everything down to the jetty. We're moving out.' Another blast stopped him, then Othello came to the top of the stairs.

'I'm to lead you to the old track. So please, leave your blankets there and follow me.'

There was no hesitation at all. Rafa led them up and through the glass-strewn kitchen, and the change in temperature as they crossed the garden was like getting a big hug from an old friend. After the cellar's dimness, the sky was now completely lit up from the direction of the army base. Othello stood by the gateway, as they all filed past and shook his hand and said their goodbyes.

Rafa and Gussy both now had lanterns and walked ahead of everyone down the track that zig-zagged its way under the trees. Monika and Killy were on either side of Alison trying to keep her steady, but she was so frightened it was making her laugh. The two of them kept exchanging glances over her head as she tried to stifle her squeals, and by the time they got to the jetty, she was getting pretty hysterical. Othello had sent all four of his house team down and they'd moved quickly, as the two big inflatables were already roped one behind the other and tied up to the red boat, all set to tow them. Enzo, Cinzia, and Bunny immediately started passing the cases of technical gear to Alain and Paddy, who'd jumped straight into the first inflatable and were making sure everything was stowed safely. Then the five of them filled the remaining space with personal baggage and settled themselves in, ready to go.

After another enormous explosion that momentarily lit everything up like daylight, Killy called out, 'Rafa, you should have room for the rest of the personal baggage. Sarah and I will squeeze in with the camera gear.' He passed one of the mooring ropes to Bunny and yelled, 'Run this through the handles of Enzo's gear, and then Paddy's as well, in case we hit bad weather.'

Bunny laughed and shouted back, 'Tell you what, Killy; if we do, it'll be women and Gaffer Sparks first, and bollocks to the gear!'

Rafa called out, 'All good on this boat, Killy! I have Victoria, Chris, and Julian with me and the remaining personal baggage, ready to go!' Gussy had Monika, Ali, Serena, Gloria, and Marta with him, so that was everyone accounted for.

Killy shouted, 'That's it, Gussy, let's go!

All the team from the house were lined up along the jetty,

silhouetted against the fire-lit sky, shouting against the noise, and waving as though this was just another group of family visitors leaving. 'Adiós, señoras y señores. Buen viaje!' Everyone was yelling goodbyes and waving back to them as two more bombs went off, and the sky again turned into a violent fireworks display. Gussy steered them away from the jetty, checking back on the inflatables and making sure his towing speed wouldn't risk any accidents. A few minutes out and he levelled the powerful engines down to a steady rhythm as the red boat rolled along through the calm, silky water.

Sarah and Killy were sitting side by side in the bottom of the inflatable, feeling the gentle undulation of the sea massaging the hard, tubular rubber walls and nudging them closer together in the silence. She finally turned to him.

'So, Killy Wilde, where exactly are they meeting us? You never said.'

He turned to her. They were nose-to-nose. 'Well we're going to be picked up by Arthur's friend's boat out in international waters, so right now we're on our way to the landing beach.'

She stared him right in the eye. 'We're not going on that fucking submarine, are we? I tell you, mate, only over my dead body.' He'd had a feeling he might get that response from Ali, but not from Sarah.

'What's the problem, darlin'? They've spent fortunes making it safe and they sail it all over the world.'

She was shaking her head like a defiant little kid. 'No way, Killy, no fucking way am I getting on that thing!'

'We don't have any choice, and it's not like we're crossing the Atlantic. We just go down …'

'Go down? Go fucking down? I'd rather go down the

toilet!' They were now eyeball to eyeball in the dark, more able to sense each other than see.

'Yes, Sarah! It's a submarine for fuck's sake. 'Course we go down that's what they do, then they come back up! And we'll be twelve miles from the shore and safe, out in international waters and on our way home.'

Her eyes were blazing, 'So we're going underwater in a World War Two submarine, driven by an old Dutch geezer who's pissed every time I see him! Tell me you're kidding, *please*, Killy.'

'Sarah, I don't know about you but the last few hours have been pretty spicy, and if it came to it I'd swim my way out of here, sharks and all. So don't worry, we'll be fine. I promise you.' That brought the discussion to a close as they sat, now shoulder to shoulder, in silence for what seemed ages. Then Killy turned to her and whispered, 'I suppose there's no chance of a quickie, is there?'

Sarah couldn't stop herself laughing. 'Very funny and no; absolutely no chance, Killy Wilde.' After another very long pause she finally said, 'So what's going on with us, Killy? Same as usual is it? Job done and kiss goodbye until the next one?' She was staring deep into the darkness, and he could sense her body pushing back against the side of the boat and easing her away from the hard warmth of his shoulder. Her head was shaking almost imperceptibly. She could tell he was looking at her. 'Still can't say anything, eh, Killy?' She paused but he said nothing. 'Well you know where I stand, I'm ready to give it a go … But it's you, Killy; you're the problem. Always were and always will be.' She carried on staring into the growing light.

It didn't matter how much he wanted to tell her that he loved her and that he wanted to be with her forever; he couldn't bring himself to say it, to commit, to make a promise he knew he couldn't go through with. He sat and said nothing.

Dawn was definitely breaking as they finally pulled alongside the sub. Lex and his ladies were waiting, and it didn't take much time for everyone to get the baggage and the kit out of the inflatables and up onto the deck, and then passed down the hatchway to Ilze and Hannah. With everything stowed below, they all stood on the deck finding it hard saying goodbye to Gussy. But there was no time to spare.

When it finally came to Killy's turn to give him a hug, it was difficult for him to say what he wanted to say, 'You sure you won't come with us? You could leave all the boats here, moored to the barge?'

Gussy hugged him, then held him by his shoulders. 'This is my world, Killy, and like you I have to take care of my people.'

Killy nodded. 'You've been incredible. Thank you. See you on the next one.'

'Thank you for changing my life, Killy. Please phone me when you're all safe.'

They hugged each other again, then Gussy climbed down into the red boat, sat behind the wheel, started the engines, then turned and gave them all a wave and a big smile as he powered his little flotilla away into the growing light.

27

Film crews don't do tantrums, or not in public anyway; they prefer to leave that to the stars. But preparing to go under the sea, in essentially a steel tube, was forcing Killy to deal with two of his closest colleagues having a major meltdown in tandem. It didn't matter what anyone said to try to calm their fears, Ali and Sarah were refusing to even get near the stairway that ran down from the hatch into the sub. Finally, it was the potential for a rerun of what they'd escaped that did the trick. Coming towards them low over the water was a sinister-looking black helicopter, bristling with guns and missiles, which finally hovered directly above the sub, blasting out a warning from a speaker. Neither Sarah nor Ali spoke a word of Spanish, but the implied threat in the voice was enough to get them to do what all the loving persuasion had failed to achieve, and the pair of them almost jumped down the hatch. Hannah followed everyone and made the boat watertight, then strode like a great blond Amazon through the living quarters where they were gathered calling out, 'Forward hatch sealed, Ilze!'

They were all very apprehensive but apart from a sense of movement, nothing unusual happened at all; no dipping forwards or backwards, no rocking side to side, just a slight change in the air pressure, like coming into land on a regular commercial flight. They were on their way and it was no more frightening than being on the London Underground.

The living space was set out with sofas and armchairs and as everyone accepted there really was nothing to worry about, they started making themselves comfortable. Which after the night they'd just left behind, meant simply crashing out wherever there was space on the plush carpeted floor.

The next thing Killy knew, Hannah was whispering in his ear, 'Killian, Papa asked me to tell you we are now in international waters.' She'd parked a really strong cup of tea on the floor next to him and, after struggling to get himself upright, he sat and sipped it, then got up and walked through to Lex.

'Hello, Killy. You'll have the honour of being first out on deck.'

'Have we already surfaced, Lex?'

He laughed. 'Yes indeed, two hours ago. We're a lot better at surfacing after all the filming.'

'You certainly are, Lex; I had no idea.'

'Ilze darling, lead Killy up please.'

He followed her out onto the deck, breathing the cool morning sea air with nothing but miles of blue water wherever he looked. Lex appeared on the bridge right above him.

'I think we might have to wait a few more minutes, Killy, we've made much better time than I estimated. Beautiful morning.'

'It certainly is. Which direction will they be coming from?'

'More or less due north.' He was pointing dead ahead. 'Do you want Hannah to wake everyone? It shouldn't be long now. Ah, excuse me.' His phone was ringing. 'Yes, it is Lex speaking. Hello, Captain. And good morning to you, sir. Just let me get my binoculars.' He was trying to hold them and his phone. 'Yes, I can see you now. OK, we'll get everyone ready to go, and yes, you too.'

By the time the gang were all out on deck, the boat they were waiting for had grown from something white and just visible out on the horizon, to what was obviously a very impressive vessel. Now Killy understood why Mr Sieglovitz had sounded slightly amused when he'd asked if there would be room for them all. It was enormous and absolutely beautiful, with at least three more levels above the main deck. It started to slow down and gradually turn sideways on to them, as obviously they would need to approach it and not vice versa. It towered above them as they all stood, absolutely spellbound, faced with the fact that the next stage of the journey was going to be aboard what was indisputably a super-yacht.

Ilze called down, 'They're taking you all onboard through that freight loading door in the side, so everyone hang on to the rail.' Then she spoke through the loudspeaker, 'All deck crew ready with the fenders please, we don't want any insurance claims for damage to that beauty!'

In the midst of all the excitement, as the gap between the two vessels narrowed, a small helicopter was gradually coming down onto the landing pad that jutted out high above them. Its rotors came to a stop, and then two members of the ship's crew ran out and attached cables to the wheels, as its side door slid open and out jumped King Arthur himself, in all his tropical glory, waving a new Panama hat.

He leaned over the safety rail and bellowed out, 'Hello, you lovely lot! Come on up, you're late for breakfast!'

The champagne started flowing as soon as they were all assembled on the canopied rear deck. Arthur was introducing everyone to the captain, who was actually more interested in talking to Lex about the dear old sub. Arthur tinkled a spoon in his glass.

'Well, boys and girls, from now on let's make sure we keep all drama strictly in front of the camera. Anyway, congratulations every one of you for finishing what I'm sure will be a very fine picture, and I'd like to thank you, Julian, for your fantastic work after having come onto the job so late.' That got a big cheer from everyone, and clearly Julian was really touched. Arthur continued, 'I'd also like to thank our rescue teams for getting us all here in one piece, so would both captains be kind enough to raise a glass with us?' The two of them managed to tear themselves away from nautical chat mode and stand up with raised glasses, which got another hearty and well-deserved cheer, and a great deal of hugs and kisses, for Lex, Ilze, and Hannah. 'And finally for Mr Sieglovitz, who couldn't be here but has so generously made all this happen. Mr Sieglovitz!'

They all joined in with that one, and then Killy decided to respond on behalf of the crew. 'Arthur, Captains, crews; I'd like to raise a glass and toast two people who have helped make this movie but who, for different reasons, can't be here with us to celebrate. First of all, our dear friend Furio, who hopefully is safe and well, and secondly our extraordinary discovery, Gussy Santini, who I'm sure right now will be looking after everyone back at his family home every bit as well as he's taken care of us. Ladies and gentlemen; Furio and Gussy!' That got another big response, and then Monika stood up.

'I just want to say yet again what a joy it has been to work with you all, and to say a really very special thank you to our leading lady, who has endured, with grace and dignity, an extremely unfortunate piece of casting. She is without doubt already a star, with a great future before her. Ladies and gentlemen;

Serena Madura!'

Everyone stood up and clapped Serena as she sat wiping the tears away, and that was where the formalities ended and the party really started. At a certain point, they all stood on the side of the deck and waved goodbye to the sub and their three saviours as they sailed on to Miami. Killy was standing right at the back of the boat, watching the *Hondssbosch* gradually sink below the horizon, when Arthur came up to him holding out an old-fashioned, saucy, seaside postcard.

'Have a butcher's at this, son; go on, read it.' It was a cartoon joke that had been funny once, a long time ago, but now wasn't funny at all. He turned it over and read the handwritten message: *Arthur. We're all having a lovely time, your friend Furious Fred*.

'Got me there, Arthur. Who is it from?'

'Furio. That's what I used to call him. This was sent to the London office from somewhere in the UK, and it's definitely his handwriting. He's letting us know he's alright, but I have to say I knew he was. Anyway that's one bit of really good news.'

Something was cooking and Killy read it in Arthur's eyes. 'So what else?'

Arthur was nodding, with a great big grin on his face. 'Mr Sieglovitz has got a picture he wants to do with us; a murder mystery set in Canada.'

'Depends what time of the year, Arthur, last time I did a job up there it was so cold the cameras froze; but summertime, definitely. I loved it.'

'Well it would certainly need to be shot in summer, son, it's about a couple who sail their yacht up there from New England every year and spend a month with all their very rich boaty friends. The year the story takes place, the husband is found dead by some local fishermen …'

Killy assumed he was going to continue. 'And? What happens next, Arthur?'

'That was as far as I read, son, but as I said it's a murder mystery, so I suppose it's all about finding out whodunnit, innit?'

'Have they got any cast attached?'

'Well it's early days yet and it won't be until next year, but it's one of the possibilities Mort is keen for us to look at.'

'Well, if it's in the summer, Arthur, and they get a couple of decent names to do it, why not? After this last one it sounds like a little bit of heaven.'

'Do you want to read the script?'

'Is there a director attached yet?'

'No but I thought it might interest Julian, and he could go straight onto it as soon as this one's all ready to go.'

'I'll tell you what, Arthur; give it to him to read and if he likes it, tell him I'll definitely be up for doing it with him, OK? Frankly though, at the moment, the last thing I want is to be reading a script. Any script.'

'OK, son, that's great. I'll talk to him.'

'So what's the deal for today, Arthur? How long is the trip?'

'The captain wants to get us back to port by about seven this evening. I've had Mort's people book us into a nice hotel for the night, and then we fly to Miami mid-afternoon tomorrow, and then back to London. I thought it would be a good idea to have dinner at the hotel and invite Mort and his wife to meet everyone. They're both interested to hear all about it; she reckons it would make a good movie!'

'Yeah it would, Arthur — a fucking disaster movie!'

'You don't know yet, Killy, let's wait and see. You never can tell.' Arthur turned and walked across the deck. 'Anyway, I'm just going to have a quick bite and then I'm off for a snooze they've put me in Mort's suite, so I don't want to miss out on that. The captain said if you want a room just ask; there's plenty of them. This is something isn't it? See you in a bit.'

'You said it, it's beautiful and I might just do that after I've had something from that barbecue I can smell.'

He looked back at what was turning into a belated wrap party, albeit with only department heads, but decided that as Arthur had put him wise to the fact there was a dinner to deal with later, it would be more sensible to walk up one of the flights of stairs and find the way to the bridge, the captain, and a place to crash. He was halfway up when one of the crew was coming down towards him.

'Excuse me, do you think you could show me to the bridge? I have to sort out a room please.'

He was obviously an Aussie by his accent; suntanned, fit, and clearly very happy doing his job. 'That'll be a pleasure, sir, just follow me. And would you like your bags brought along once you're settled in? I can organise that for you, if you'll just tell me your name.'

'Killian Wilde. There are two large bags and a small one, all labelled; I only need the smaller one, thanks.'

'No problem, sir. Here we are; here's the bridge.' He tapped on the door, opened it, and indicated Killy should step in. 'Captain. Mr Wilde would like to rest, so I'm going to go down and get his bag.'

The skipper was standing in the middle of what looked like a sci-fi space station; a waist-height control table that ran from one side of the bridge to the other, under a wall of windows that were obviously light sensitive and kept the sun's intensity under control, as the change in brightness inside was noticeable straight away. He was another antipodean, although Killy thought probably a Kiwi.

'Hello again, Mr Wilde. Killian, isn't it? Can't remember what you do on the movie but your name stuck. Welcome to the bridge.' He turned to the guy who'd brought Killy up. 'Fraser, we'll put Mr Wilde in the Bay Suite, so you sort out his bag and I'll send him down with Leah.'

Fraser nodded. 'OK, sir,' and took off.

'So, Killian; bit of an adventure you've had, eh? I got an idea of what had gone on from Lex, and from what he told me you were lucky to get out. And seemingly, it's not got any better.'

That wasn't what Killy wanted to hear. 'Yes, and I've tried to call one of my colleagues who had to stay behind, but I'm not getting a signal that lasts more than a second or so.'

'You're welcome to call on the satellite phone; use my office over there. The glassed-in area.'

'That's great, Captain, thank you.'

'John please. I like to keep it formal with the crew, or it all gets a bit too familiar if they call me by my first name.'

'Do I just pick it up and dial?'

'Just dial 9 then the country code, and off you go. Pull the door shut if you want a bit of privacy.'

He didn't bother to close the door but just sat in the very comfortable leather-covered chair, scrolled up Gussy's number, and dialled it into the old-style phone. 'Gussy, it's Killy calling from … somewhere safe at sea. How is everything?'

There was a bit of static crackling on the line but his

voice came through really clearly 'Everything is OK, Killy… well, sort of. There was a last big explosion that blew in the remaining windows over the terrace, but fortunately nobody was injured and no other damage. It appears to be quietening down; just occasional bursts of gunfire but no more big stuff. So how are you all? Where are you? How did it all go?'

'We're on our way to the US Virgin Islands on a big, beautiful ship, and being very well looked after. And everything went perfectly, even the underwater cruise. Do you know how things are at Los Zapateros?'

'I phoned Rosalia and she told me they were all fine and I had a call from Uncle Philip, and apparently the government forces have regained control and things are beginning to calm down across the island. He says he'll probably be flying home with my mother in two or three days.'

'So where are you now, in the house?'

'Yes, I'm actually in the kitchen, drinking tea from Linda's giant teapot. Something I've definitely picked up from you; I'm hooked! Othello is keeping all the staff down in the old boathouse until we're sure it's safe for them to come back up here. I'll text you when we get word. What are your plans, are you flying directly to the UK?'

'No, we overnight at Saint Thomás and then fly to London via Miami the following day.'

'And do you start work on another film immediately?'

'Definitely not! I'm going home and sleeping for at least a week, and then I'll look in and see how Julian is getting on in post. And then start thinking about what's next.'

'Sorry, Killy, *post*?'

'Post-production; putting the film together now it's all

shot. In actual fact, it would be interesting for you to see that happening, having lived through it from day one.'

'Can I come over there and watch, Killy? I'd love to see how it all works.'

'Well you'd be more than welcome. I'll see what I can sort out.'

'I have family in London, I'm sure I can organise accommodation.'

'OK. Give me a call tomorrow. We'll be around the hotel until just after lunch. And let me know what's going on there, and I'll have a chat with Arthur. Look after yourself, and pass on my thanks and best wishes to Othello and all the staff.'

'I will do, Killy. And do the same for me please; tell them I really miss them.'

Another crew member, a young woman dressed in the uniform of blue polo neck and white shorts, was chatting to the captain as Killy came out of the office.

'Leah, this is Mr Wilde and he's going to be in the Bay suite, so perhaps you could show him along there and get him settled. We're making good time, Killian, and we should be docking right around 7pm. Do you envisage sleeping that long? Perhaps if you do, we should give you a heads-up before we arrive?'

'Perfect, John, that would be great. Thanks a lot. OK, Leah.'

She led him into a corridor that ran directly away from the bridge. 'The Bay Suite is right along here, Mr Wilde, and two of your colleagues are already neighbours.'

'Oh yeah, who?'

'Mr du Clos, is it, the French gentleman? He's in this one

here, the 'Miami', and the script supervisor, Sarah I think she said, wanted this one, the 'Jamaica'. Everyone else seems to be partying so far.'

The Bay Suite was absolutely stunning. Leah opened the door and showed him in.

'This is terrific, Leah, thank you. What a wonderful place to work. Have you been here long?'

'two years now, Mr Wilde. It's fabulous, eh? I'm going to have to move on soon or I'll never be able to tear myself away; it's like living on another planet, and Mr Sieglovitz is a dream to work for. I'll wake you when we're an hour out from port. Sleep well. From what I hear, you need it.'

'I'm absolutely shattered, so knock hard.'

As exhausted as he was, he couldn't resist going out onto the terrace that ran the length of his quarters, pulling a sun lounger into the shade and stretching right along it, staring out over the flat calm sea. But then knowing Sarah was just a couple of doors away took over his thoughts, and that was it. He walked along the corridor, pressed the doorbell and, as there was a good chance she'd be sound asleep, he prepared to wait. It opened quite quickly and Sarah stood in the doorway, wrapped in a bathrobe, seeming not long out of the shower.

'Hello, Mr Wilde. I was just thinking about you. Everything alright?'

'Would you like to come and look at my beautiful digs?'

'Well I'm not exactly slumming it here, Killy. Is that all?'

'No ... Actually, I wanted you to share them with me.'

'Blimey that's a bit bold for you isn't it; aren't you scared I might say yes?'

'No. That's what I want you to say, Sarah. Or if you

don't, that you'll—'

—let you share mine?' she cut in. He smiled.

'Yeah. But as long as you let me show you mine, first.'
Now she smiled.

'Hmm, that old line.' She stood back and waved her arm
to take in her room. 'Well you can see all of mine from here,
Killy. Let's have a look at yours.' She closed her door behind
them and followed him along the corridor.

She did share them but left a couple of love-filled hours
later, and scribbled on the bedside notebook:

Better and better Killy boy xx S

He woke to find Leah standing at his feet, smiling.

'I've brought you a cup of tea, Mr Wilde. I was knocking
for about five minutes, so excuse me for breaking in on you.
Good sleep?'

'I'm *still* asleep. Yeah, a cuppa would be great thanks,
Leah. Sun's almost set; how long have I got?'

She looked at her watch. 'You're fine, we're a tiny bit
behind; say forty minutes. And we certainly won't be chucking
you off, so take it easy.' She put the tea and some biscuits by the
bed. 'There you go. We'll all be out there to see you off. Bye for
now.'

He poured himself a cuppa and walked out onto
the terrace, and stood sipping it and looking out at the sea as
Arthur's voice came from behind him.

'Hello, Killy boy. We're next door neighbours.'

He turned round and there was his Majesty's freshly-
showered head looking over the top of the deep coloured glass
panel that divided the two terraces. 'I dunno what your side's
like, Arthur, but I could definitely get used to living like this.'

'Yeah me too, boy; he must have done very well to have this sitting around waiting for him to come and have a ride on.'

'Really well, Arthur. I'm looking forward to meeting him.'

'He's quite a bloke. And you'll meet his wife; she's really something, and a good bit younger than him. They've obviously been together for years and I think she's definitely the power behind the throne. I only had dinner with them but I really liked her; she's dead straight, no bullshit, just like him. Anyway, let's go down and have a look at the wreckage. When I finally got away, Bunny was trying to get everyone to have a knees-up, including the captain!'

To their surprise, it appeared people had been sensible and taken up the offer to sleep through the afternoon, and they were all gathered back on the rear deck as the ship pulled into the beautiful bay that sheltered the port. The only person missing was Bunny but he suddenly popped up from beneath one of the tables, looking very much the worse for wear.

'Killy. Give me a hand could you, mate? I'm feeling a bit rough. Just can't party like I used to.' Arthur and Killy helped him up and escorted him to the gents, and did as he insisted and left him there. 'Sorry, Arthur, I got a bit too fired up. So apologies. I'll see you in the morning.'

Arthur looked at Killy and shook his head. 'You can take the boy out of London, right …'

Once they'd dropped anchor in deep water about a quarter of a mile or so out, they were transferred onto two smaller vessels and ferried to the steps that ran up the side of the dock just opposite their hotel. Their bags were going to be waiting for them in their rooms. Arthur and Killy were the last ones up on the quayside. They stood looking back at the ship out in the bay and Arthur put his massive arm around Killy's shoulders.

'What an ending to the adventure, eh, son? Finished a lot better than it started.' Then he took a long, pensive pause. 'Well, I suppose I did eventually choose a great director but we owe this picture to you, Killy.'

'And a top-notch crew, Arthur.'

'But then they only come when there's someone like you to lead them, Son. Anyway, thank you, we did it.'

Killy smiled, then nodded to Arthur,

'All wrapped up.'

The End

Acknowledgements

I was very fortunate to have a group of people who, each in their own way, made this book happen.

Helen Wild, who convinced me I could do it.

Dave Ferris, for patiently reading the endless original and spurring me on.

Richard Carlisle, for giving me hugely valuable professional encouragement.

Emily Kitchin, for making me believe it had commercial potential.

Anna Barrett, for her incredible direction as editor.

Camilla Barnes, for her crucial critiques.

Michael Foster, for boosting my lost confidence.

Meryl Hoffman and Ruth Morrison for being there.

Steve Roberts, for allowing me to watch a master at work.

Paul Cox, for encapsulating it all.

Thanks to all at Softwood Books, and Jason Best.